NEW GIRL

in

LITTLE COVE

NEW GIRL in GIRL LITTLE COVE

DAMHNAIT MONAGHAN

HarperCollins*Publishers*Ltd

New Girl in Little Cove

Copyright © 2021 by Damhnait Monaghan.

All rights reserved.

Published by HarperCollins Publishers Ltd

First edition

HarperCollins books may be purchased for educational, business or sales promotional use through our Special Markets Department.

HarperCollins Publishers Ltd
Bay Adelaide Centre, East Tower
22 Adelaide Street West, 41st Floor
Toronto, Ontario, Canada
M5H 4E3

www.harpercollins.ca

Library and Archives Canada Cataloguing in Publication information

Title: New girl in Little Cove : a novel / Damhnait Monaghan.
Names: Monaghan, Damhnait, author.
Identifiers: Canadiana (print) 20200385984 | Canadiana (ebook) 20200386026
ISBN 9781443462693 (softcover) | ISBN 9781443462709 (ebook)
Classification: LCC PS8626.O515 N49 2021 | DDC C813/.6—dc23

Printed and bound in the United States of America
21 22 23 24 LSC 10 9 8 7 6 5 4 3 2 1

For my mother, Gabrielle Monaghan,
who brought us to Newfoundland and loved it as much as I do.

1

September 1985

Little Cove: Population 389

The battered sign came into view as my car crested a hill on the gravel road. Only 389 people? Damn. I pulled over and got out of the car, inhaling the moist air. Empty boats tilted against the wind in the bay below. A big church dominated the valley, beside which squatted a low, red building, its windows dark, like a row of rotten teeth. This was likely St. Jude's, where tomorrow I would begin my teaching career.

"You lost?"

I whirled around. A gaunt man, about sixty, straddled a bike beside me. He wore denim overalls and his white hair was combed neatly back from his forehead.

"Car broke down?" he continued.

"No," I said. "I'm just . . ." My voice trailed off. I could hardly confide my second thoughts to this stranger. "Admiring the view."

He looked past me at the flinty mist now spilling across the bay. A soft rain began to fall, causing my carefully straightened hair to twist and curl like a mass of dark slugs.

"Might want to save that for a fine day," he said. His accent was strong, but lilting. "It's right mauzy today."

"Mossy?"

"Mauzy." He gestured at the air around him. Then he folded his arms across his chest and gave me a once-over. "Now then," he said. "What's a young one like you doing out this way?"

"I'm not that young," I shot back. "I'm the new French teacher out here."

A smile softened his wrinkled face. "Down from Canada, hey?"

As far as I knew, Newfoundland was still part of Canada, but I nodded.

"Phonse Flynn," he said, holding out a callused hand. "I'm the janitor over to St. Jude's."

"Rachel," I said. "Rachel O'Brien."

"I knows you're staying with Lucille," he said. "I'll show you where she's at."

With an agility that belied his age, he dismounted and gently lowered his bike to the ground. Then he pointed across the bay. "Lucille's place is over there, luh."

Above a wharf, I saw a path that cut through the rocky landscape towards a smattering of houses. I'd been intrigued at the prospect of a boarding house; it sounded Dickensian. Now I was uneasy. What if it was awful?

"What about your bike?" I asked, as Phonse was now standing by the passenger-side door of my car.

"Ah, sure it's grand here," he said. "I'll come back for it by and by."

"Aren't you going to lock it?"

I thought of all the orphaned bike wheels locked to racks in Toronto, their frames long since ripped away. Jake had been livid when his racing bike was stolen. Not that I was thinking about Jake. I absolutely was not.

"No need to lock anything 'round here," said Phonse.

I fumbled with my car keys, embarrassed to have locked the car from habit.

"Need some help?"

"The lock's a bit stiff," I said. "I'll get used to it."

Phonse waited while I jiggled in vain. Then he walked around and held out his hand. I gave him the key, he stuck it in and the knob on the inside of the car door popped up immediately.

"Handyman, see," he said. "Wants a bit of oil, I allows. But like I said, no need to lock 'er. Anyway, with that colour, who'd steal it?"

I had purchased the car over the phone, partly for its price, partly for its colour. Green had been Dad's favourite colour, and when the salesman said mountain green, I'd imagined a dark, verdant shade. Instead, with its scattered rust garnishes, the car looked like a bowl of mint chocolate chip ice cream. Still, it would fit right in. I eyeballed the houses as we drove along: garish orange, lime green, blinding yellow. Maybe there had been a sale on paint.

As we passed the church, Phonse blessed himself, fingers moving from forehead to chest, then on to each shoulder. I kept both hands firmly on the steering wheel.

"Where's the main part of Little Cove?" I asked.

"You're looking at it."

There was nothing but a gas station and a takeout called MJ's, where a clump of teenagers was gathered outside, smoking. A tall, dark-haired boy pointed at my car and they all turned to stare. A girl in a lumber jacket raised her hand. I waved back before I realized she was giving me the finger. Embarrassed, I peeked sideways at Phonse. If he'd noticed, he didn't let on.

Although Phonse was passenger to my driver, I found myself thinking of Matthew Cuthbert driving Anne Shirley through Avonlea en route to Green Gables. Not that I'd be assigning romantic names to these landmarks. Anne's "Snow Queen" cherry tree and "Lake of Shining Waters" were nowhere to be seen. It was more like Stunted Fir Tree and Sea of Grey Mist. And I wasn't a complete orphan; it merely felt that way.

At the top of a hill, Phonse pointed to a narrow dirt driveway on the left. "In there, luh."

I parked in front of a small violet house encircled by a crooked wooden fence. A rusty oil tank leaned into the house, as if seeking shelter. When I got out, my nose wrinkled at the fishy smell. Phonse joined me at the back of the car and reached into the trunk for my suitcases.

"Gentle Jaysus in the garden," he grunted. "What have you got in here at all? Bricks?" He lurched ahead of me towards the house, refusing my offer of help.

The contents of my suitcases had to last me the entire year; now I was second-guessing my choices. My swimsuit and goggles? I wouldn't be doing lengths in the ocean. I looked at the mud clinging to my sneakers and regretted the suede dress boots nestled in tissue paper. But I knew some of my decisions had been right: a raincoat, my portable cassette player, stacks of homemade tapes, my hair straightener and a slew of books.

When Phonse reached the door, he pushed it open, calling, "Lucille? I got the new teacher here. I expect she's wore out from the journey." As he heaved my bags inside, a stout woman in a floral apron and slippers appeared: Lucille Hanrahan, my boarding house lady.

"Phonse, my son, bring them bags upstairs for me now," she said.

I said I would take them but Lucille shooed me into the hall, practically flapping her tea towel at me. "No, girl," she said. "You must be dropping, all the way down from Canada. Let's get some grub in you before you goes over to the school to see Mr. Donovan."

Patrick Donovan, the school principal, had interviewed me over the phone. I was eager to meet him.

"Oh, did he call?" I asked.

"No."

Lucille smoothed her apron over her belly, then called up the stairs to ask Phonse if he wanted a cup of tea. There was a slow beat of heavy boots coming down. "I'll not stop this time," said Phonse. "But Lucille, that fence needs seeing to."

Lucille batted her hand at him. "Go way with you," she said. "It's been falling down these twenty years or more." But as she showed him out, they talked about possible repairs, the two of them standing outside, pointing and gesturing, oblivious to the falling rain.

A lump of mud fell from my sneaker, and I sat down on the bottom step to remove my shoes. When Lucille returned, she grabbed the pair, clacked them together outside the door to remove the remaining mud, then lined them up beside a pair of sturdy ankle boots.

I followed her down the hall to the kitchen, counting the curlers that dotted her head, pink outposts in a field of black and grey.

"Sit down over there, luh," she said, gesturing towards a table and chairs shoved against the back window. I winced at her voice; it sounded like the classic two-pack-a-day rasp.

The fog had thickened, so nothing was visible outside; it was like watching static on TV. There were scattered cigarette burns on the vinyl tablecloth and worn patches on the linoleum floor. A religious calendar hung on the wall, a big red circle around today's date. September's pin-up was Mary, her veil the exact colour of Lucille's house. I was deep in Catholic territory, all right. I hoped I could still pass for one.

"Do you have other boarders?" I asked.

"I only takes one at a time," said Lucille. "You're the first mainlander."

A steady heat emanated from the wood stove and the smell of freshly baked bread almost masked the odour of stale cigarettes. Lucille dropped a tea bag into a mug, lifted a large kettle and splashed in boiling water. Then she plonked the mug in front of me, along with a can of evaporated milk. I'd seen it in grocery stores, but never tasted it.

"You take sugar?"

I shook my head, then, following Lucille's lead, dribbled the canned milk into my mug. I took a cautious sip, wincing at the sickly sweet taste.

"Too hot, is it?" asked Lucille.

I nodded.

She sliced into a thick, white loaf of bread and my stomach growled in harmony. Then she pushed a jar of homemade blueberry jam and a tub of margarine towards me before sitting down and lighting a cigarette, turning her head to blow the smoke away. The familiar gesture and the smell of smoke were like a slap in the face. It was too soon after Dad's death. But this was Lucille's house, and she didn't know about Dad, so I swallowed my outrage, washing it down with the tea.

I was on my second slice of bread when Lucille said, "I s'pose you heard what happened to the last French teacher?"

"No."

Her lips tightened for a moment, then she said, "She run off with the priest."

"What?" I might be a lapsed Catholic, but a priest running off with a parishioner will always be good gossip. I needed all the details, if only to share them with Sheila when next we spoke.

But Lucille pushed herself up from the table and said it was time I headed into school. "Besides you as the new teacher," she said, reaching for my plate, "we got a new priest in the bargain. Don't be getting any notions about him, now, he's the back end of sixty."

I opened my mouth, ready to swear to a lack of interest in any man of the cloth, no matter what his age, then shut it again when Lucille winked at me.

As I drove to the school, I couldn't stop thinking about the runaway priest. No wonder Patrick Donovan had grilled me on my Catholic background during our telephone interview. He'd started by emphasizing the importance of faith for teachers in Catholic schools. Then he said, "Are you a practising arsey?"

"Pardon?"

"R.C. Roman Cat'lic."

I had crossed my fingers behind my back before answering. "Baptized and confirmed. I attended Catholic schools and my father taught in a Catholic high school for thirty years."

I hadn't directly answered his question, but I hadn't outright lied either. While he carried on talking about the vacant teaching position, I'd walked over to the kitchen bookshelf, the telephone cord uncurling behind me. I flicked through the worn pages of Dad's old atlas and found the map of Canada. I traced the route from Toronto to Kingston, then Montreal, and on to Quebec City—the farthest east I'd ever been. My index finger splashed into the St. Lawrence Seaway and drifted over to Newfoundland, the tenth province and a place I'd never much contemplated, beyond the tired old jokes: "The world will end at ten o'clock, ten thirty in Newfoundland."

Now I was actually in Newfoundland and on my way to meet the man who'd brought me here. The gang of teens was gone from MJ's takeout and few people were around. But as I pulled into the schoolyard and parked beside a red pickup truck, caked in dust, two young girls appeared. They were perhaps thirteen and strolled down the road, arms linked. When I got out of the car, one of them hollered, "H'lo, Miss O'Brine," before they ran off giggling.

O'Brien, I said to myself, enunciating all three syllables.

A tall man in his forties stood at the school entrance, his broad frame filling the doorway. "It's Patrick," he said, holding out his hand. "Good to meet you. I heard your car on the gravel."

I followed him into the foyer, where the smell of bleach mingled with that of ditto-machine fluid. Straight ahead, in a small alcove, was a statue of a saint with a flame wreathing his head. He wore the obligatory brown robe and sandals.

"There's himself," said Patrick, following my gaze. "Been trying to get rid of him since I got here, but no luck."

I glanced at St. Nondescript. He seemed fine to me, if you were into that sort of thing.

"Come on," said Patrick, striding down the hall. "I'll show you 'round."

The school was small: staff room, office, classrooms; all were deserted. We stopped at the end of a corridor and Patrick showed me the small library.

"We didn't have a library when I took over the school," he said. "It was a real priority for me."

"I'll be sure to make good use of it," I said. But the room was in stark contrast to the well-stocked libraries I was used to back home. It seemed unlikely there'd be much of interest to me on those half-empty shelves.

The tour finished in my classroom. Patrick sat down on top of a desk and motioned for me to do the same. I took in his faded corduroys and scuffed construction boots, then forced myself to concentrate on what he was saying. He took me through class lists, policies and procedures, and a huge planner.

"I hope you enjoys your time with us," he said. "Most of the youngsters are right keen to learn. There's some lives in Little Cove, but most are bused in from other small communities. There's seventy-four students spread across the six grades. They're allowed to drop French after grade nine, so we gets a big dip then, but sure you'll change that, won't you?"

It seemed my first goal had already been set for me.

Patrick was still talking. "A few bad apples in grade nine this year. If there's any problems, see me sooner, not later. And look out for Calvin Piercey—he can be a right pain in the arse. He's in grade nine. Again."

"Calvin Piercey," I repeated, writing down the name.

"Another thing."

I waited, pen poised. There was a long silence while Patrick rubbed his sandy beard and looked past me out the window.

"There's not a lot to keep a young one like you occupied 'round here."

That had already become abundantly clear, but I didn't say so.

"And there's not much privacy," he continued. "I already knows you stopped to get directions at the gas station on the way out here. Heard you bought some postcards, too."

"Who . . . what?" I couldn't even begin to phrase an appropriate question.

Patrick roared laughing. "There's very few secrets in Little Cove, my dear. People knows what you had for breakfast before you've brushed your teeth." He waved a finger at me. "So you've got to keep yourself in line, hey?"

My cheeks burned. Was this some kind of lecture? But then I remembered Lucille's comment about the teacher running off with the priest and decided not to take it personally.

There were more questions. "Have you got family here in Newfoundland?"

I clenched the pen a little tighter. "I . . . I don't really know anyone here, actually."

We were quiet for a minute, the only sound the rain splattering against the windows. I could hear the unasked question; I knew he was dying to know why I'd taken this job so far from home.

After a minute, he cleared his throat and said, "Well, I don't know your circumstances, but maybe it doesn't matter. I'm thrilled someone with your credentials is joining us."

He stood up, then rapped his knuckles on the table. "I'll see you tomorrow." At the door, he turned back and said, "I knew you were the right one as soon as I saw your name. My wife was an O'Brine."

Alone in the classroom now, I paced the aisles and looked out the window. Then I sat down at the huge teacher's desk—my desk. Its wood was pockmarked, like the cheeks of that girl who had given me the finger. Had my predecessor sat here, dreaming of her priest? I shuddered at the very thought of it.

Looking out at the empty desks, I tried to imagine faces to match the names on the class lists.

Belinda Corrigan.

Cynthia O'Leary.

Calvin Piercey.

I picked up my pen and drew a circle around this last one. He didn't know it yet, but Calvin "pain in the arse" Piercey was about to become my project. It was something Dad had repeated many times. Sometimes you come across a student who seems past help, but when you finally reach them, it turns out that the trouble-maker is merely a lost soul. They're the ones you stick with, Dad used to say. They're the ones who need you most.

Dad. If only I could talk to him. Tell him about the school, my desk, Patrick. I reached into the pocket of my painter pants and pulled out Dad's silver lighter. I ran my fingers across the engraved initials: J.O'B.—Joseph O'Brien. When Dad's colleagues had given him the lighter, Mom commented that the initials also spelled Job and could be a reference to Dad's unlimited patience with students. I'd taken it after he died, hoping some of that patience would rub off on me. But a part of me hated the lighter too, because it was what Dad used every day to light the cigarettes that eventually killed him. I flicked the flame briefly, then shoved it back in my pocket.

I wrote my name on the blackboard, in my very best teacher writing, then turned to face my invisible students. They were exceedingly attentive, if devoid of personality. The classroom too was dull; its only adornments were tiny pinpricks on the bulle-tin boards and paper remnants stuck to the walls. The boxes I'd shipped from Toronto were neatly stacked in a corner; it was time to make my mark.

An hour later, autumnal displays and vocabulary posters had lifted the decor. But I spotted an errant pink ribbon dangling like a pig's tail from the ceiling, high above my desk, too high to reach. I poked around the supply cupboard at the back of the room, find-ing notebooks, rulers, erasers and, aha, a pointer. I was ready to duel with the offending ribbon.

I climbed onto the desk and repeatedly swiped, pinata style, at the ribbon, but still it taunted me. I put down the pointer and balanced one foot on the chair back. I had just put my other foot onto the blackboard ledge when the chair wobbled. I managed to complete my transfer to the ledge before the chair crashed to the floor, the noise resonating in the silence. Spread-eagled against the blackboard, I had no idea how to get down, let alone grab the damn ribbon.

Chalk particles tickled my nose. What would happen if I sneezed? Would the force knock me backwards off the ledge? Above me, the clock ticked loudly as the seconds slid past. Prickles of sweat bloomed on the back of my neck. How badly would I hurt myself if I jumped backwards? Or could I land, ninja-like, on the desk?

There was jaunty whistling now, and then footsteps in the hall. Phonse? A janitor could get a ladder. Then again, did I want anyone, even an old man like Phonse, to see me squashed up against the blackboard like a swatted fly?

The wooden ledge began to creak beneath my feet, focusing my mind.

"Excuse me," I called.

The footsteps came closer, then a deep voice boomed, "Jaysus God tonight, woman. You trying to be Spider-Man?"

It wasn't Phonse, and whoever it was, I hated him already. "I'm about to fall!"

In seconds, a hand was on either side of my waist, gently supporting me. The warmth from his hands penetrated my shirt and my cheeks grew hot.

"Okay, you can let go," he said.

But it felt like I was superglued to the blackboard. "I, I can't."

"Relax, I got you."

I took a deep breath, dropped my arms and let go, sliding slowly down the length of him. I smelled soap, wool and the sea. When my feet were on the floor, he released his grip. I turned around and saw a red sweater first. I had to look way up before I found a face. His blue eyes held my gaze until I looked down, brushing chalk from my shirt and pants.

"Do you work here?" I asked.

"Starting tomorrow." He offered his hand. "Doug Bishop. Science and phys ed teacher."

"Rachel O'Brien," I said. "French teacher."

"The mainlander," he said. "What in the name of God were you doing perched up there?" He gestured towards the ledge.

"I'm a new teacher," I said. "It's my first classroom."

Doug nodded as if that made perfect sense, then said, "I'm a new teacher too, but I didn't get the memo about testing the strength of the blackboard ledge."

When I explained my ribbon fixation, he righted my chair, stood on it, and pulled down the ribbon. Then he bowed low, presenting it with a flourish. His dark curls were inches from my hand and I nearly brushed them reaching for the ribbon.

"Thanks," I said.

"T'anks," he said.

"Pardon?"

"That's lesson one. Newfoundlanders don't say thanks. We says t'anks. Usually followed with b'y."

"Bye, like goodbye?"

"No, girl. B'y like boy, or someone might say to you, t'anks, maid."

"Made? Like thanks, I've got it made?"

He laughed, "I'll stay away from duckie for now."

I had no idea what he was talking about.

"Stick with b'y," he said. "Go on, give 'er a go."

"T'anks, b'y," I said.

"Proper t'ing," he said.

"What?"

"Never mind. That's lesson two." He gave me a wave as he left, calling over his shoulder, "No more climbing without a safety net, okay, Spidey?"

I found myself hoping that the nickname wouldn't stick.

Back at the boarding house, there was a cold plate on the table, along with a note from Lucille. She was gone to a neighbour's and I shouldn't wait up. I pulled the plastic wrap off the plate—chicken breast, potato salad and coleslaw. The radio was on low; a mournful country singer lamenting about a man who'd done her wrong was the soundtrack to my solo meal. I could relate all too well.

I clattered my dishes into the sink, then wandered outside and thought about all the street noise I wasn't hearing, unlike back home in Toronto. Eventually, a blue sedan drove slowly past and the driver waved. A boy in the passenger seat stared at me, craning his neck, until the tail lights disappeared down the hill.

When I went back inside, the phone was ringing. I followed the noise into the living room, where matching floral couches were smothered in doilies and the lampshades retained their plastic wrap.

"Hello?" I said.

"Rachel? It's Sheila."

I sat down. "Do I know a Sheila?"

She played right along. "Let me refresh your memory. Best friend? Since kindergarten?"

For a minute I was that shy little girl who'd clung to Dad's hand until Sheila Murphy dragged me over to the dress-up corner, where she plunked an old veil on me and asked me to marry her. Her teddy bear had performed the brief ceremony.

Now I said, "Oh, that old bag."

Sheila laughed. "So?"

I filled her in on Little Cove and its bleak consumer outlook. Then I moved on to the runaway priest.

"Wow! I bet he's gorgeous. Is he? Is he dreamy?"

Classic Sheila question. In grade twelve she had lusted after an earnest young seminarian; more recently we'd watched *The Thorn Birds* miniseries together. It had revived Sheila's fascination with priests while at the same time confirming my disgust at their inherent hypocrisy.

"How would I know what he looks like?" I said. "He ran away, remember?"

"True," she said. "Just like you."

I had nothing to say to that, and after a brief pause, Sheila carried on talking.

"Big day tomorrow. You ready?"

"I'm nervous," I said. "No, make that terrified. And I have PMS."

"Perfect," said Sheila. "You can be the bitchy new teacher that all the kids hate."

There was another pause, then she said, "Have you heard from your mom?"

"No, but don't forget the time difference between here and Australia."

"I can't believe she went," Sheila said.

"She promised my dad she would take the sabbatical," I said.

"Still."

"On his deathbed, Sheila."

"I know. Still."

Mom was a law professor who also took on casework. I knew Sheila thought Mom was selfish to take the sabbatical so soon after Dad died, and part of me agreed. But Dad *had* made her (and me) promise. And above all else, I wanted to honour Dad's wishes.

After Sheila said goodbye, I clutched the receiver to my chest, wanting to keep the connection for a minute. Then I hung up and went upstairs to unpack.

My room was fiercely tidy. The narrow bed was topped with a thick quilt, a repeating pattern of evergreen trees in each square. On the floor was a hooked rug, depicting a boat out at sea. They were the loveliest things in the room. There was a peg on the back of the door with a few hangers, and I hung what I could there. The rest of my clothes went in the pine dresser.

When I got under the covers, shifting in the unfamiliar bed, Lucille was still not home. A sliver of moonlight curled around the curtains, and in the distance a dog howled. I closed my eyes and tried to picture myself in front of a class of eager students, their hands raised like pointers. Instead I saw myself teetering on the ledge, flattened against the blackboard, having to be rescued by Doug. I found myself hoping that he wasn't going to tell everyone. Then again, after what I'd been through with Jake this past summer, I was used to public humiliation.

2

The next morning, a slow rumble shook the stage as the students pushed into the gym for assembly. I tried to make out individual faces, but it was a blur of freckles. Onstage, I forced myself not to fidget, but instead to project a non-existent inner calm. I crossed my legs, then uncrossed them again quickly when my skirt rode up. I tugged the fabric back down as inconspicuously as possible. The skirt hadn't seemed so short when I tried it on. Then again, it was Sheila who convinced me to buy it, and she tended to err on the side of vamp.

To my right, Judy Doyle, the vice principal, was wearing pants and a blouse with huge shoulder pads. I had met her briefly before assembly. She looked confident and at ease, as opposed to easy, which seemed to be the look I was projecting. A glance to my left, and my fears were confirmed. A nun, lips pursed, was looking with disdain at my thighs. The ratio of thigh to skirt was clearly not to her liking. What was it? Two-thirds thigh to one-third skirt? I never was very good at fractions.

Patrick walked to the microphone, yesterday's casual look replaced with a suit and tie. He told the students to settle down; they moved more quickly then, organizing themselves, cross-legged, into rows. A few older boys lounged at the back, but when Patrick called out, "Look lively now, b'ys," they sat up straight. Patrick welcomed them all back, singling out the grade sevens, new arrivals to the high school. He was a natural speaker, confident and funny.

"Some changes to the teaching staff," he said. "You all knows Mr. Bishop, of course. He'll be whipping our sports teams into shape in no time."

I was confused. Doug had said he was new, like me. But Patrick was already moving on. He caught my eye, then turned back to the students. "And this year, we has our first mainlander. How about that, a CFA?"

While the students hooted, I tried to parse this acronym. CFA: *F* would obviously be French, maybe *C* was certified . . . but what was the *A*? Not assistant. I might be probationary, but Patrick knew I was a fully qualified teacher.

"Yes, Miss O'Brine is a come from away," Patrick said. "They don't grow them very tall up in Toronto, do they?"

My face burned, causing him to add, "She only landed here yesterday, so I don't know too much about her, but she goes some red."

Which, of course, made me blush all the harder. Judy discreetly rolled her eyes at me. The nun clenched the rosary beads that hung from her belt; my first day and she was already praying for me.

Patrick briefly noted my double major honours in French and education, my student teaching award, the year I'd spent in

Quebec City, and my glowing academic references. I looked out at the student body. Were they wondering how, with all I apparently had going for me, I'd wound up in Little Cove? Or was that just me?

Once he'd introduced all the staff and finished his remarks, the assembly ended and we teachers filed out ahead of the students. Judy touched my arm as she passed. "Let's catch up at lunchtime, Rachel," she said. "Good luck."

I knew I might need it. My first-ever lesson as a qualified teacher was grade nine French, the very class Patrick had warned me about. There were only ten pupils in grade nine, but the noise they made in the hall as they approached my classroom sounded like a hundred. I waited at the blackboard, smiling hard, as they sauntered in, sat down and continued talking with each other.

The register shook in my hands. I tried unsuccessfully to make eye contact with someone.

"Peter Cahill," I said.

No one replied.

"Peter Ca—" I stopped. No one was paying attention. Most of the grade nines were huddled in groups, whispering, some glancing over their shoulder in my direction. As the seconds ticked by, the noise level rose, in tandem with my heart rate.

I decided to try again. "Peter," I called, as a paper airplane floated in from the left and landed on the register.

"Who threw that?" I said, then wished I hadn't. No one was going to claim responsibility. I threw the paper airplane in the garbage, then walked over to shut the classroom door.

"Quiet, please," I called loudly, followed by "Silence, s'il vous plaît." My remonstrations were in line with Canada's bilingualism, while the students' indifference seemed to mirror the views of many Canadians about that policy.

Finally, I climbed up on my chair. "Hey," I yelled, abandoning bilingualism and maybe self-control. "Shut up, right now. Or you'll all have detention."

Was I even allowed to give detention? And had I really told a class to shut up in my very first lesson? Sheila's prophecy had come true; I was the bitchy new teacher. But it worked. They began to settle, turning around and opening pencil cases and notebooks. "Don't smile until Christmas," one of my teaching professors used to say. It seemed unlikely I'd be tempted otherwise with this crew.

"Peter Cahill."

"Here, miss." Skinny and gap toothed.

"Trudy Johnson."

"Yeah." The corner of her lip curled upwards, as if reaching for the pockmarks on her cheeks. She wore a scarf in her hair, lace leggings and stacks of bangles on each arm, in clear homage to Madonna. I briefly wondered where she'd managed to find clothes like that around here.

"Calvin Piercey."

No one answered but a tall boy raised his hand in the air, middle finger extended. I looked away, shocked. When I looked back, the hand was down and so was he, slouched so low in his seat, he was practically horizontal.

"Can you sit up, please?"

He muttered something under his breath and a few students snickered. Had he sworn at me? With that accent, who could tell? I let it go. If I was going to help Calvin get out of grade nine, I might have to let a few standards slide.

"Miss," said the boy behind him. "Can I ask you how to say something in French?"

"Oui!" I exclaimed.

My first opportunity to impart knowledge and demonstrate the importance of learning a second language! Who said the grade nines were difficult?

"How do you say *seal*, miss?" he asked. "Like in the seal hunt, right?"

My head filled with images of seal pups, their eyes pleading with the camera. In the weeks since I'd accepted the job in Newfoundland, the topic of the seal hunt had come up a few times. Some of my friends thought it was barbaric, others defended it as an important regional industry. Either way, I didn't know how to say *seal* in French. I'd always excelled at French, which had driven my decision to study it at university, but in all those years of study, this was not a word I'd ever come across.

For a minute I was stuck. Then I remembered Dad saying that a teacher should never be afraid to admit a gap in their knowledge. No one ever had all the answers and that was an important lesson, too.

"I'm not sure," I said. "But we can learn it together." I picked up my *Collins-Robert French-English Dictionary* and flicked through the pages until I found the entry: seal 1. *n*. phoque *m*.

In other words, a masculine noun, pronounced *fuck*.

That little phoquer had clearly known exactly what he was doing when he asked the question, but I wasn't going to play along. Further up the page I spotted the French for *sea lion* and seized upon it.

"Lion de mer," I said, writing it on the blackboard for good measure and ignoring the jeers of "That's not right, miss."

Somehow I managed to get through the rest of the lesson, talking above their chatter about my plans for the year and my expectations of them. Then it was straight on to two more lessons with grades seven and eight. Mercifully, those students weren't such hard work.

Still, by lunchtime, I was exhausted and starving. At breakfast Lucille had mentioned that Patrick always treated the staff to lunch from the takeout on the first day of school. The smell of deep-fried fish wafted from the staff room. I would've killed for a burger.

My fellow teachers sat around the table, reaching for cardboard cartons and passing around packets of ketchup and vinegar. Doug motioned vigorously at the empty seat beside him and pushed a carton towards me. Did I have to sit beside him?

"Proper scoff on the go, right," he said.

I tilted my head, trying to figure out what he meant. From across the table, Judy spoke. "You'll have to get used to our Newfinese."

"Is that what you call the Newfoundland accent?" I asked.

"You mean Newfunland," said Doug.

It hadn't been much fun so far, but I kept quiet.

"It's pronounced *Newfunland*," he repeated. "Like *understand*. Understand Newfunland."

I nodded, then opened a cardboard carton and poked at the fish with a plastic fork. It was soft and flaky and, I quickly discovered, the best fish I'd ever tasted.

Judy was watching me. "You like?"

My mouth was full, so I gestured with my hands.

"So good you're speechless?" When she smiled, a gold tooth gleamed.

I swallowed and said, "I have died and gone to fish heaven."

There was a *tsk*ing sound on my right. It was the nun from the morning assembly. Her black veil framed a sharp face and square glasses. Two strikes against me and it was only lunchtime. At least my offending thighs were hidden under the table. I pasted on my placid Catholic schoolgirl smile and introduced myself.

"Yes, it's quite obvious who you are," she said.

I had a long history of bad relationships with nuns and it seemed this one would be no different. Why was it that most brides of Christ seemed to be stuck in such an unhappy marriage?

Judy leaned across the table for some ketchup. "Sister Mary Catherine is our grade seven homeroom teacher, and of course she teaches religion across the grades," she said.

The door to the staff room opened and Patrick strode in, rubbing his hands together. "I'm so hungry I could eat the leg off the Lamb of God," he said.

My laughter died when I heard more *tsk*ing from Sister.

"Don't encourage him, Rachel," Judy said. "And for the love of God, don't get him started on the fish puns."

Dad had been a punster; I was pretty sure I knew all the fish ones.

"I don't want to rise to the bait," I said, "but I love puns."

Patrick was reaching for a carton, but stopped. "They has their plaice."

"Whale," I replied, "too many give me a haddock."

Judy slapped Patrick's arm. "She might know more puns than you, Pat."

"You cod be right," he said.

"Speaking of cod," Doug interrupted, "any seconds on the go or wha?"

"Yes, b'y." Patrick pushed a brown bag towards Doug. "Sure this fish is so fresh it practically swam to the takeout."

I had been sneaking sideways glances at Doug, and he caught me staring. Our eyes held for a few seconds, then he said, "I've been wondering, Rachel."

Maybe it was my proximity to the nun, but I found myself praying he wouldn't mention the Spider-Man incident. He didn't. Instead, he asked, "What brings a mainlander down this way?"

His question coincided with a lull in the conversation; everyone turned to hear my response. I didn't exactly blend in around here. I reached for my drink and took a long sip.

"Ah, I'm just here for the halibut," I said.

Taking advantage of the scattered laughter, I made my exit, tossing the paper plate in the garbage and making a mental note to come up with a better answer before I was asked again. This job had been my only option, but they didn't need to know that.

After school, I stopped for gas on the way back to Lucille's. That morning I had briefly toyed with the idea of walking to school, but the rain changed my mind. Now I was glad to have my own little space, even if only for a few minutes.

I pulled in behind a huge pickup truck that was blocking the pumps. Its mud flaps had not lived up to their billing. I'd arrived only twenty-four hours earlier, but my car was caked in a thin layer of dust, like most of the vehicles in Little Cove.

Visible through the window of the gas station, a stocky man in a jean jacket and baseball cap leaned over the counter, his face inches from that of the woman at the cash register. When I pushed open the door, the tinkling bell above me was barely discernible over his loud voice.

"I got the wrong change in here last night," he said. "You owes me three dollars."

The woman behind the counter leaned away from him, hands planted on her hips. "Nothing to do with me, b'y," she said. "I wasn't working yesterday."

I cleared my throat loudly and he jerked his head around. "What the Christ do you want?"

"Gas," I said. "But your truck's in the way. Would you mind moving it, please?"

"Who do you think you are, talking to me like that?"

"Excuse me?"

"*Excuse me?*" he mimicked. "Miss Hoity-Toity, come from away, taking our jobs."

"Oh, so you're a French teacher?" I blurted out before I could stop myself.

The woman behind the counter covered her mouth to hide a smile.

He stared at me for a good minute before finishing his transaction with the cashier. Then he brushed past me, a little too close, muttering, "Comes down from the mainland and thinks her shit don't stink."

He slammed the door and the bells jangled frenetically. "Well," I said. "Someone's in a mood."

There was the sound of an engine being revved, and then his truck peeled out onto the road, a trail of dust rising in the air behind it.

The woman shrugged. "That's Roy Sullivan for you," she said. "He's the most contrary man you ever laid eyes on."

She began slotting chocolate bars from a large box into the display below the counter. "You're Miss O'Brine," she said. "Did you meet my Cynthia today? She's right mad for the French."

That didn't sound like any student I'd met so far, but much of the day had been devoted to administrative tasks. I told her I hadn't met everyone yet, but would be sure to look out for Cynthia.

"You gonna pump yourself?" she asked.

It took me a minute to realize she meant gas. Back outside, I shoved the gas nozzle in, wondering if Roy Sullivan had any children at the school. Then I noticed a piece of paper tucked under my windshield wiper, flapping in the breeze. I pulled it out. In big, black capital letters, someone had written, "You're not wanted here. Go on back home."

I slumped against the car. This *was* my home. At least for the next year. And who had left the note? Roy Sullivan had driven off immediately. He wouldn't have had time. There was no one but me on the gas station forecourt. The dark windows in the cluster of houses across the road gave no clue. I crumpled up the note, shoved it in my pocket and went inside to pay.

3

H ow was your first day?" Lucille called from the kitchen
before I'd even shut the door.

Not bad, just the one piece of hate mail, I thought,
but didn't say.

She was feeding sheets through a wringer, her face ruddy with
exertion. I'd only ever seen a washing machine like that in a museum.

"Be back the once," she said. "There's a fine breeze so I wants
to get these out."

I said I'd help her peg, but she said no and pointed me to the
table, where a cup of tea and a blueberry muffin waited. When
she came back inside, she sat down opposite me, lit a cigarette and
returned to her half-finished crossword.

"Classes all good?" she asked.

I considered telling her about the seal question, but then I wondered if hers was a trick question too. Hadn't Patrick said that

everyone knew everything around here? Besides, for all I knew, that particular French scholar was her nephew. I would have to save my stories for Sheila. And maybe Doug, although I wasn't sure about him yet. So it seemed safest to say that everything had been fine. Lucille didn't need to know that in the O'Brien household *fine* was code for "I don't want to talk about it."

"Ah sure Pat Donovan runs a tight ship," she said. "Smooth sailing with himself at the helm. Hang on, girl." She stubbed out her cigarette and disappeared into her bedroom off the kitchen, returning almost immediately with a framed picture. She gave it a polish with the skirt of her apron, then thrust it in my hands.

A younger, slimmer Patrick and a curler-free Lucille flanked a girl with short, dark hair, holding a certificate.

"That's my Linda," said Lucille. "The day she got her scholarship to go to the university. She was the only one in her year that went. She's a teacher now, like you. Up in Labrador."

"How old is she?" I asked.

"Twenty-five. Same age as I was when I had her."

I coughed to hide my surprise. Lucille was the same age as my mother, but to my eyes, she looked decades older.

"She's two years older than me," I said, taking one last look at the photo before handing it back. I had a similar one of my university graduation upstairs on the dresser. It was just me and Sheila. Dad was already gone and Mom had been in Washington, the keynote speaker at a conference.

Lucille propped the picture frame on the table and went back to her crossword.

"Five across," she said. "That's one for you." She pushed the paper towards me, her yellowed finger pointing at the clue: "A quality not easily described (French, 2, 2, 4, 4)."

"Je ne sais quoi."

"Je ne say wha?"

I took the pencil from her and filled in the answer. As she scowled over the next clue, I said, "I might go for a walk."

Lucille reached for the purse hanging on the back of her chair. "If you goes left down the road, you'll come to a little store. A can of milk would be good."

"Keep your money," I said. As I grabbed my jacket from the bannister, I found myself wondering if the store sold fresh milk. A few hundred yards down the road, I passed a woman pulling sheets from a clothesline.

"Hallo, Miss O'Brine," she called. "Fine day on the clothes. Where you off to?"

When I mentioned the store, she shouted directions, and I soon arrived at the large brown house she had described far better than Lucille. A hand-lettered sign in the window read, "No tea bags 'til Thursday." A few kids were hanging around outside, smoking.

"H'lo, miss," one of the boys said.

I said hello back and walked up the steps, ignoring their whispers. No one was at the cash register, but behind it, a half-open door led to a kitchen. A few rows of white-painted shelves held random grocery items. Toilet paper was stacked beside cans of soup; cardboard boxes on the floor displayed potatoes, carrots and turnips. I saw cigarettes, matches, balls of yarn and chocolate bars. I'd secretly hoped for a celebrity magazine, hell, even a tabloid, but there were no magazines, and I didn't see a fridge for fresh milk either. I grabbed a can of milk and was heading to the counter when several girls smirked their way inside.

"Whatcha buying, miss?" asked Trudy Johnson.

I'm looking for tampons, Trudy. Any particular brand you can recommend? I waved the can of milk at her. Would I be on display like this for the entire year, my every move and purchase critiqued? I rang the bell and a woman came out from the kitchen, folding her freckled arms when she saw me.

"You're that new French teacher from the mainland," she said. From the corner of my eye, I saw Trudy elbow her friend.

"That job belongs to a Newfoundlander," the woman continued.

"Then maybe she shouldn't have run off with the priest." I winced, not wanting to have said it out loud.

I put the so-called milk on the counter and the woman snatched my five-dollar bill and made change. Then she picked up a broom and began sweeping her way out from behind the counter, the dust chasing me to the door.

I dragged my feet back towards Lucille's house. The wind was up and it blew grit from the road into my eyes. I blinked hard. First Roy Sullivan, then the note, and now this awful woman. Why had I taken this job?

At the top of a hill, I paused to catch my breath. Behind me, a bicycle bell tinkled.

"There's herself," said Phonse, drawing alongside me. "How's she going?"

I sniffed, looking away into the distance.

He put down one rubber boot, then the other, straddled the bike, and reached into the chest pocket of his sweater vest. Like a magician, he pulled out a clean, white handkerchief.

"It's the wind," I wailed, dabbing my eyes.

"Yes, girl, she's blowing a gale." He looked past me out to the sea, his gnarled fingers still gripping the bike handles.

"Phonse, can I ask you something?"

"Fill your boots," he said.

I looked down at my shoes.

"Ask away."

"Do people mind me being here?"

He ran a hand over his chin. "Maybe some."

"What about the woman in the store?"

"Bertha?" He grimaced. "Don't mind her. She's not fond of mainlanders on account of her son."

"Did he lose his job to a mainlander?"

"Worse." His smile grew so big, his eyes disappeared. "He married one. He went out west four years ago and he's not been home since."

"And that's my fault?"

Phonse put a foot back on his bike and began to pedal. "Seems like it might be," he called over his shoulder. "Chin up, girl."

Back at Lucille's I wondered where to put the milk. Not in the fridge, obviously. Lucille was on the phone in the living room. She kept saying, "I knows, girl," every fifteen seconds. Eventually she hung up and joined me in the kitchen.

"Jaysus, Mary and Josephine," she said. "That was Bertha Peddle. She's after threatening to bar me from the store. Says you were right saucy."

"But I . . . she . . ." I stopped talking as, really, there was no excuse for my rudeness.

But then Lucille said, "Let her try and bar me." She took the can from me and put it on a shelf. "I got more dirt on her family than muck on a pig. Sit down now, for the love of God. We needs to eat early. I got a meeting over to the church."

She went to the wood stove and began lifting food from an iron frying pan. "Fish cakes," she said, putting a plate down in front of me.

I wasn't thrilled at the prospect of fish twice in one day. But these deep-fried golden discs were a delicious blend of potato and fish. A feeling of warmth spread from my stomach to my extremities. "Lucille," I said, putting down my fork. "The fish from the takeout for lunch was really good. But this"—I gestured at my plate—"this is amazing."

She waved her hand. "Go 'way with you, maid." But the curve of a smile softened her features for a moment. She took down a pack of cigarettes from a shelf over the stove and lit up. Then she lifted the smallest lid from the stovetop and dropped in the match.

"Tell me about your people," she said, sitting down on the day-bed in the far corner.

As she blew a long stream of smoke up to the ceiling, it didn't feel like the best time to talk about Dad's death from lung cancer just a few months prior.

"Actually, Lucille, I'd love to hear more about the teacher I replaced."

She scratched her head between the curlers and sighed. "Brigid Roche. Her husband, Paul, died last year. He was only twenty-eight."

"Oh my God, what happened?"

"He was driving home from Mardy with Ron Drodge, Brigid's brother, and they hit a tree. Not a scratch on Ron, but Paul died straight away. People said Ron was drinking that night, but no one knows for sure. Police never made it out this way until hours after the accident."

"Poor Brigid," I said. "Imagine being widowed so young."

Lucille came over to clear the dishes, stubbing out her cigarette in the leftover ketchup on my plate. "There's many left a widow too soon around here, myself included. But you don't see me running off with the priest, now, do you?"

She returned with a dishcloth and began wiping the table with quick, hard strokes.

"Seemed like Brigid was coming out of herself by Easter. And everyone said Father Jim was a big help with his grief counselling." She sniffed. "Grief counselling with a priest? I never heard the like. You buries your man, you gives it up to God and you gets on with life."

I thought about Mom sitting in Dad's leather chair for weeks after he died, stroking the worn arms, deaf to any attempts at conversation.

Lucille took a few more swipes at the table, though I could see no crumbs. Then she threw the dishcloth in the sink.

"Do you think Brigid will ever come back?" I asked.

"I expect she'll stay well clear," Lucille said. "She's brought too much shame on this parish."

She reached for a scarf lying on the daybed and wrapped it around her head. "I'm off to see Father Frank, now," she said. "He's got some fancy notions he needs to be set straight on right quick."

After Lucille left, I went upstairs and pulled Dad's school sweatshirt from the bottom drawer of my dresser. I put it on and lay down on my bed, thinking that grief counselling didn't sound like such a bad idea.

4

"Bonjour, mademoiselle."

A girl in jeans and a sweatshirt stuck her head in my classroom. I was mid-gulp of a cup of coffee, so I beckoned her in. She chattered her way up to the desk, telling me, in perfect French, that her name was Cynthia and she was in grade twelve.

"Bonjour, Cynthia," I said. "I think I met your mom at the gas station."

She nodded. "She told me. Oh miss, I loves French," she gushed. "It's my favourite subject."

"Mine too," I said and we both laughed.

"I wants to be a French teacher," she said. "I'm trying for a scholarship to get to university, like Doug did." She covered her hand with her mouth. "Mr. Bishop, I mean. We're not allowed to call him Doug at school."

"Wait," I said. "Is Do—Is Mr. Bishop from Little Cove?"

She nodded. "His family lives two doors down from us. But I won't come back to Little Cove like he did," she said. "I wants to see the world."

The bell rang then, so I told Cynthia I'd see her later that morning. "Can't wait, miss," she said.

I quickly scanned my lesson plan, waiting for the grade nines to arrive. I could hear the shrieks and staccato bursts of laughter as they approached. The noise continued as they took their seats in the classroom. Calvin was semi-horizontal at his desk and Trudy was blowing the biggest bubble I'd ever seen. I willed it to burst all over her face, but she sucked it noisily into her mouth.

"Trudy," I said. "Get rid of that gum, please."

She sauntered past me to the corner, stood over the garbage can and spit. There was a soft thunk as the gum hit bottom.

"Miss," Trudy said. "Can I just say something?"

She was clearly destined to be a teacher because all of a sudden, she had everyone's attention.

"What is it?"

"Bertha Peddle says you're a proper slut."

I heard myself gasp as shouts of laughter erupted, and I looked around to a mass of braying mouths.

"Get out," I said, my voice trembling.

"But, miss," she protested.

"Right. Now." I pointed to the door, my fingers jabbing the air. "Go see Mr. Donovan and don't you dare slam the door on your way out."

I turned on the class, snarling. "Get out your books and do some exercises."

"Which ones?" a few of them asked.

"Any," I said. "Just get to work. I don't want to hear another word. From any of you."

Maybe I was good at French, but I couldn't control these feral teenagers. I sat down at the desk and stared at the planner where last night I'd set out a carefully constructed learning objective. "Students will demonstrate an understanding of the negative." Bonus marks for Trudy on that one.

There was a tap at the door and Judy came into the classroom. "Miss O'Brine, a word in the hall, please." Her voice was crisp, but it softened when I shut the door behind me and joined her outside, one hand still resting on the knob.

"Patrick wants you in his office in five minutes," she whispered. "I'll cover the lesson."

I took a detour to the women's bathroom. My face was blotchy in the mirror and my eyes were full. I splashed water on my cheeks and scratched them dry with a paper towel. Taking a deep breath, I went to Patrick's office, ready to defend my honour.

He rose from behind his desk and motioned me into a chair, then handed me a steaming mug of tea from a side table.

"Where's Trudy?" I asked, hoping she'd been suspended, or even better, expelled.

"I'm after sending her back to class," he said. "I had a word, but to be fair, she was only repeating what Bertha Peddle said."

I put down the mug lest I spill it. "So it's okay for a student to call me a slut?" My voice was tight.

Patrick choked mid-slurp, spitting tea onto his desk. "Jumping Jaysus," he said. "Is that what you thought Trudy called you?"

"She did call me that."

Patrick put down his mug. "I can see why you tossed her out, but no, my duckie. Bertha said you were a scut. S-C-U-T."

It didn't sound much better. "What does it mean?"

"Mean."

"What?"

"It means *mean*, like you're a mean person."

"I'm not mean," I said, pulling a tissue from the box on Patrick's desk and wiping his spill. "If anything, Bertha was mean."

"Maybe so," he said. "But it's you that needs to fit in around here."

Behind Patrick's desk was a table covered in neat piles of paper. Above it, on the bulletin board, was a yearly planner and a to-do list, which included the notation—"Probationary Reviews—Rachel and Doug."

I imagined my review thus far: "Takes offence easily; struggles to understand students; no classroom control." I put my head in my hands.

"Chin up, girl. The first few weeks are hard but you'll get the hang of it."

"But what do I say to Trudy next class?"

"Not a God-blessed thing."

"But what if she says something to me?"

Patrick drained his tea noisily. "Do you think you're the first teacher ever got mad at a youngster for no reason?"

I thought about my own time as a lippy young thing. To be fair, when the nuns used to get mad at Sheila and me, it was usually for a very good reason.

After school I lingered at my desk long after the bell had rung. Students thundered down the hall, conversing loudly, some rushing for buses that would take them to outlying communities. The footfalls subsided, car doors slammed, engines turned over, and then, there it was, blissful silence. I put my head on my desk and replayed the conversation with Patrick. *It's you that needs to fit in*, he had said. But how?

Gradually I became aware of my foot tapping along to music. I lifted my head. It sounded like a violin, but the tune was much jauntier than any I'd ever learned. It built to a crescendo, then after a final thrust of the bow across the strings, there was silence.

Had I dreamt it? But then a slow, melancholy tune filled the air. It was the soundtrack to my mood, and I followed it down the hall and around the corner to an open door I'd not noticed before.

I peeked inside the small room, barely bigger than a closet. Wearing a faded but spotless green coverall, Phonse sat in a chair, eyes closed, arm swaying back and forth as he played. A neat assortment of mops, buckets, brooms and cleaning supplies surrounded him. When the tune ended, I clapped softly and his eyes jolted open.

"Jaysus, girl," he said. "You scared the life out of me. I thought everyone had cleared out."

"I didn't know you played the violin," I said.

"I don't." He raised his instrument in the air. "This here's a fiddle."

"Whatever it is, you play beautifully."

He ducked his head. "Ah, sure I learned at me fadder's knee," he said. "Do you play anything yourself?"

I thought about all the tears and tantrums that had accompanied my violin lessons. Those Thursday-afternoon sessions had lasted long after my passion for the instrument had waned.

"You're away with the fairies, sure," said Phonse.

I gave my head a shake to dislodge the memories. "Sorry," I said. "I used to play the violin."

He thrust the fiddle at me. "The violin's cousin," he said. "Have at it."

"Do you have any sheet music?"

Phonse tapped the bow to his head. "It's all in there, girl." Then he handed me the bow and said, "Have a go, sure."

I drew the bow across the strings, flinching at the high-pitched squawk.

"Sounds like a chicken getting its neck wrung," Phonse said.

I wanted to give up, but was reminded of Patrick's challenge to fit in. I forced myself to try again, the squawks gradually turning to notes. And suddenly it came back to me: Vivaldi's "Spring," the last piece I mastered before I quit. I closed my eyes and concentrated, picking up speed and making fewer errors.

When I finished, I kept my eyes shut, remembering how Dad used to sit in his armchair, newspaper tossed aside, and listen to me play. Phonse's soft clapping brought me back.

"I don't know that tune," he said, "but it was wonderful grand."

I felt my cheeks pink as I passed him back the fiddle. "I used to play it for my dad," I said.

"Well here's to our fadders," said Phonse. "I think we've earned a cup of tea. Will you do me the honour?"

Dad always said that support staff were a teacher's most important ally, and I found myself thinking he would've liked the down-to-earth Phonse.

In the corner of the room, a hot plate sat on a rickety table, a can of milk beside it. When the kettle boiled, Phonse made tea, handing me a mug emblazoned with a slogan.

"World's Greatest Teacher," I read aloud.

"Now, don't be getting ahead of yourself," said Phonse. "It's only your first week."

That evening Mom called from Australia, except it was already the next day for her. She filled me in on her life in Sydney—the classes she was teaching, her new neighbourhood and the quirks of her apartment. She asked lots of questions about Little Cove, which I tried to answer as neutrally as possible, aware of Lucille in the kitchen. It wasn't the most satisfactory conversation, but we were still renegotiating our relationship following Dad's death and what she deemed my disappointing behaviour afterwards. But she promised to call me regularly, and we said our goodbyes.

5

Lying on the bed listening to Bruce Springsteen sing "No Surrender," I could feel my stomach vibrating in time to the music. Why were no delicious supper smells wafting up the stairs from the kitchen? I removed my earphones and went downstairs, where I met Lucille at the front door, coat on and scarf over her curlers.

"I was about to holler up to you, girl," she said. "I forgot to tell you this morning. I don't cook on Fridays. It's my ladies' night."

"Okay," I said, wondering if I was meant to cook for myself.

"There's cold meat in the fridge," Lucille continued. "Or, I s'pose you could get fish and chips from the takeout."

Decision made. Like Pavlov's dog, I was. I watched Lucille walk out of the yard, wondering how late she'd be. It was my first weekend in Little Cove and I was spending Friday night alone. Dad used to say start as you mean to go on, but I hoped this wasn't how I'd be going on all year.

I debated walking to the takeout, but in the end, I decided to drive so the food would stay warm. A girl of about sixteen, hair in a messy bun, leaned on the counter, chin resting on one hand. Her petite frame was dwarfed in a man's shirt. Dark eyeliner highlighted an odd puffiness around her eyes. I placed my order and she wrote it down. Her nails were bitten right off.

"You're Miss O'Brine," she said. "My sister Belinda is in grade nine. I'm Georgie."

"I haven't seen you at school, Georgie. I guess you don't take French?"

"I did," she said softly, "but I had to drop out." Then she turned to put my order on the pass-through and I saw she was pregnant.

I was silent, unsure of the correct response given the fact that I was teaching in a Catholic school. I left the counter and went to sit in a nearby booth.

"I'll wait here," I said. Then I fixed my gaze out the window, suddenly fascinated by the wildflowers growing up through the carcass of a rusted-out car in the field opposite.

"Order's up," Georgie called a few minutes later. But when I reached the counter and went for my food, she didn't let go. Grease stained the brown paper bag, which shook slightly in her hand. "Do you think it's fair?" she asked, her voice quivering.

"What?"

"I got pregnant, so I had to drop out. I didn't exactly get like this on my own. Only the Blessed Virgin managed that, to my knowledge." She made a sound, more bark than laugh. "My boyfriend, Charlie, is still at school."

She let go of the bag and it sat between us on the counter, the grease spreading slowly across it.

"I don't want Charlie to be kicked out," Georgie said. "He needs his certificate." Then she lifted her chin, face defiant. "But I needs mine too. It's not fair."

Behind her, in the pass-through, a woman wearing a pink hair-net lifted a basket of chips from the fryer and threw them on a large tray. "Chips up," she called. "Come and bag 'em, Georgie, and never mind the chit-chat."

Georgie's eyes were pleading with me now.

"You're right," I said, picking up my order. "It's not fair. In fact, it sucks out loud."

She smiled weakly. "T'anks, miss. Belinda said you were right cool."

Calvin Piercey was standing at the bottom of the steps beside my car when I went outside. His open palm revealed a scattering of coins.

"You hungry?" I asked.

When he didn't answer, I thrust my supper in his hands. "Have this," I said. "I've lost my appetite."

Then I saw a note stuck under my windshield wiper. I snatched it and slid into the driver's seat. My hands fumbled and I cursed—it was the same block lettering as the first note. "Batter to Jesus." I wasn't sure what it meant, but it didn't sound like a call to prayer. Could Calvin be leaving the notes?

Someone rapped on the window and I jumped, crumpling the paper in my fist, then relaxing when I saw who it was.

"Hey," I said, rolling down the window.

Doug leaned in, his elbow pushing the window down further.

"How's she going?" he said.

"The car? Seems fine."

He grinned. "Nah, I meant how's things."

"So much to learn," I said. "And I'm supposed to be a teacher. Although the grade nines might debate that point."

"Rough week?"

Tears welled in my eyes and threatened to spill over, so I started the engine. "Gotta go," I said, aiming for a breezy tone.

"Wait. You free tomorrow morning?"

"Think so," I said. There would be no need to check my diary, but I didn't want to advertise the fact.

"Great. I'll take you jigging."

"Jigging? Like folk dancing?"

He burst out laughing. "Ah, Rachel, I dies at you. Cod jigging."

My confusion remained. He spoke loudly and very slowly. "Fish - ing. Out . . . at . . . sea."

"Oh," I said, trying to hide my horror. "Can I just watch?"

"Mandatory participation. The wharf's just behind Lucille's." He straightened up and I put the car in reverse. "I'll see you there at six."

"Six a.m.? On a Saturday?"

"If we leaves it any later, the fish'll all be gone."

I wasn't sure if he was joking, but I said I'd see him at six.

I spent the evening washing and straightening my hair and reviewing my wardrobe options. Practicality won and I laid out jeans and a sweater. It wasn't a date, and besides, it was sure to be cold and wet.

It was still dark when I got up, but Lucille was banging around at the stove. "I made bacon," she said. "You'll get hungry out on the water."

Clearly the all-points bulletin of my plans had circulated overnight in Little Cove.

She slid my breakfast onto a plate and was making for the table when she stopped cold. "What's after happening to your hair?"

"Is it that bad?" I ran to the hall mirror. Curls had sprouted overnight.

"Just different," Lucille said, her head of curlers appearing behind me in the mirror. How did she sleep with them in? Didn't they hurt? We were like mismatched twins. I was trying to get rid of my curls and she was determined to make some. After breakfast, I ran upstairs and put my hair in a ponytail, shoving on a baseball cap for good measure.

"I'm glad you're keeping Doug company fishing," Lucille said. "Gerry won't go with him."

Before I could ask who Gerry was, Lucille was pushing me out the door so I wouldn't be late. "Bring me back a big one now, girl," she said.

The footpath behind her house led right down to the sea. It was growing lighter already. I could see the wharf, and beyond it, little fishing dories anchored about the bay. A few men were working on a larger boat that was moored about thirty yards out—splashes of yellow overalls against the blue boat. One of them waved and I waved back.

There was no sign of Doug so I sat down on the edge of the wharf to wait, dangling my feet over the edge. All around me were stacks of lobster traps, along with bits of old rope and empty plastic containers. I heard a chugging and a small yellow boat with red trim approached. As he got closer, Doug cut the engine and glided alongside the wharf.

"Here," he said, tossing over a smaller version of the green bibbed overalls he was wearing. "These looks about your size."

"Oh, I don't need them."

"You don't want fish all over your jeans." I looked at the blood, guts and other detritus scattered around the wharf. The man had a point. I wrestled my way into the overalls, pulling the straps over my coat, then accessorized with a bulky orange life jacket. My aggressively curly hair didn't seem to matter much all of a sudden.

I eyed the boat. It looked tiny compared to the sleek motorboats that plied the cottage lake back home.

"Is it safe?"

"Built her myself."

"And that's meant to reassure me?"

"Stop stalling."

I sat back down on the wharf edge and slid into the boat, grabbing the side as it pitched. "I got you," said Doug.

His hand closed around my upper arm and he guided me to a wooden seat at the front. Then he started the engine and we cruised out of the bay, slowly at first, then gaining speed so that the colourful houses of Little Cove blurred into a rainbow that grew smaller and smaller, disappearing when we rounded a rocky bend in the shore. The waves were bigger now, but we hugged the coastline. Evergreen trees sprouted from rocks; I spotted a bald eagle high up on a branch.

Doug shouted something that I didn't hear. He held up a thumb and I nodded, grabbing the side of the boat as it sped up suddenly. We were headed away from shore, out to the wider sea. After a few minutes, we slowed, then Doug cut the engine. The waves slapped hard against us, and the boat swayed like a drunk while I held my stomach and stared hard at the horizon. Eventually we gained a slower rhythm or maybe I got used to it. As far as I looked, in every direction, there was nothing but sea.

"Goes like the clapper when she wants, wha?" said Doug.

"Um, sure."

He took a flask from his backpack and poured a hot chocolate, spilling none as he passed the plastic mug over. Then he poured more into a mug for himself.

"Does your family fish?" I asked.

His face changed briefly; his lips set in a thin line. Then with a slight shake of his head, his habitual smile returned. "Most everyone around here does," he said. "It's in our blood."

A boat flew past, its occupants shouting across the waves at us, but their words were lost to the air.

"They weren't wearing life jackets," I said.

"Lots don't."

"Why not?"

He rubbed the side of his mug absently. "Habit, maybe. Plus, if you ends up out here in this water, miles from nowhere, maybe you're better off drowning."

We finished our drinks in silence. When I handed back my empty mug, I asked where the fishing rods were stored.

"Rods?" Doug's voice rose theatrically, lightening the mood. "Sacrilege."

He pulled a burlap bag towards him and removed two wooden bobbins strung with fishing line. A meaty hook sprang from the end of each line.

"Mind she don't bite you," he said. I gingerly took the nearest one, holding it away from my body.

"Unfurl your line and toss it over," Doug said. "All of it. It's right deep out here."

He threw his hook overboard and began twisting the bobbin back and forth so the line spilled into the sea like water from a tap. My hand jerked clumsily as I copied his movements. But I was watching his line, not my own. Soon mine was in a tangle, around my feet. Doug hadn't noticed and was still shouting out instructions.

"Now you starts hauling it back in, giving little tugs, like this, every few seconds. That's jigging." Then he whooped. "Got one." He pulled the line rapidly in, then held up a huge fish.

"That's a cod?" I had imagined something the size of the battered fish from the takeout.

"I've caught bigger." He unhooked it and threw it in the blue plastic bucket beside him. Then he threw his line back overboard again, spooling it through his fingers, and repeated the process, hauling up another fish. I managed to untangle my line and throw it overboard while Doug was busy with his catch.

"You got any yet?" he asked.

"Maybe there's no more fish around here," I said.

"There's enough fish in this ocean to last ten lifetimes."

I jiggled—jigged—my line every few seconds, my fingers stiff in the old gloves Doug had insisted I wear. The line felt heavy now, and harder to pull.

"You got one," shouted Doug. "Haul 'er in."

As the fish breached the surface, I leaned over the side and pulled it in with both hands. Sea water dripped from my catch, landing on my sleeve.

"She's a beaut," Doug said. "Lucille will be some pleased. That's your dinner sorted."

I looked at the fat mouth and dull eyes of the fish dangling from my hand. I barely managed to put it down before I retched repeatedly over the side of the boat. I slumped down, burying my face in my hands. But Doug couldn't have been sweeter. He told me to put my head between my legs and take deep breaths until the queasiness passed.

"Plenty of fish on board now," he said. "Probably time we heads home, if that's okay with you."

If it was obvious he was lying, I didn't mind. I nodded and Doug started the engine and motored slowly back, talking aimlessly, somehow managing to never say anything that required a response. Back on shore I struggled out of the life jacket and overalls and sat down on the grassy hill while Doug cleaned and gutted the fish, whistling to himself. He handed one over; I didn't ask how he knew it was mine.

"You all right to get back on your own?" he asked.

I nodded, then mumbled my thanks and headed up the hill towards Lucille's.

"Rachel," he called.

When I turned around, he said, "You done good." He paused a beat, then added, "For a mainlander."

6

The bathtub at Lucille's was a large claw-footed beast. I topped up the hot water twice, my toes resting on the tap, trying not to race through my novel. Unless I found a library soon, I'd be reading the Bible for pleasure at this rate. I reluctantly pulled the plug only after repeated shouts up the stairs from Lucille. When I descended, Our Lady of Perpetual Smoke was pacing up and down in the hall, practically chewing her cigarette.

"Jaysus, Mary and Josephine," she said, her voice high. "What's after taking you so long? It's getting late."

"For what?"

Her eyes widened and she forgot to exhale. After a prolonged bout of coughing, she wheezed, "Mass."

I looked from Lucille's frilled red blouse and black skirt to my ratty sweatpants and ran back upstairs. Dammit! The only time I'd been inside a church in the last five years was Dad's funeral.

But even a Catholic as lapsed as me should have realized that in a small community like Little Cove, there would be no escaping the Lord.

Lucille bellowed up the stairs. "We needs to go."

I grabbed my trench coat. It could hide a multitude of sins, as Mom would say. And God knows I had plenty of those as far as the Church was concerned.

Nothing was far away in Little Cove, so I drove slowly. Nonetheless, Lucille clung to the grab handle with one hand and braced herself on the dashboard with the other. I glanced across at her hair. The curlers were gone, replaced by a tall curly mound, the hairspray on it glistening like dew. A tornado wouldn't shift it.

The wooden doors of the church were propped open and the small parking lot was full. Lucille blessed herself as we came level with the church, then gestured to a small lay-by on the roadside.

"Park there, luh. That's for stragglers. We'll not leave it so late next Sunday."

We hurried up the steps, slipping in just ahead of Phonse, who was closing the doors. "Evening, ladies," he said, winking. Lucille scowled at him and I regretted my role in this minor embarrassment.

The central aisle was heavily scuffed; the wooden pews on either side were mostly full. I tried to slink into the back row, but Lucille prodded me on towards the front. Students were dotted through-out the congregation, the younger ones sitting with parents, the older teens pressed in together at the back. I looked straight ahead, but from the corner of my eye, I could see elbows poking ribs and heads tilting in our direction.

We were getting so close to the front of the church that I decided Lucille must be heading for the altar to say Mass. But at the last minute, she steered me to the left and into the front pew. She creaked to her knees and I followed suit. I'd taken the job at St. Jude's because I'd missed the entire Ontario recruitment process, having parked my job search when Dad got sick. I hadn't given the Catholic angle much thought, not fully appreciating that it would necessitate regular attendance at Mass. I wasn't sure I could handle a year of that and bowed my head to pray for a solution.

The organist began playing a vaguely familiar hymn and the congregation rose as one. I recognized the two altar boys walking solemnly up the aisle. Behind them was Sister Mary Catherine, holding the Bible like a shield. A fat priest, in full regalia, brought up the rear.

During the service, I mumbled half-remembered prayers and responses. Periodically I glanced around. I saw Doug two pews over. Judy was in the row behind him and lifted a hand discreetly in greeting.

I was a long way from a state of grace when I went up for Holy Communion, but it seemed safer to risk the wrath of the Almighty than the shame of Lucille. Father Frank stood before me, the host in his hand.

"The Body of Christ," he intoned, looking at me intently, as if to ferret out my sins.

"Amen," I croaked, adjusting the collar of my trench.

When I returned to the pew and kneeled to say my post-Communion prayer, memories of Dad's funeral came back to me. He'd been a much-loved English teacher; the church had been packed with weepy girls and stoic boys. Mom and I had been overwhelmed by it all. I pinched the skin on my inside wrist and began counting backwards in my head, to push the sadness away.

When Mass was over, Lucille whispered, "Father Frank wants a word with you. He says to wait here for him. I'll see you later back home."

I found myself wondering how Father Frank had managed to communicate all of this to Lucille when he gave her the host. Still, I sat and waited while the church emptied. The sun streamed in through the stained-glass window behind the altar. In an alcove to the right, rows of votive candles flickered. I glanced back to the church doors, flung wide like outstretched arms, but there was no sign of the priest. I began to think he'd forgotten until he surprised me, coming out from a door to the right of the altar, now wearing the simple black garb of everyday priesthood.

He walked towards me, his broad stomach rising like dough over his belt. He was nearly bald with scattered wisps of grey hair.

"Miss O'Brine," he said, holding out a hand. There was a large gold ring with a ruby stone on his fourth finger, and for a second, I wondered if I was expected to kiss it.

"Rachel," I said, taking his damp hand in mine.

He sat down beside me in the pew, drawing his hands into his lap. "So, you're out here to teach French," he said. "Now tell me this. Do the young people of outport Newfoundland need to be learning French?"

Before I could say anything, he answered his own question. "I have my doubts. It seems to me that there are far more important matters that could be taught."

"Like what?"

"Manners, for starters. And faith."

He unfolded his hands and raised them into the prayer position. "As a teacher in a Catholic school, Miss O'Brine, you will be expected to demonstrate a high code of moral conduct and set an example for the young people of this parish."

"Yes, Father."

"There is also the vexing problem of chastity." He over-enunciated this final word while his eyes bored into mine as if seeking a confession of my full sexual history. "Do you know, Miss O'Brine, we have girls in this parish who have to leave school because they fall pregnant?"

"That is indeed shocking," I said, choosing my words deliberately.

He looked sharply at me but I smiled back. If going to Catholic school all those years had taught me anything, it was how to suck up to a priest.

"You are young, Miss O'Brine," he continued. "Some of the girls may therefore look to you as a confidante." He straightened in the pew. "However, that is *my* role in this community. If any of the girls seek you out to confess to any sexual impropriety, you must refer them to me."

When hell freezes over, I thought.

"Now, do you have any questions about your teaching position?" he asked.

"Mr. Donovan has briefed me on all my responsibilities," I said, standing to go. "If there's nothing else, Father, Lucille will be waiting for me." It wasn't a complete lie. She *was* waiting for me. At home.

There were a few stragglers outside the church when I left, pockets of women chatting to each other, some with small children pulling on their arms. I crossed the road to my car, sighing loudly when I saw the note fluttering in the soft breeze. Was it too much to ask that hate mail be banned on the Sabbath?

But when I opened the note, it said: "Hope it wasn't the company that made you sick. You'll get your sea legs yet. Doug."

As I drove back up the hill towards Lucille's, the sun shone on the water and I spotted a boat heading out of the bay, its wake trailing behind like a bride's veil. Then a cloud crossed over the sun and the sea turned dark, the wake becoming shroud-like. I remembered what Doug had said about life jackets, and shivered.

7

After a few weeks, I knew my schedule by heart, including the sad fact that every Monday morning I had grade nine French first period. It was not the best way to start the week, and no sooner had I reached the front of the classroom than Calvin Piercey bellowed, "Can I go to the bat'room?"

I slammed my books down on the desk. No sign of a *please*, in either official language. And the golden rule from day one had been that anyone who wanted to go to the bathroom had to ask in French, no exceptions. God knows we'd practised that sentence enough times that the entire class should have been able to waltz their way across France without fear of being caught short.

But Calvin had his own rules, one of which seemed to be, *I'm not saying nothing in French. You can't make me.*

I gritted my teeth. "En français, s'il vous plaît, Calvin."

His habitual scowl intensified. "Come on, miss, I'm bursting."

There was a buzzing in my ears and I fought the urge to run screaming from the classroom straight to Patrick's office and quit. It was too hard. I couldn't win against Calvin or any of this cohort. Dad was wrong. Sometimes a troublemaker was just a troublemaker.

I was about to tell Calvin to just go when I looked around the classroom. For once, all eyes were on me. Trudy was smirking, willing me to fail. But the expressions on other faces looked sympathetic or embarrassed on my behalf. Belinda, who seemed to enjoy French, nodded her head slightly, as if to say, *You got this, miss.*

I breathed out and counted backwards from three in my head.

"You're bursting?" I said, my voice a mix of honey and venom. "Oh dear, I hope you don't have an accident right here in the classroom." I repeated my command. "En français, s'il vous plaît."

Glowering, Calvin stood and mumbled something, eyes down. I had no clue what he said and he probably didn't either. He might have asked me to banish homework forever, or to sacrifice myself at dawn. Maybe he asked me to the prom. Whatever *bon mots* had dripped from his lips, from a distance, it sounded enough like French for me to smile, magnanimous as a queen, and grant his request.

After school, on my way to the staff room, I heard the steady thwack-thwack of a ball being dribbled in the gym. Making a detour, I stood on tiptoe and peeked through the window of the double doors. Doug was playing pickup basketball with a student. The boy was heading towards the basket, his left arm up to thwart Doug's attempted steal. Doug forced him back, and the boy turned and dribbled the other way.

The sequence was repeated again, amidst mutual laughter and jeering. Then Doug grabbed the ball away mid-bounce. He deked past his opponent, performed an impressive layup and scored. He raised his arms triumphantly in the air and whooped. I pushed one of the doors open slightly, my nostrils twitching at the blend of sweat and testosterone.

Doug began imitating a sports announcer: "That basket puts Bishop ahead by two points, folks. Time's running out. It's not looking good for Piercey. Can he make a comeback?"

Piercey? Did Calvin have a twin? That seemed the only plausible explanation, because I did not recognize this energetic, enthusiastic—dare I say joyful?—teenager.

Doug passed the ball to Calvin and began guarding him. Calvin dribbled the ball more slowly, as if biding his time. He worked his way around the court with an easy grace, then, with one quick dart, managed to get past Doug and score. He grabbed the ball as the net released it and bounced it hard on the ground. Then he flexed his biceps and pranced in a circle around Doug.

I went into the gym and clapped. When Calvin saw me, he dropped his arms and his smile vanished. Doug picked up the ball and began dribbling towards me. Then he grinned and threw it hard.

"Let's see what you got, Miss O'Brine."

My hands stung on contact, but I held on. Calvin threw himself onto a low bench along the wall, but from the corner of my eye, I could see him watching me.

Thankfully I was wearing flat shoes. I dribbled the ball towards the net. When I got close to Doug, he thrust his lanky arm in my direction, but I broke quickly to his left. I could hear his feet pounding after me, so I stopped short and took aim. As the ball sailed through the net, I heard the familiar swoosh and sent a silent thank-you to Dad for all the Sunday afternoons we'd spent in the backyard shooting hoops. I turned around and flicked my hair like a supermodel. Then I started humming the *Rocky* theme. Loudly.

Doug stood where I'd left him, scratching his jaw, but Calvin was on his feet, whooping.

"Good on ya, maid!" he yelled.

Maid didn't seem like the most appropriate form of address for a teacher, but I'd take praise from Calvin however it came. I picked the ball up from the floor, ready to challenge Calvin, but he called, "See yez," and jogged off towards the exit.

"I hope I didn't break up the party," I said, as the double doors swung back in on their hinges.

"Nah, his mudder will be after him if he doesn't get home. Geez, I'm thirsty. Wanna grab a beer?"

"Is that even possible in Little Cove?"

"Patrick keeps a stash in the staff room. We used to try to raid it when I was a student."

"Is it weird to be back here as a teacher?" I asked as we walked through the deserted hallway.

"Not really. It's been a few years and there's been some changeover."

In the staff room, I cleared a space at the table, while Doug squatted in front of a minifridge in the corner. "Holy frig, he's got black arse," I heard him say.

"Pardon me?"

"It's Patrick's brand." He slid a bottle of beer down the table and it stopped right in front of me. When I read the label—Black Horse—my confusion dissolved.

"Is it special?"

"It's a Newfoundland beer! Don't you know there's a beer strike on? All we've been able to get lately is American suds. Patrick must have stocked up ahead of time, the sleeveen."

I took a sip of the beer. It tasted like any other beer to me, but I kept my thoughts to myself.

"Why did you come back home to teach?" I asked Doug.

"After Dad died, I felt like Mudder needed me. But she

wouldn't let me give up my studies. So when the local job came up, I went for it."

I put my beer down. "I didn't know your father died," I whispered.

Doug shrugged. "It's not something you brings up all the time, I guess."

"No," I said. "You don't. My dad died in April. He was the one who taught me how to play basketball."

Doug moved his chair closer to mine. "Well, he taught you some good. Can I ask how he died?"

"Lung cancer," I said. "He couldn't seem to quit, even after . . ." I stopped talking and looked out the window for a bit. "What about your dad?"

"Drowned," said Doug, his voice clipped.

I thought about the boat that had raced past us the day Doug took me fishing. I wanted to know if his father had been wearing a life jacket. But I also knew how hurtful those kinds of questions could be. So instead, I crept my hand across the table and gripped Doug's, and we sat in silence drinking our beer.

8

Having won the battle of the bathroom with Calvin the day before, I set my sights on the rest of the recalcitrant grade nines. I met with Patrick before school to get some advice. He suggested I assign worksheets to anyone who was being disruptive. It went against every pedagogical method I'd been taught, but those ivory tower thinkers had clearly never had to wrestle with the likes of Trudy Johnson.

"Tell them the worksheets needs to be done in my office," said Patrick. "They'll soon learn."

I put in time at the ditto machine, running off worksheets on every topic known to French teachers: vocabulary, verb tenses, the negative. I inhaled the heady fumes, hoping it was the smell of another victory.

Later that day, brandishing a sheaf of worksheets in one hand and raising it above my head, I outlined my behaviour expectations going forward and the punishment that would be meted out were they not met. Minutes later, when I called on Trudy, she ignored me. I reiterated the new rules and told her that if she didn't answer, she would get a worksheet.

Trudy didn't respond when I posed the question a second time, so I dropped a worksheet on her desk.

"I'm not doing that," she said.

I put another worksheet on top of the first and she muttered something. We repeated our little ditto sheet dance a third time. Then I picked up the three worksheets from her desk and made a show of straightening them into a tidy pile.

"Oh," I said, smiling sweetly as I placed the pile on her desk. "I forgot to mention that the worksheets have to be completed in Mr. Donovan's office. He said he couldn't wait to see who'd be keeping him company first. I guess it's you, Trudy."

Trudy blanched. "Yes, miss," she said. "I mean, oui."

It was the first time I'd ever heard her say anything in French. Hopefully, it wouldn't be the last.

Little victories like these, some accomplished on my own, some with Patrick's guidance, helped me get through my first month at St. Jude's. I was also discovering that Patrick was a bit of a maverick. Instead of traditional parent-teacher meetings, St. Jude's held an informal session on the last Friday of every month.

"I lures 'em in here with tea and cake," Patrick explained, rubbing his hands together like some kind of evil magician. "But then, once they're here, bam, we talks to them about their youngsters." Judy told me that parents tended to gravitate towards the teachers of core subjects like math and science, but that attendance at the monthly meetings was mandatory for all teachers.

I stood alone in the cafeteria on that first Friday-night session while parents and some students mingled with Doug, Judy,

Patrick and even Sister Mary Catherine. The edge of my name tag began to curl away from my top, as if it, too, wanted nothing to do with me. As I patted it back down, I found myself wondering why I was even wearing a name tag when everyone within a fifty-mile radius seemed to know who I was, even if they couldn't pronounce my surname properly.

I bristled when angry Roy Sullivan from the gas station arrived, but he made a beeline for Doug, and within seconds they were deep in animated conversation. I mentally reviewed my class lists. Sam Sullivan was a sweet, shy boy in my grade ten class. Could this be his father? Surely not. Then I saw Calvin on the other side of the room, stooped over, listening intently to a middle-aged woman. At one point he looked over at me, then quickly away again. But the woman's eyes had followed his, and after a minute, mother and son crossed the room.

"Miss," said Calvin. "Me mudder wants a word."

She launched straight in. "Tell me now, is he behaving in class?"

Calvin kept his gaze down, a scuffed brown shoe digging into the floor. I looked at his mother's neat skirt, sturdy shoes, and faded but impeccably ironed blouse. Her hopeful look was the decider.

"Calvin is trying," I said. *Very trying*, I didn't add.

He looked up, puzzled, and mouthed, "T'anks."

"Calvin, you go on, now," his mother said. "I've got more to say that you don't need to hear."

We watched him lope off, then Mrs. Piercey said, "Calvin is the last of my youngsters at the school. Now, tell me, Miss O'Brine, will it be third time lucky this year?"

I said I didn't understand.

"It's Calvin's third year in grade nine. French is one of the subjects that holds him back."

"How old is Calvin?"

"Seventeen."

How did she get him to stay in school when I couldn't even get him to say bonjour? Mrs. Piercey was obviously a persuasive woman.

"Mr. Donovan wanted to put him up to grade ten this year, but I said he's got to get there on his own steam."

It felt to me like Calvin had run out of steam a long time ago.

"Mrs. Piercey," I said, struggling to find the right words. "Do you think it's in Calvin's best interest to stay at school? He doesn't seem very happy here."

"Happy?" She frowned. "My dear, happy don't get you a job. Calvin's staying here 'til he gets his piece of paper and that's all." She gripped my arm tight. "There's a young fella up our road who quit school and you know what he's at every day?"

I shook my head.

"He's hauling wood. I wants better than that for Calvin."

I admired her determination, but for the first time, I felt sorry for Calvin. A high school certificate seemed beyond his grasp, and I couldn't think of a single job for which he'd be qualified. But I told her that I'd do what I could to help. She said goodbye and went to join Calvin on the other side of the room. He smiled down at her, took her arm and escorted her out of the room, like a true gentleman.

Then Cynthia pitched up, tugging along the woman I'd met at the gas station. In flawless French, she introduced us to each other and we two adults beamed at her.

"I got no clue what's she saying," Mrs. O'Leary said, laughing. "But all the teachers says she's doing some good at school. That scholarship's looking like a real possibility, so we're going out to celebrate." She put her arm around Cynthia, and my heart hurt as I thought about Mom in Australia. A year without her suddenly seemed really long. I decided to tell her about Cynthia and Mrs. O'Leary when she next called.

"We're going to Tony's in Clayville, miss." Cynthia's face was alight. "They does the best pizza."

"Do," I said.

"Wha?"

"They *do* the best pizza."

"Yes, miss, that's what I said."

There were several bright pupils in the senior French class, but Cynthia was the shining star. Her accent was good, her grammar stellar. But like many of the students, her English was another story. What had she said? *They does the best pizza.*

I said goodbye and wished them bon appétit, but my mind was already on a new extracurricular activity. When the last parent had left, I went looking for Doug and found him at his desk, eating an apple.

"How's she cutting?" he said.

"Like the knife."

He grinned. "You're learning." Then he flicked his apple core into the garbage can, pushed aside his planner and began stacking notebooks on his desk, ready to leave.

"Can I run something by you?" I asked.

"Shoot."

"I was thinking of starting a remedial English club. You know, so the kids make less mistakes when they talk. And, I guess, when they write too."

"Fewer," said Doug.

"Pardon?"

"You just said so the kids make less mistakes. But it's fewer. So the kids make *fewer* mistakes. I guess you made a mistake there too."

"Oops, ha ha, you're right."

"Ha ha?" Doug put down his notebooks, now giving me his full attention. "Have you mentioned this idea to Patrick?"

"Not yet, but do you think he'll go for it?"

"Oh yeah, it's a real beaut." There was an edge to Doug's voice that I hadn't heard before. He stood up and roughly pushed his chair in. The legs squeaked in protest.

"I thought you were okay, Rachel. I thought you got it."

"What do you mean?" I asked. "Got what?"

He opened his mouth, then closed it, as if afraid of what he might say.

"Doug, what is it?"

He put up a hand as if to push away my questions. And me. Then he spoke with slow, controlled calm.

"I sees who you are now. Little Miss Mainlander wants to help us poor dumb Newfoundlanders talk nice, is that it?"

Prickles of heat burst on my neck and chest. "Doug," I began. "I'm not sure what . . ."

But he talked right over me. "Bet you didn't know our linguistic history has roots in Irish and Scottish Gaelic, did you? Or that our dialect has been the subject of academic papers by eminent folklorists? Or that—"

"Doug, please." I covered my face and he stopped talking.

Silence fell like a heavy weight between us. After a minute, I peeked out from between my hands. Doug was leaning against the blackboard, arms folded, looking down at the floor. I lowered my hands and he looked up. Our eyes met and he crooked his finger at me.

"Come with me."

Heart thudding, I followed him down the hall, walking quickly, trying to match his stride. But by the time I reached the library door, he was already inside, over at the reference shelf. He pulled out two books and put them on a study table.

"Sit," he said.

I sat.

"Read," he said.

And before I could say anything else, Doug left the library without saying goodbye.

I picked up a heavy yellow hardback book—*Dictionary of Newfoundland English*—surprised to find they had their own dictionary. I flipped through the pages, randomly reading entries. The discourse on *arse* went on for two columns, and the entry for *seal*, and related words and expressions, lasted more than seven pages. A *bazz* was a blow or a slap. To *blear* was to utter prolonged complaints. Blearing. Is that what I'd been doing about Little Cove and its people?

On and on I read, marvelling at the strange and wonderful words. Eventually I took the books to the deserted staff room and made a cup of tea, amazed to see it was after seven o'clock. It didn't matter, Lucille was out. I could have read that dictionary cover to cover, but after a while, I set it aside.

The other book was a faded folder, labelled a dissertation for a master of arts degree from Memorial University of Newfoundland. I flicked idly through it. A footnote explained that the impetus for the thesis had been a summer spent in Toronto, where the author's dialect had been relentlessly mocked. The rationale read in part: "I determined that a substantive study of the history of the Newfoundland dialect would demonstrate that the manner in which we speak is neither wrong nor ignorant, but the result of our distinctive history, culture and geography. It is a cause for celebration, not derision."

The dissertation was a thoughtful analysis of Newfoundland's distinct dialect. It was well written and persuasive; the author's pride in the local culture gleamed through every word. I flipped back to the cover page to see who had written it. The author was Patrick Donovan.

Shame roiled in my gut as I imagined Patrick's reaction had I proposed a remedial English club to him. Slowly, like fog lifting from the bay, I made the connection that had eluded me until now. My snooty aversion to the local parlance and my lack of appreciation for their distinct dialect was no different than the attitude of many French-speaking purists towards the Québécois. I was no better than the French tourists who had complained to me about the Québécois accent the summer I worked in a bar in Quebec City. "Ça vient du nez," a Parisian man had said, dismissively. "It comes from the nose."

At the time, I had no riposte. But I did now. And it applied equally to the accent and vocabulary of Newfoundland. "Non. Ça vient du coeur. It comes from the heart."

9

Over the weekend I tried to find the right words to apologize to Doug, but when I saw him pull into the parking lot ahead of me on Monday morning, I still wasn't sure. I decided I would have to wing it. But by the time I got out of my car, he was already at the school door.

"Morning, Doug," I called, racing over and grabbing his arm. "Listen, I read Patrick's paper and—"

He brushed my hand off his sleeve. "I'm late for a meeting with Patrick, actually."

He walked down the hall, then turned the corner heading in the opposite direction to Patrick's office. Obviously, he was still mad at me. I would have to figure out a way to fix things.

For a school as small as St. Jude's, there were plenty of places to hide. And Doug sure knew all of them. I barely saw him all week, and when I did, he always seemed to be either deep in conversation with someone or rushing off somewhere. He left the school for lunch every day too. Then on Friday, Patrick called a brief staff meeting over lunch. I put my purse on the seat next to mine to save it for Doug, but he didn't sit, just lounged against the wall eating a sandwich.

That afternoon, after the final bell had rung, I headed to Doug's classroom as soon as I could, but it was already deserted. There wasn't much on display apart from a poster of the human anatomy on the bulletin board near his desk. A biology assignment was written on the blackboard in big, bold strokes.

I looked up and down the hall and saw no one, so I went over to Doug's desk. It was exceptionally tidy, the planner already turned to Monday's date with brief lesson plans neatly jotted down for each period. Doug would have the weekend off, while I would still be planning my lessons.

In my car, heading back to Lucille's, I fiddled with the radio trying to get some kind of reception. Culture Club's "Do You Really Want to Hurt Me" crackled in briefly, and I turned it off so roughly the knob came off in my hand. The hell with Doug. Had he never made a mistake? Judge not lest ye be judged. Let he who is without sin cast the first stone. I might not be big on religion, but I could quote chapter and verse with the best of them.

I flung open the door at Lucille's and stomped in, almost knocking her over.

"My God, girl," she said. "You looks some crooked. What's after happening?"

Crooked? I looked at myself in the hall mirror, rebalancing my shoulders.

"Bad day?" she asked.

I grunted something, then sulked past her up to my room, flopping onto the bed. After a few minutes I heard Lucille in the living room, talking on the phone, no doubt alerting the local authorities to my mood.

Much later, when the room had grown dark, there was a soft knock at the door and Lucille stuck her head in to tell me she was going out.

I wasn't sure I could face another Friday evening on my own. I sat up abruptly, causing the bed to bounce and shake.

"Where do you go on Friday evenings, Lucille?"

"Hooking," she said.

She's a hooker? No. I tried to figure out what she could possibly mean.

"Want to come?" she asked. "Might do you good to get out."

"Lucille, when you say hooking . . ."

"Rugs," she said. "We hooks rugs. What did you think?"

I thought it best not to answer. "Like this one?" I tapped a foot on the cozy rug beside the bed.

"Yis. And we makes quilts like the one you're sitting on."

"Who's we?" I asked.

"The Holy Dusters."

"Is that a euphemism?"

Lucille laughed. "We cleans the church together," she said. "I don't know where the name came from, but I've been a Holy Duster these twenty years."

"They don't have staff to do that?"

"The Church provides for us. It's only right we does our bit for her."

I agreed to come along and we set off into the dark evening. Lucille steamed ahead while I dawdled, admiring the abundant stars, shining like sequins on a black velvet cape.

Finally, Lucille shouted back up the road at me. "Come on, if you're coming."

I walked quickly to catch up. "Sorry," I said, whispering for some reason. "We don't have stars like that in Toronto."

"Stars is stars, sure," she said.

But as I crept along, head back and eyes skyward, I couldn't agree with Lucille. These stars were like the ones at our summer cottage. These stars were magical.

We stopped outside a small orange house surrounded by a white picket fence.

"No sulking in here, now," Lucille said. "These women are my dearest friends, more like sisters, they are."

I stiffened at her words. Lucille was telling me off. But I had to admit, I kind of deserved it.

When we reached the side door, Lucille didn't knock but went straight in, after giving the door a hard shove. I followed her into the kitchen, where three women were surrounded by strips of colourful wool and fabric. Each of them held a wooden frame on her lap.

"Now me duckies," said Lucille. "I hope ye all brought your patience because I brought Rachel."

"We're some glad you did," said the woman nearest the door. She had a large purple birthmark, like Gorbachev's, covering one side of her face, but what stood out for me was her welcoming smile. "Hello, Rachel," she said. "I'm Biddy Cormack and this is my house. Lucille and I went to school together. Don't pay her no mind."

Lucille took off her coat and hung it on a hook. I followed suit. Biddy introduced the other women, Flossie and Annie, who were obviously sisters.

"Right then, Rachel," said Biddy. "Do you want to start in on your own piece or just watch us and have a natter?"

I said I would watch and sat down beside Lucille on the day-bed. "How do you do it?" I asked.

"You fits a piece of burlap sack between the top and bottom, see?" She touched the material trapped between the two sides of the frame. The bottom third of the burlap was covered in various shades of blue with scattered grey flecks. Sketched crudely above and waiting to be filled in was a fisherman, standing in a dory with his back to us.

"Watch now," said Lucille. "I takes the hook"—she held up a small metal hook with a wooden handle—"and I holds it like a pencil, luh, or how you might hold a bit of chalk. Then I puts the length of wool in my other hand underneath." She became bossier then. "Coopy down underneath now, Rachel girl, and take a peek."

I knelt on the floor and tilted my head to look up under the frame. The tiny holes in the burlap shone in the light. When the tip of the hook broke through, Lucille said, "I dips down with the hook, see? And I pulls the wool through." Lucille was a fantastic cook, and now I could see she was also an excellent teacher and craftswoman.

I sat back down beside her. She held the wool in her left hand and fed it smoothly through her callused fingers. The tip bobbed in and out of the burlap, bringing a wool loop through each time. When she reached the end of the strip of wool, she put a fresh one under the frame and started again. Lucille worked quickly and methodically, the hook moving across the burlap in neat, even rows.

"I guess that's the sea?" I pointed at the bottom of the canvas.

"Yis." The back of her hook traced the outline of the fisherman. "And that's my John in his dory."

"God rest his soul," the other women said in unison.

"It's for Linda," Lucille said. "For Christmas."

"She loved her dad," said Biddy.

I knew what that was like. I sat slowly back on the daybed.

"Ah, he was a good man," Lucille said. She stopped hooking and twisted her wedding ring. "He used to plait Linda's hair every morning before school, remember?"

The other women nodded. Then Biddy said, "He used to say he was practising his knots, but sure we all knew he did it for Linda. She always had the most complicated concoctions in her hair."

Lucille sighed. "She made me cut it all off after he died."

"He was taken too soon," Biddy said.

"What happened?" I whispered so low I wasn't sure anyone would hear.

"He went out fishing one day and never came home," said Lucille, her voice matter of fact. "Like his father and his brother."

"Like too many," said Biddy.

"Like Doug's father," I said.

The four women exchanged glances at this, and I thought I saw Lucille shake her head a little.

"My dad died this year," I said, surprising myself with this disclosure.

"My dear," said Lucille, putting down her handiwork and putting an arm around me. "I can't believe you never said. I thought he was in Australia with your mother."

I stayed quiet, conscious that tears were forming in my eyes.

"Tell me something about your dad, now," Lucille said, patting my shoulder. "Grief is best shared. Like laughter and music, I s'pose."

"He was a teacher," I said.

"Well, isn't it grand that you're a teacher too?" said Biddy. "My dear, he's looking down at you and he's some proud."

It felt good to have talked about Dad, however briefly, with these women. After a minute, Lucille picked up her hooking again. Biddy caught my eye and nodded at me as if to say, *You're safe here.* I pushed myself off the daybed to go inspect her handi-work and the other women's.

Flossie and Annie sat side by side, their hooks moving in time. Flossie was working on a small house with the ever-present sea behind it. Annie's rug was much more detailed: a woman in a red dress and a white apron stood in a grassy yard, pegging sheets to a clothesline. Flossie and Annie hooked like Lucille, row by row. Biddy hooked freestyle. Her design featured a woman kneeling in a wooded area, picking blueberries. I marvelled as her hook roamed the surface of the burlap.

When I remarked on her style, she said, "Ah sure, as long as you fills it in, it don't matter how. I likes to meander."

As the women hooked, the scenes unfolded rapidly. It amazed me that they were creating such vivid works of art from bits of burlap, recycled wool and cast-off garments. But they brushed aside my words of praise.

"Ah, go on with you," said Lucille. "It's only a bit to rest your toes on."

"You knows yourself," said Flossie.

"Sure anyone could make these," added Biddy.

"Well, I couldn't," I said. "They'd make great Christmas presents."

"I've yaffles of them upstairs," said Biddy. "You can have any you want, sure." She put aside her frame. "Come on up and take a gander."

"Smoke break, then," said Lucille. I startled, but then I remem-bered I hadn't said *how* Dad had died. Lucille lit cigarettes for Annie and Flossie, then for herself, inhaling, then exhaling with a contented sigh.

I was glad to follow Biddy upstairs. "You don't smoke?" she asked.

"No. Do you?"

"No. That's what killed me brother. Lung cancer."

I grabbed the bannister. "My father too."

Biddy stopped climbing. "It's a terrible way to go," she said. "I'm sorry for your loss."

After a minute we started climbing again.

"You don't mind them smoking here?" I asked, gesturing down the stairs.

"Ah sure, they've few enough pleasures," said Biddy. "Widows, the lot of them."

"Not you?" I asked, figuring when in Rome.

She was waiting at the top of the stairs now and touched the bloom on her cheek. "I got a face only a mother could love," she said. But I loved it already.

An old iron bed dominated the small bedroom to the right of the stairs. A faded pink-chenille bedspread was laden with hooked rugs. I ran my hands over them, exclaiming at the fish, birds, dories and rural scenes.

"They're gorgeous," I said. "I couldn't possibly choose."

"Think on it," she said. "Come back next Friday if you've no plans."

If? I nearly said.

On the way back down the stairs, I was ahead of Biddy, and she patted my back softly. "You come back to us any evening you likes," she said.

Once we were back downstairs, Biddy asked the other women, "How're ye all getting on? Is it time for a drop?"

When they concurred, Biddy took a bottle of sherry down from the cupboard and laid it on a tray of glasses, which tinkled as she slid it along the table. Lucille sloshed sherry into her glass and returned to the daybed. Flossie poured slowly, alternating between two glasses, stopping to ensure her careful measures were equal, before giving one to Annie. Biddy handed me the bottle. "You do the honours, my dear." I poured a serving somewhere between modest and generous.

I sipped the sherry, trying not to shudder visibly at its sweetness. By my second glass, the shudders were gone.

"Tell us now," said Biddy, "how are you making out over to the school?"

Leery of possible relations or other connections the women might have with the school community, I spoke generally. I said it was good to put into practice the theories I'd learned at teachers' college. I didn't mention my difficulties or the loneliness I felt, especially now that Doug seemed to hate me. I bypassed the frustration of teaching someone like Calvin and the thrill I felt when Cynthia spoke French so beautifully.

During a subsequent lull in the conversation, it occurred to me that Cynthia and Calvin were the yin and yang of my teaching. Calvin loathed French, me and school, while Cynthia loved all three. Calvin's future was uncertain, Cynthia's looked golden.

I was jolted back to the conversation when Flossie said she'd heard that Brigid Roche had been seen in St. John's and asked what would happen if she came back to Little Cove.

"I wouldn't be surprised if she landed back here with the Irish toothache," said Annie, brandishing her glass for a refill.

Biddy tutted. "Annie, you're shocking, you are. Don't mind her, Rachel."

Lucille said, "Rachel, when you're done pouring for Annie, pass 'e over."

I topped up Annie's glass, then Lucille's, but Flossie and Biddy both demurred.

"What's an Irish toothache?" I asked, filling my own glass.

Lucille breathed out a stream of smoke as she answered. "Bun in the oven." She drew an exaggerated pregnant belly in the air.

"But what if Brigid do come back?" Flossie persisted. "What'll happen to Rachel?"

Lucille stubbed out her cigarette and reached for her hooking. "Rachel's got a one-year contract with the Board," she answered on my behalf. "If Brigid comes back, I allows she'll have to wait 'til Rachel's year is up."

"Speaking of bun in the oven," said Annie. "Georgie's is starting to rise."

"It's such a sin for Georgie," said Lucille.

Anger flashed in me as I wondered if I'd misjudged these women who had seemed so kind. But then Biddy said, "Yis, maid. She has to drop out and Charlie gets to stay on. It's a proper sin."

"'Twas ever thus," said Annie.

"And ever shall be," Flossie replied.

"But it shouldn't be," I said, mostly to myself.

10

The women went back to their hooking and chatting. I was knocked flat on the daybed wondering what proof the sherry was. My mother sometimes reminisced about her single days when she used to sip sherry on the front porch with her own mother. I had a whole new respect for their livers. That made me wonder what time it was in Australia and what my mom was doing right then.

Isn't it odd, I realized. Mom and I are alone, far from home, and separated from each other in our grief. Lucille was right—grief was best shared. I hoped my mother had found someone in whom to confide over in Australia. I made a mental note to ask her when she next called me. If we were going to repair our relationship, at some point we'd have to speak about the tough stuff.

A faint knocking had been going on for a while in the background, but as none of the women reacted, I decided it must be a branch tapping on a window. Then it became more of a banging.

"Who in God's name is at the door?" said Lucille.

"No one knocks with good news," Flossie said. "Must be some bad, else they'd be in here by now."

They were still debating the best course of action when the door finally opened, sending gusts of wind into the kitchen.

"Geraldine!" cried Biddy, rising nimbly from the rocking chair to embrace the blonde in the doorway. "My dear, you're too long in St. John's picking up them fancy ways. Imagine knocking at your own aunt's door."

Biddy's niece was beautiful. There was no other word for her. Her hair was impossibly straight, her complexion flawless, her smile wide.

"You needs to get that door fixed, Biddy," said Geraldine. "It was stuck."

"I'll have a word with Phonse, by and by," said Biddy. "Now come in out of it 'til we gets a look at you."

I fought my way up from the depths of the daybed, waiting to be introduced. The women clustered around Geraldine, exclaiming over every part of her.

"Loves your coat," said Annie. "Some style on ya, girl."

"How's the hospital?" Lucille asked. "You running it yet?"

There was laughter and more questions.

Then Geraldine fetched a chair from the hall and sat down beside her aunt.

"I'll not stop long," she said. "Mam will be waiting."

"My little sister can wait," said Biddy. "She's into town to see you all the time. I haven't set sight on you in weeks."

I stood up and put a steadying hand on the wall. "I should go."

Biddy clucked. "Here's me forgetting my manners. This," she

said, putting a hand to Geraldine's cheek, "is my lovely niece Geraldine who's a nurse in St. John's."

"Call me Geri," she said. "Please. It might convince Biddy." She smiled and patted her aunt's hand. "I've only been asking her for six months. You must be Rachel. Doug's told me about you."

"He has?"

"Well, sure. He's some glad to have another new teacher, so it's not just him that's a rookie, right?"

"Is Doug your . . . ?"

"He's her boyfriend," said Biddy.

Geri grimaced briefly and seemed about to say something, then stopped herself. But maybe I was wrong; my head was spinning from the sherry. "I'll see you at home, Lucille," I said, then waved goodbye to everyone and lurched towards the door.

As I staggered up the road to Lucille's, a cloud crossed over the moon, rendering the night darker and my progress slower. I fumbled with the gate latch, then made for the house. Once inside, I didn't bother turning on the hall light, but felt my way along the wall to the living room. I flung myself on the nearest couch, doilies scattering like snowflakes. I grabbed the phone, my finger shaking as I turned the dial. When Sheila answered, I shouted down the line at her.

"He's got a girlfriend."

"Who? Jake?"

"No!" I said. "Doug."

"Who's Doug?"

"He's a teacher here."

"The one that took you fishing?"

"Yes. But he's mad at me now, because of the English club. And he's got a girlfriend called Gerald."

Sheila said nothing.

"And she seems really nice, too," I added.

"Who?"

"Gerald! Keep up, Sheila."

There was a long silence and then Sheila said, "Rachel, have you been drinking?"

"Just some sherry with the hookers," I sniffed.

"What hookers? Rachel, you're making no sense."

I closed my eyes, my grip on the receiver loosening, my thoughts drifting. Sheila waited for further details that never came. After a minute, she jumped in.

"Okay, so Doug has a girlfriend. Do you like him?"

"Not exactly."

"Then why does it matter? And what's this about an English club? I thought you were teaching French?"

I told her about my gaffe.

"Oh boy, you do like to stick your foot in it from time to time."

"I know."

"How bad is it?" she asked.

"I don't think he'll tell anyone," I said. "But he's mad at me. My head hurts. I'm going to bed now."

"Okay," Sheila said. "But listen, cut yourself some slack. You've been through so much—your dad, Jake, the move down there and all the other stuff."

I listened to Sheila make excuses on my behalf for a while longer before saying goodbye.

I staggered up the stairs and onto my bed, fully clothed, wrapping Lucille's quilt around me. I replayed all the conversations I'd had with Doug since my arrival in Little Cove, the sherry helping me skip lightly over the remedial English incident. Why hadn't Doug or anyone else mentioned Geri? Then I remembered Lucille saying Geri wouldn't go fishing with Doug, but I'd heard it as Gerry.

What had perfect Geri said tonight? Doug was glad to have another rookie teacher so he wasn't alone. I was a teammate, or had been, until Doug put me in the penalty box. Now I had to find a way to apologize. So far, Doug seemed to be my best bet for a local friend. I didn't want to lose that over my own stupidity.

My thoughts turned to Jake. Hearing Sheila say his name had brought back the awful scene on the night of my graduation party. Mom had insisted on throwing a party to mark my graduation from university even though neither of us felt like celebrating so soon after Dad's death.

"Your dad would've wanted you to celebrate your achievements," she'd said. And in the end, I'd agreed.

The party had started so well. It was a warm evening in late May, with a slight breeze that rattled the patio lanterns in time to the music. Clusters of friends and family chatted and sipped champagne. My cousin Pete was tending the makeshift bar and Uncle Scott was at the barbecue ready to grill. Jake and Sheila were standing by the pool chatting, and I remember thinking how lucky I was to have those two people in my life: my best friend since kindergarten and the kindest, most thoughtful guy I'd ever met. They had both propped me and my mother up in the sad days following my father's diagnosis, and all the way through his deterioration and death.

When I checked in with Pete at the bar, he held up an empty champagne bottle and I said I'd get some reinforcements. As I opened the fridge in the kitchen, I heard my mom talking to someone at the front door. Well, my mom was talking, the other person was shouting.

"I'm sorry," Mom said, "you seem quite upset, but I don't know you, so I'd like you to wait here while I get Rachel."

Champagne bottle in hand, I reached the hall, but by then the girl was pushing past Mom. She fixed her wild eyes on me and I stepped back against the wall. Then, following the noise of the party, she ran towards the patio doors, screaming Jake's name. Mom took the champagne from me and we quickly followed her outside. We found her on the deck, scanning the crowd. There was a patch of damp on her red tank top and a large birthmark on her left shoulder. I reached out and tapped it.

"Hey," I said.

But then she spotted Jake and bolted. He had his back to us, but Sheila didn't. As the girl got closer to Jake, Sheila's smile shrank away.

"You fucking bastard," the girl screamed. "You said you were breaking up with her."

Jake turned around, lips screwed up. He looked from her to me, and I knew this girl was not lying. People were pointing and whispering behind their hands to each other. Then the stranger shoved Sheila hard, sending her into the swimming pool.

There was a collective intake of breath, and then Jake screamed, "That's not even her!" As if that changed anything. The song "I Want to Know What Love Is" was playing in the background, and I remember thinking, I thought I knew.

Jake and my cousin Pete escorted the girl out of the backyard. I averted my eyes as they walked past. Sheila emerged, dripping, from the pool, and my mom handed her a towel.

"Are you okay?" I asked.

"You know I always like to make a big splash," she said.

I just about managed a smile before I started shaking. My mom put her arm around me. One by one my friends approached, murmuring platitudes and saying goodbyes, despite my mom's pleas that they should at least eat something.

Sheila went up to my room to borrow some dry clothes. Then the few of us who remained—Mom, Sheila, Uncle Scott and

Pete—collected bottles and glasses. Uncle Scott insisted we eat some of the food he'd barbecued. We sat down to eat, but I kept getting up for things from the kitchen: more napkins, a jug of water, ketchup. When I came back from yet another trip, Sheila pulled me into the seat beside her and rubbed my back. We were picking at our food when Jake walked around the side of the house.

"He's got some nerve," Sheila said.

"Someone make him leave, please," I said.

Uncle Scott stood up and walked towards Jake. He kept coming, palms raised, as if approaching a wild beast. "Rachel, please let me explain."

"Unless you can tell me that girl was delusional and there's nothing between you, I never want to see you again," I shouted.

Pete went over to join Uncle Scott and Jake. Shortly, the three of them left the backyard. I said I was tired and was going to bed, but once I got upstairs, I stood under a hot shower crying until the water ran as cold as my heart. Now, I fell asleep, wondering if Jake and that girl were still together. Not that I cared.

11

A folded note lying on my desk first thing in the morning gave me pause. Did my tormentor have access to the school? But when I opened it up, it was Patrick's scrawl asking me to meet him during the morning break to discuss my first probationary review. If I wasn't so nervous, I might've smiled at the terminology. Probationary, like I'd already screwed up.

When I arrived at Patrick's office, Doug was already sitting in a chair. I took the other one and said hi. While Patrick talked, Doug stared straight ahead, while I risked a few sideways glances. Doug seemed to be transfixed by Patrick's frankly boring remarks. I tried to imagine him with Geri.

"So that date's good, Rachel?" I half heard Patrick say.

I flushed. "Sorry, can you repeat that?"

Patrick repeated a date a few weeks hence and said that Judy would also be conducting class visits to see how Doug and I were getting on.

When we left Patrick's office, I wanted to ask Doug how he planned to prepare for his first review. But he headed straight for the men's bathroom, no doubt to escape me. It wasn't the best place for me to loiter outside. It seemed I'd be preparing on my own.

That evening, I mentioned my upcoming probationary review to Mom during our weekly call.

"Are you nervous?" she asked.

I am now, I thought.

"You'll be great. Remember to engage the students. Don't try to cover too much and don't repeat the content of the reading materials."

"Mom, it's high school French."

She wasn't listening. "Oh, and ask the students for feedback at the end of the lecture."

It was predictable from Mom. All good advice, but none of it was applicable to my situation. I was teaching high school, not university students. And no way would I be asking the likes of Calvin Piercey for feedback. I wished I could speak with Dad, but I already knew what he would have said: "Be prepared, but have fun with it."

I decided it wouldn't hurt to prepare extra worksheets and lesson plans in advance of any reviews. So after breakfast on Saturday, I told Lucille I was going into school to do some work.

"My dear," she said. "You needs time off on the weekend. You looks right frazzled. I've half a mind to phone Pat Donovan and tell him he's working you too hard."

I knew her heart was in the right place, but sometimes Lucille's fussing went too far.

There were no cars in the school parking lot, but as soon as I opened the front door, I heard Phonse playing. I dumped my bag in the classroom and went to the janitor's room to listen. Phonse was wearing a plaid shirt and denim overalls. This seemed to be his weekend attire. He smiled but carried on playing, the bow flying back and forth over the strings while the fingers of his left hand moved up and down the fingerboard. His left foot tapped along with the beat; he was almost dancing. Then he ended the piece with a flourish and, bow still in hand, wiped the sweat from his forehead.

"That was so much fun to listen to!"

"Plenty more reels where that one comes from. They gets you hopping, me fadder always said."

"Could you teach it to me?"

"I can try." Phonse took another fiddle from a cupboard and handed it to me, then repositioned his own, the wood gleaming like a brooch against his shirt.

I assumed the position so familiar to me after years of violin practice. Phonse tutted.

"No. Not like that, girl," he said. "See how it's resting on my shoulder? It's got to be loose, but at the same time like a part of you."

I mimicked him, aiming for a looser hold. Phonse played a few bars slowly, his movements exaggerated for my benefit. I watched carefully. Then he pointed his bow at me. "Have at 'er, girl."

I drew the bow slowly across the strings, copying Phonse. We repeated the sequence a few times, working through the song. Once I'd mastered a line, we would repeat it. Phonse would play, then I would mimic. Line after line. His playing sounded fluid, soft and floaty. Mine sounded staccato, laboured and stodgy.

"I'll never crack it," I said.

"You got the talent, all right," he said. "But you're stiff as a plank, maid. Loosen up."

Even as he spoke, I could feel my shoulders hunch forward and my right arm tighten. I wriggled my shoulders, then started over from the beginning. Phonse set aside his fiddle and sat with his head down, listening to me. I was glad I couldn't see his face.

"Better," he said when I'd finished. "Give 'er one more go, now."

I closed my eyes and concentrated, swaying to the music. Was it a bit better? Maybe. When I got to the end of the piece, there was a long whistle of appreciation and I flushed, happy to have pleased Phonse. But when I opened my eyes, it was Doug leaning in the doorway, staring at me.

I thrust the fiddle at Phonse. "That's enough for today."

"That was grand," he said. "It's brought the colour to your cheeks, too. Sign of a good player."

He gave me back the fiddle. "Hang on to that one, sure. I got a few spare."

"Now then, sir," he said to Doug. "Will we be seeing you tonight?"

"You might," said Doug.

"What's happening tonight?" I asked. The last few Saturday nights, I'd been in bed before ten. Something had to give.

"Phonse and the b'ys are playing in the pub," Doug said. It was the first time he'd spoken to me in what felt like forever.

Phonse said he had a regular gig in the pub "with a few fellas."

"Wait, there's a pub in Little Cove?"

"Mardy, next town over."

"You should come see us," said Phonse. "The b'ys are right good. I does me best to keep up."

Doug was having none of that. "Go on, Phonse. You carries them." Then he said to me, "Think you'll go?"

"Yes, b'y," I said, pleased to see a brief smile in return.

"Might see you there," said Doug.

After he left, I asked Phonse for more details. Then I said, "If I'm going out tonight, I better crack on with my work."

"Got to keep on top of it," he agreed.

"Well, some of it seems pointless," I said. "I mean, when you're dealing with students like Calvin Piercey . . ." I threw my hands up in the air dramatically, waiting for Phonse to sympathize.

Instead he frowned. "There's more to Calvin than maybe meets the eye, Rachel. He has other gifts."

Heat rose from my chest and I blushed. I wasn't used to disappointing Phonse.

"Maybe you're right," I said. "See you later." I walked down to my classroom thinking maybe there was more to Phonse than I'd thought.

I worked extra hard on my lesson plans for the next few weeks, then headed back to Lucille's and offered to take her on a night out to the pub in Mardy. She looked up from her crossword.

"To hear the b'ys?"

I nodded. "Phonse asked me to go."

"I don't know, girl." She stretched her legs out and wriggled her fluffy slippers. "I'm right cozy now. And I'd have to do me hair."

"You have to do it anyway for Mass tomorrow," I said.

But she was back to her crossword. "Three across, four letters, place of torment and punishment."

"Mass," I said.

Lucille looked up, her mouth agape.

"Ha ha, no, that was a joke, Lucille. Hell, the answer is hell."

"That's where you'll end up if you keeps up that sauce," she said.

I brought her back to the matter at hand. I didn't want to go on my own, and while Lucille wasn't my ideal drinking partner, she did have local knowledge. "You'd actually be ahead of the game if you did your hair tonight, Lucille. And we won't stay late, I promise."

"That's what they always says. One set, then."

We retired to our respective bedrooms to get ready, then met at the front door and gave each other the once-over. Lucille had removed her curlers and sprayed her hair silly, while I'd re-straightened mine. Each seemed satisfied with the other's efforts.

It didn't take long to drive to Mardy, but I was glad of Lucille's directions, especially as she warned me about various potholes.

"Hard left now, missus," she said at one point, going so far as to grab the steering wheel. "They calls that one 'the killer.' No tire has ever been known to survive contact."

It felt like years since I'd been in a bar. A rush of heat, smoke and loud music swirled around us like a storm when we went in. Lucille walked ahead of me, waving at people like a visiting dignitary. Which maybe she was. I stopped to watch Phonse up on stage, eyes squeezed shut, fingers flying. Beside him were two more fiddlers, and to the left of the stage, a huge man with a long beard squeezed an accordion.

Then Lucille waved at me from the other side of the room, indicating she'd nabbed a table. I joined her and she took her cigarettes out of her purse, pulled the ashtray close and sent me off for drinks. Doug and Geri were side by side at the bar, but Doug's stool was facing the stage; Geri had her back to the musicians. Doug's right knee jiggled in time to the music, but he raised his beer bottle in greeting. Geri was chatting to the bartender. I sidled up beside her to place my order.

"Hiya, Rachel," she said. "We never got to talk much over to Biddy's." She gestured dismissively at the stage. "What do you think of that racket?"

"I love it."

She arched an eyebrow. "I hates it almost as much as fishing. Wham!, Madonna, Simple Minds. That's my music. I wish I'd stayed in town this weekend but Mam wanted me to come home."

The bartender came back with my drinks so I said goodbye to Doug and Geri and walked back to the table, where I handed Lucille a rum and cola. I sipped my American beer while admiring a couple waltzing nimbly around the dance floor. Over in the corner, an older man danced by himself. His arms were rigid at his side, but his feet moved so quickly they were blurred. "That's Ambrose," said Lucille. "He's shy as a bat, but he's got some moves on him."

Around us, people sat at tables and listened to the band. Many of them joined in lustily with the singing as if they were part of the show. The singer had a clear, strong voice; the lyrics mostly involved life at sea. With the strains of a tin whistle as an introduction, he sang about being a cook on a trader:

> *I can handle a jigger, I cuts a fine figure*
> *Whenever I gets in a boat standing room*
> *We'll rant and we'll roar like true Newfoundlanders*
> *We'll rant and we'll roar on deck and below*
> *Until we strikes bottom inside the two sunkers*
> *When straight through the channel to Toslow we'll go.*

I had no idea what Toslow or the two sunkers meant, but it didn't matter. And the extra *s* on words like *cuts* and *gets* didn't bother me anymore. I got it now. Hell, I liked it. When the chorus came around a second time, I joined in with the crowd:

> *We'll rant and we'll roar like true Newfoundlanders*
> *We'll rant and we'll roar on deck and below*

Most of the audience were on their feet by the end of the song, drinks aloft and shouting more than singing along. After a few more songs, the band announced a short break. Phonse stopped by our table on his way to the bar.

"Lucille Hanrahan, it's a keen spell since I seen you in this pub."

Lucille tilted her head at me. "This one got me on the go, right."

"Proper t'ing."

I was still buzzing from the music. "Phonse," I said. "I love this music! Will you teach me properly, so I can play songs like this? I'll pay you for lessons."

"You will not," he said. "It would be my pleasure."

On impulse, I kissed him on his cheek. He smiled awkwardly. "Best get me drink and head back to the stage."

Lucille tutted. "You haven't got a hope there, girl," she said. "Phonse is a confirmed bachelor."

She was teasing of course.

Wasn't she?

12

The pelting of heavy rain against the window and eaves woke me the next morning. Out the bathroom window, the sea was churning grey. Sundays were tough in Little Cove; I couldn't imagine a rainy one. I dressed quickly and went downstairs. Lucille was already installed at the kitchen table, drinking a cup of tea.

"I'm dropping from last night," she said. "But it was some fun, girl."

I told Lucille I didn't want breakfast and would be out all day.

"But what about Mass?" she called after me as I slipped out the door.

An hour later, just as the rain stopped, I saw the sign for Clayville. Its population was 4,500, much larger than that of Little Cove. Just past the sign, the road turned from gravel to pavement. When my car made the transition, it stopped juddering. I'd assumed it was the car's age that made it so sluggish, but now it rolled smoothly through the town. As I approached an intersection, the light turned red and I was slow to brake, almost forgetting how. It had been so long since I'd seen a traffic light, let alone traffic.

I cruised Clayville for twenty minutes to get my bearings, spotting the fabled Tony's Pizza opposite a coffee shop. On the next street over there was a grocery store and a library—a library! Both were shut, but I knew I would be returning to Clayville as soon as possible.

I circled back and parked in front of the coffee shop. It was small, with five or six tables, and smelled of fresh bread and cinnamon. I walked up to the counter and ogled the baked goods.

"Date square and a coffee, please," I said to the middle-aged guy behind the counter. He wore a spotless white apron and a hairnet that must have shifted, because I could see a red line running across his forehead, just under the edge of the net.

"You're not from around here, are you?"

I decided it might be time to start wearing a mainlander sash.

"I've just driven over from Little Cove."

"You on holiday or something?" he persisted.

"No. I work out there. I'm a teacher."

I waited for him to "Miss O'Brine" me, to say that he was Cynthia's uncle or Calvin's older brother, that he'd heard all about me, and then to ask me how Lucille was keeping. But he just nodded, then poured the coffee, fetched my date square and rang up the bill.

I sat at the table nearest the window and took a sip of coffee. It was delicious. I sniffed it, then took another sip.

"Excuse me," I called over to the counter. "Did you put fresh milk in my coffee?"

"Yeah, did you want this?" He held up a can of the ubiquitous evaporated milk.

"No!" I half shouted. "I wondered where you got it, that's all."

He gave me a suspicious look, like I was trying to trick him. "Over to the corner store."

"The grocery store?"

"No, they got it there too, though."

"In Clayville?" I could hear the note of hope in my voice.

Again with the look. "Uh-huh."

My taste buds cheered.

I opened my purse, pulled out *The Handmaid's Tale* and hunkered down for the morning. Periodically, I glanced out the window. Outside on the street, cars passed each other heading in opposite directions. Had I even seen that happen in Little Cove? And then, I swear I heard a horn beep. Two men in suits stood on the sidewalk in animated conversation. A woman in a bright-yellow slicker walked past. She was carrying a magazine with the headline "Madonna Weds Sean." Okay, that news was weeks old, but it was still news. And she looked like fun. The woman, not Madonna. Seeing her made me think of Sheila, and I wondered what she was doing. Then I remembered the time difference. She was probably still asleep or, knowing Sheila, heading home after a big night out.

I had the café to myself until midway through my second coffee, when a young family came in. After ordering, they sat at the table beside mine. Two girls, maybe six and eight, slurped hot chocolate and coloured while their parents talked in low tones about unemployment insurance and mortgage payments. As they got up to leave, the woman's coat grazed the table, knocking a pamphlet to the floor. By the time I picked it up to return it to her, they were already out the door. It was a Mass bulletin for Holy Redeemer Catholic Church in Clayville: "Sunday service: 10 a.m."

My prayers had been answered. Henceforth, I would follow God's call to Clayville on Sundays, bypassing the church to worship at the café. I slipped the bulletin inside my purse. It would be prominently displayed on my car dashboard all week.

I was contemplating a third coffee when, to my surprise, Doug walked in. A swarm of butterflies took up residence beneath my sweater. Was he still mad at me?

"Whaddya at?" he said.

"Not much."

"Can I join you?"

"Only if you let me buy you a coffee," I said. "Peace offering."

"Is it still peace if it's hot chocolate?"

"Sure." I stood up and pulled out the other chair for him.

"With marshmallows."

"You drive a hard bargain," I said, heading to the counter.

I returned with two hot chocolates and a selection of butter tarts, muffins and cookies. Doug's eyes lit up. "I'm gut-foundered."

I took a butter tart—I mean it was practically lunchtime—and handed the rest to Doug. The hot chocolate was delicious and the butter tart a perfect mix of gooey and flaky. Doug was on his second blueberry muffin before I found the right words.

"About that crazy idea I had for an English club," I began.

"Never mind, girl," he said, brushing crumbs from his shirt. "I was right contrary that day."

"I don't know about contrary," I said, "but you were right."

"I usually am." There was that easy smile. Things were back to normal.

"Maybe a French club would be better," Doug added. Then he bit into a butter tart, making appreciative noises. "How come you're in Clayville?"

I sipped my drink. "I needed a change of scene."

He nodded. "I guess Little Cove seems pretty small after Toronto. My sister couldn't wait to get out of Little Cove."

"Where did she go?"

"Boston. She used to come home every summer, but she's got three youngsters now, so she hasn't made it back the last few years."

Then he grabbed another muffin and leaned back in the chair. "What's your story?"

"*The Handmaid's Tale*," I said, holding up my book.

He ignored my flippancy. "Seriously, what brought you down this way?"

"A bunch of things," I said. "I told you about my dad. Then I had a bad breakup and my mother went off to Australia on a sabbatical."

Doug cocked his head. People obviously didn't like this story about my mother. The truth is, even if Dad hadn't made her promise, she might've gone. She's very career driven. But I took the time to explain the deathbed promise to Doug.

"Anyway, I hadn't applied for any teaching jobs because of Dad, and then I missed all the deadlines. I was really surprised to see the St. Jude's advertisement in the newspaper."

"Yeah," said Doug. "Brigid's situation was a real shock and it took them awhile to get their heads 'round what to do. And of course, a new priest was the bigger priority. Tell me about the breakup."

Normally, I might not have, but he seemed genuinely interested, so I said that Jake and I had met at university.

"He was amazing when Dad was diagnosed with cancer. Sometimes I think Mom leaned on him as much as I did." I looked out the window, remembering how Jake had raked leaves and later shovelled snow at our house.

After a minute, Doug said, "So, what happened?"

I looked away, biting a nail. Then the words came out in a rush. "He cheated on me. He started seeing someone else and she actually crashed a graduation party at my house looking for Jake."

"Ouch."

I took a sugar packet out of the bowl and began flicking it back and forth. "Yeah, it got pretty ugly."

"So that was it?"

I threw the sugar on the table. "Pretty much." Anger flared as I remembered Jake's justification for the affair. "You know what he said to me later, when I asked him why?"

Doug shook his head.

Tears filled my eyes. "He said it wasn't fun anymore. That I was too sad all the time. My goddamn father had just died." My voice cracked on the word *died*. I was quiet for a minute and then I whispered, "I mean, who says things like that?"

"Jerks," said Doug, handing me a paper serviette. "Jerks says things like that."

After a minute, I said, "He wasn't a total jerk, actually."

"No," said Doug, "or you wouldn't have been with him. People does stupid things every day of their lives. I guess at some point we needs to forgive them."

I decided he must be talking about me and the remedial English club. Because although I could concede that Jake wasn't a total jerk, I hadn't yet reached the point where I was ready to forgive him.

13

A few weeks after our girls' night out, Lucille said, "I thought we might go over to Mardy. Johnny's Crew is playing with Phonse and the b'ys tonight."

I could think of no good reason not to go, but I inwardly bristled at her use of the word *we*. As much as I liked Lucille, I was already spending most Friday nights with her and the hookers. I didn't want to hand over my Saturday nights too. Then again, it wasn't as if I had any plans besides reading a library book or listening to music.

Lucille went to get dolled up. I roused myself enough to brush my teeth.

But my spirits lifted on the drive over as I thought of the jaunty music I'd soon hear. Phonse was warming up onstage when we walked in, and he sat a little taller when he saw me. Or maybe he was stretching. The usual assortment of musicians was gathered around him, but front and centre of the stage were three familiar-looking teens.

Lucille went off to talk to a woman in the corner. I bought her a drink and myself a beer, and wandered over to the stage.

"Hiya, miss," said Beverley, who was adjusting the microphone stand. She was one of the brighter senior students. She was no Cynthia, but she was smart. Behind her, Roseanne was tuning a fiddle, and to her left was Jerome, holding a guitar. All three were in the senior French class.

"You guys," I squealed. "I didn't know you played. I'm excited to hear you."

"You might change your mind when you does," said Beverley, in what I had come to recognize as her habitual self-deprecation.

The bar was filling up rapidly and Lucille was waving an agitated arm at me. Yet again, she had managed to find a table. It was clear this was her superpower. I went over to join her and mentioned the students who were up on stage.

"I knows," she said. "That's Johnny's Crew, that's the name of their group."

I'd forgotten that Lucille knew everything.

Then although she was the one talking, she shushed me as the opening bars of a familiar song filled the room. Up on stage, a barefoot Beverley, eyes closed, began to croon the folk song "Four Strong Winds."

Beverley was shy in class and blushed easily if called upon. But up on that stage, she looked completely at ease, her voice caressing the words.

I'd heard the song many times, of course. Dad used to have the Ian and Sylvia version, and more recently Neil Young had released it. But hearing it sung live heightened the significance of the lyrics, somehow. That's what it had come down to for Jake—the good times were gone, and he'd moved on. And maybe, just maybe, I was ready to forgive him after all.

Lucille leaned in, her breath reeking of cigarettes. "You've gone right quiet."

"I'm fine," I said, patting her arm. We both turned our attention back to Beverley, who swayed softly on the stage, seemingly oblivious to the crowd. As she reached the final chorus, many in the audience crooned softly along, the odd baritone wending its own way through the lyrics.

Amidst the prolonged clapping, Beverley and Jerome hopped down from the stage, threading their way through the crowd. They left Roseanne in conversation with Phonse. She glanced my way once and her head bobbed enthusiastically.

"That was amazing," I said when Beverley and Jerome reached our table. "You're all so talented."

Beverley rolled her eyes, a physical manifestation of "this old thing."

"Miss," she said, "Phonse is after telling us that you plays the fiddle. Will you play a tune with us?"

"Oh, I couldn't, Beverley. I'm not that good."

"Please, miss," she wheedled.

"S'il vous plaît, mademoiselle," Jerome simpered, batting his eyelashes.

"I haven't got a fiddle," I said.

"Phonse has a spare."

"He does, eh?" I caught Phonse's eye up on the stage and shook my finger at him.

"C'mon, miss, it'll be fun." Beverley tugged my sleeve and I stood up, allowing myself to be gently pulled towards the stage.

"Thought it was time you showed them yer stuff," Phonse said, handing me a fiddle.

As I quickly tuned the instrument, the pub went quiet.

Beverley spoke into the microphone. "By special request, our teacher Miss O'Brine is going to play a tune with us."

A male voice bellowed from the back of the room, "Heave it out of ya, miss."

There was laughter and the thumping of bottles on tables. I squinted into the crowd; there was nothing but friendly faces smiling back. I leaned into the microphone. "Only one song," I said, pausing for effect before adding, "That's all I know."

There was more laughter as I took my place next to Phonse. We'd been working on a piece called "Sweet Forget Me Not" and it was fresh in my mind. I was grateful that he'd chosen that one for my debut.

I nestled the fiddle beneath my chin. Beverley counted down, mouthing *three, two, one*, and as we began to play, I shifted my focus to Phonse. But even as I concentrated on my playing, I was enthralled by the lyrics, which I'd not heard before.

> *She's graceful and she's charming, like the lily in the pond*
> *Time is flying swiftly by, of her I am so fond*
> *The roses and the daisies are blooming 'round the spot*
> *Where we parted, when she whispered, "You'll forget me not."*

I mostly kept my eyes trained on the clock behind the bar, but occasionally I glanced over at Phonse. Once he caught my eye and winked, and when I smiled back, it stayed. I couldn't think of a single violin recital where I'd smiled as I played. After, sure, but not during. Despite my inexperience, this music and these people pleased me so much more than all the classical violin recitals of my youth.

By the time we finished the song, the beer bottles were banging so hard on the tables, I worried they'd break. Phonse patted me on the shoulder.

"Some good, girl. You've been practising."

I was glad not to be a disappointment this time.

"But why did you say you only knows one song?" he asked. "Sure you've got half a dozen under your belt now."

"Always leave them wanting more."

He slapped his knee. "Proper t'ing, my dear. But I hope you'll come and play with us again some time."

"Try and stop me."

When I got back to the table, Lucille was wiping her eyes with a tissue. "My John used to sing that song to me," she said. "You did us proud, girl."

I was so used to seeing Lucille on her own that I sometimes forgot she had her own grief to bear. I shuffled my chair closer to hers as the band began another tune.

During a break, I was pleased to see Judy approaching our table. She sat with us for a while, introducing her husband, Bill, before sending him off for a round.

"Rachel, that was something," she said. "I had no idea you were so musical. I was minded to put you in charge of the yearbook after Christmas, but now I've got a better idea. I wants you to organize a group of students to play at the garden party in June."

"Um," I said. "I'm not sure, I . . ."

"You knows she'll do it, sure," said Lucille. And the matter seemed to be settled.

Then Lucille began discussing the upcoming funeral of someone I didn't know with Judy and Bill.

The band started up again with a jaunty reel and people headed for the dance floor. There was a tap on my arm and a swarthy young man I didn't recognize waggled a beer bottle at me and said, "Fancy a scuff?"

I was getting good at Newfinese but this was a new one. Still, if a scoff was a big feast, then a scuff was probably a drink.

I waggled my bottle back at him. "Thanks, but I've got one and I'm driving."

He wandered off shaking his head, as Judy and Lucille burst into laughter.

"A scuff is a dance, you ninny," said Lucille. "That's what buddy was after."

"Oh." I was glad of the dark to hide my red cheeks. "Maybe I can dance with him later."

Judy said, "If you dances with him, you'll have them all lined up for a go."

"I wouldn't know how to dance to this music anyway," I said as a couple whirled past, inches from our table.

"Ah sure, it's easy enough," said Lucille. "You catches the beat, and off you goes."

I wasn't convinced.

As soon the music stopped, the trio of students from the band came to our table.

"Miss," said Roseanne, "you were some good."

"Never mind me, you guys were fabulous. If you bring your instruments to school, we could play together."

Jerome looked down at his feet. "Nah, sure we only plays here 'cause we're made to."

"What do you mean?"

"My dad owns the pub," said Beverley. "He's their uncle." She jerked her thumb at the others.

"We'd rather play rock music, not this stuff," said Beverley, casting such a disdainful look at Roseanne's fiddle that I wanted to cradle it. "But Dad says we has to play sometimes, so . . ." She turned her palms up. "We does."

Roseanne said, "Anyway, we're done now, sure. Let's get a drink."

After they'd gone, I said to Judy, "So much for your idea."

"Uh-uh," she said. "You can't give up so soon. I'm counting on you to deliver."

Bill arrived at the table with a round of drinks and he, Judy and Lucille returned to their earlier discussion about the funeral. I picked at the label of my beer bottle. I had enjoyed being up on stage. Maybe I *could* get those students to play at the garden party. I just needed to figure out how.

14

The frequency of my visits to Clayville had increased over the autumn. I was often there both days of the weekend, visiting the library and the coffee shop.

"Good morning, Wilf," I said as I entered his establishment on a bitterly cold November morning. I inhaled the smell of baking and my shoulders relaxed.

"You mean great morning," Wilf said. "Better than great. Excellent morning!"

"Why?"

"Beer strike's over. I'm closing up early today to go buy some."

"You can buy beer in Clayville?"

He nodded. "Beer, wine, liquor. There's a liquor outlet attached to the gas station. In the back of the store."

What other delights were yet to be discovered in Clayville? I wondered. I waited at the counter while Wilf poured my coffee and put a date square on a plate. Then, as usual, he added a butter tart when he thought I wasn't looking. In retaliation, I stuffed a dollar into the tip jar when his back was turned.

As I settled in for the morning, I allowed myself to fantasize that Wilf would open a branch in Little Cove so I could get up in the morning and walk over for a cup of coffee excellence. When I shared with him my idea for his world domination, he said he was happy with the one coffee shop.

"You could move to Clayville, right?"

"Yeah," I laughed. "I spend enough time here."

Then it dawned on me. Maybe I *could* move to Clayville.

"Wilf, any apartments for rent around here?"

"You could check the board." He pointed to a notice board on the wall near the bathroom. I took my mug of coffee over and scanned the notices while Wilf served another customer. There was a scrap of paper with "Free Kittens" written in swirly purple writing, a business card for "Bud's Taxi" and a recruitment poster for the RCMP, "bilingualism an asset." Damn straight. Guaranteed job security for French teachers.

Then I saw it, tucked in the bottom corner: an ad for a one-bedroom house to rent. I ripped the card off the board and kept reading. "Would suit couple or single professional."

"Wilf," I said. "Can I use your phone?"

The realtor, a woman named Ellen, agreed to meet me at the property. I jotted down the address and showed it to Wilf. He said it was a five-minute walk and drew me a crude map on the back of the card.

As soon as I turned off the main street, I was in a residential area. The houses were bigger than those in Little Cove and the roads were studded with streetlights. A few of the houses had the same bright paint colours as in Little Cove, but many were plain white or beige and seemed a bit dull in comparison.

Mill Street was a quiet cul-de-sac with few houses. I spotted the "for rent" sign hanging outside a tiny sunshine-yellow house at the end of the road. A large bay window faced the street.

Ellen was parked out front, engine running. She turned off the car and got out.

"Mind the ice," she said, leading me up the driveway.

The front door opened into a narrow hall, which led to a combined living, dining and kitchen area.

"This was three pokey rooms," Ellen said. "The owner knocked them together. Much more spacious now."

I admired the newly varnished hardwood floors. Besides the bay window, there was a smaller one near the kitchen. Ellen pointed out a tiny footpath beside the house that led down to the sea.

"What do you think?" she asked.

I thought about how much I liked Clayville. I thought about how Lucille sometimes came and stood in the hall when I was in the living room, talking to my mother or Sheila on the phone. I ran my hand over the smooth finish of the kitchen's pine table. The four matching chairs had blue-striped seat cushions. In the living room, a wooden rocking chair sat in the corner, tucked away from two loveseat sofas and a coffee table.

"There's not much room for anything else," Ellen said as I gave the rocking chair a test run. "Do you have a lot of furniture?"

"None," I said. "I'm staying in a boarding house."

She took me up the narrow stairs. To the left, in the bathroom, was a claw-footed bathtub like Lucille's, but smaller. To the right was the bedroom. I bounced on the bed and peeked in the closet. Then I looked out the window: less than ten feet away was a graveyard.

Ellen came over and adjusted the muslin curtains. We stood for a minute, looking down at the cemetery. Only a few orange leaves remained on the trees, the branches bowing down at the gates.

Back downstairs, I looked across the bay where the whitecaps rode to shore.

"I'll be honest," Ellen said. "There's not many wants to live so close to the graveyard."

I thought about all the high school bike rides with Sheila through leafy Mount Pleasant Cemetery. "I don't think that would bother me. I'll take it."

"You never even asked about the rent!"

When she named the price, I tried to hide my shock. Sheila was paying three times as much for a pokey one-bedroom apartment in the Beaches back in Toronto.

We agreed to meet the next day to do the paperwork. Ellen said if I brought along postdated cheques, I could move in right away.

"So, I'll see you here tomorrow morning after Mass," she said.

Well, you won't see me *at* Mass, I thought. Driving back to Little Cove, my stomach fizzed as I wondered how best to explain to Lucille that I was leaving and why so suddenly. Would she be annoyed? Or hurt? Then I thought about the loss of rent money, a month before Christmas. I took my foot off the gas, less keen all of a sudden to reach Lucille's.

When I arrived, I heard voices in the kitchen as I shut the door. Biddy and the other hookers were sitting with Lucille around the table. Lucille was taking notes.

"Didn't you do enough hooking last night?" I said.

"We're having a meeting of the Holy Dusters," Biddy said. "Father Frank has some special jobs he wants done before Christmas. The archbishop might come for a visit."

"The archbishop is always coming for a visit," said Lucille.

"Yis," said Flossie, "he's always coming, but he never comes."

"Right," said Biddy. "Are we done? Sure we all knows what to do over to the church anyway. Don't we run it?"

"More or less," said Lucille. "You'll be saying Mass soon enough, Sister Biddy."

The women chortled.

"Now, then," said Flossie. "Georgie Corrigan is due before Christmas, so we needs to plan some gifts for her."

"I'm after finishing a lovely rug with ducks all 'round it," said Lucille. "The perfect size for a baby to roll 'round on."

"What about a quilt, now?" said Flossie. "Can we put one together before Christmas?"

"You knows we can," said Lucille. She retrieved a bag of rags and wool from under the daybed and began rummaging. "There's your old tablecloth, Biddy, girl," she said, pulling out a soft yellow fabric. "We could use that as a border."

Flossie chuckled. "I minds the day you got blueberry jam all over it, Annie."

Annie took the tablecloth from Lucille and turned it over, looking for the stain and displaying it triumphantly when she found it. "Yis, maid, I was that tired. Sure we was after staying up all night."

"Hooking rugs?" I asked. "That's dedication."

"No, girl," said Annie. "We was having a time."

"A hard time?"

The women burst out laughing.

"A time," said Lucille, "a do . . . a party," she elaborated.

"A soir-ee," trilled Biddy, getting up and twirling around the room.

My eyes widened. "And the four of you stayed up all night?"

"The four of us and half of Little Cove," said Lucille. She clasped the bag of wool to her chest, as if lost in memories of their big night in. Then she said, "Listen now, me duckies, we could show Rachel a time this evening. Give her a proper send-off before she disappears off to Clayville."

"Who told . . . how did you . . . ?" I spluttered.

"My cousin Val was into Clayville today to visit her husband in the hospital. She went into that coffee shop near the town hall to get him some baking. He loves their date squares, right? She said she heard you talking about a place to rent. And since you've been back, you're twitchy as a cat, so I figured."

"I was going to move out tomorrow," I said softly. "If . . . if that was okay with you."

"Not a bother," said Lucille, batting her hand at me. "I had a call yesterday from the fisheries crowd in St. John's. Some fella coming out to do some research needs a place for most of December. I'll call them back and tell them yes." She reached for a cigarette. "Now girl, you already paid me for the next month."

"Lucille," I said, "I'm giving you no notice at all, so I would expect you to keep that money."

She clapped her hands and said, "Now that's another reason for a kitchen party."

"Don't you need to plan a party?" I asked.

"Not really, girl," said Biddy.

"This is me planning it," said Lucille. She went to the living room, and I heard the clicks as the rotary dial circled again and again on the phone. "That you, Phonse?" she said. "Come 'round this evening for a drop, if you're free."

There was a pause, then she said, "Yes, b'y, I knows, sure she's sat here with us. She's leaving tomorrow so we're giving her a send-off."

Another pause. "Right, we'll see you the once."

She hung up, then dialled another number, inviting more people over. "Yes, maid," I heard her say. "Round that crowd up, too."

"Now, then, Rachel," she said, coming back into the kitchen, "there'll be a party here before you knows it."

"C'mon now, Floss," said Annie. "We'll nip over the road and get some provisions." Biddy left with the two sisters as well, saying she'd see us later. I went upstairs to pack.

An hour later, the women were back, laden with food and drink. People began to arrive, in groups of two or three at a time. Judy and Bill had been first, arms full of Newfoundland-branded beer.

"My God, you should've seen the lineup outside the Clayville liquor store," Bill said.

"He was first in line, though," said Judy. "Got in there at seven thirty this morning. Initiative, right?"

Bill laughed. "Desperation, you mean."

Judy introduced me to so many people that I lost track of their names, though I recognized a few from those early days of enforced church attendance. As more people came, chairs were pushed back against walls wherever they fit.

Phonse and a few other musicians began setting up in a corner. A stooped old man was installed in an easy chair dragged in from the living room. Biddy handed him a battered black case from which he pulled an accordion. When he started to play, an ancient couple began creaking slowly around the crowded room, somehow mostly avoiding contact with all who filled the kitchen.

Platters of food covered the table—crackers and cheese, sliced meat, cakes and cookies—and bottles of every shape and size. Lucille began slicing a loaf of bread, cigarette dangling from her lips.

On the daybed, squished between Annie and the wall, I sipped a warm rum and cola. It wasn't half bad. Biddy poured more rum in, despite my protestations. Annie held her glass out for a refill, pressing the bottle down again when Biddy lifted it from her glass too soon. When the accordion music stopped, the dancers bowed to the applause, as if it was meant for them too, which maybe it was.

A tall dark-haired man strode into the centre of the room and Annie elbowed me. "That Jacko Parsons got some voice on him." The accordion player started up and Jacko began to sing:

I'se the b'y that builds the boat and I'se the b'y that sails her
I'se the b'y that catches the fish and takes it home to Liza

The song was instantly familiar. I'd learned it in grade six, thinking the lyrics sounded almost like a different language. I'd had no real concept of Newfoundland back then, or fish for that matter, apart from fish sticks. Now, of course, I knew that it was all about the fish in Newfoundland—catching it, eating it, singing about it.

When Jacko reached the end of the song, there were cheers and someone called out, "Good man, yourself."

Biddy handed Jacko a beer. "You got the voice of an angel, my son."

"And the thirst of the devil," he said, tipping his bottle in thanks.

"Or a drunken sailor," quipped Lucille. Within seconds, the musicians had started up again, and everyone, including me, sang at the top of their lungs:

What do you do with a drunken sailor, what do you do
with a drunken sailor
What do you do with a drunken sailor, ear-ly in the
morning?

The easy banter and joyful celebration of music almost made me question my imminent move to Clayville. But, as much as I had come to like Little Cove and its inhabitants, I had needs! I wanted good coffee, fresh milk, pizza, a liquor store, a library. None of that was available in Little Cove.

Towards the end of the evening, Lucille asked Phonse and me to play "Sweet Forget Me Not." To my surprise, she and the other hookers linked arms and sang along, their soft voices rising sweetly in the air. I couldn't have been the only one to wipe away tears.

My head was right sore (as the locals would say) the next morning, but I forced myself to rise early, determined to leave before Mass. When I dragged the suitcases downstairs, Lucille was in the front hall, straddling a large cardboard box, a bracelet of duct tape around her wrist.

"What's that?" I asked.

"A few bits and bobs to get you started."

I gave her a hug, her curlers pressing into my neck.

"I'll miss you, girl," Lucille said. "But a young one's got to live. Don't be a stranger now. You come and see us anytime." She followed me outside as far as the gate and waved goodbye as I drove off. When I looked in the rear-view mirror, she was still waving. Then my car dipped down the hill and I lost sight of her.

I met Ellen at the coffee shop to exchange cheques for keys. Entering my new home, any niggling doubts disappeared. I leaned against the front door, inhaling furniture polish and bleach, instead of cigarettes and deep-fried fat. Ellen had left a box of chocolates and a bottle of wine on the table. I threw off my coat and danced wildly around the room like Kevin Bacon in *Footloose*. A teenage boy strolling down the path towards the sea saw me and walked more quickly, no doubt wanting to distance himself from the crazy lady.

I spent the next half hour exploring the house, opening cupboards and turning lights on and off. I stood at the bedroom window and looked down at all the gravestones. It was a bright day and the cemetery looked benign. Would I still feel that way tonight? I shrugged off any feelings of unease and walked into town to explore.

That evening, I ate Tony's takeout pizza at the kitchen table, revelling in the smoke-free meal. The pizza wasn't quite as good as Luigi's, where Sheila and I often dined back home, but it came close. Afterwards I opened Lucille's box and found a fresh loaf of bread, a jar of her famous blueberry jam and a can of evaporated milk. I put the so-called milk in the centre of the mantelpiece, a souvenir of my time at Lucille's. A carton of fresh milk was stowed in my fridge and I vowed to never run out.

Digging further in the box, I found a hooked rug and a quilt, neither of which I had seen before. The quilt featured a simple pattern, blue and red fabric squares in repeating rows. But the rug was a heavily detailed winter scene: a frozen bay, on which dozens of children played while dogs jumped between them. Beyond the bay, a series of colourful houses spread up the hill, a long plume of white smoke rising from each chimney. It was far too beautiful to go on the floor. It was a work of art. That evening I hung it on the living room wall and toasted its creator, lifting a mug of hot chocolate, made with fresh milk, of course.

15

A week into my new commute to Little Cove, I was still leaving Clayville quite early in the morning, honing my mental map of the numerous potholes along the way. On the Monday of the second week, I pulled over at the same spot where I'd first met Phonse. The bay was the calmest I'd seen since my arrival, reflecting the hues of the houses curled around it. Although still low in the sky, the sun cast a soft light. It was a glorious November morning, heralding great things: all homework would be handed in, the grade nines would pay attention, and Calvin flipping Piercey himself would stand up and tell me he'd spent the weekend reading Proust's *À la recherche de* . . . who's kidding who.

I thought I would arrive at school before anyone else, but there was already a car in the parking lot—Judy's. She met me in the foyer.

"Morning, Rachel," she said. "I'll be observing some lessons today."

"Oh. Patrick mentioned a date later in the month."

"Yes, he likes to be organized with his reviews," Judy said. "I likes . . ."

Ambush? I wanted to say.

". . . to keep it casual." She consulted her planner. "Let's see, what class can I visit this morning?"

I didn't answer but crossed my fingers that she wouldn't pick . . .

"I'll start with grade nine."

I must have winced, because she added, "I'm sure it will all be grand. But if not, we'd better nip any problems in the bud."

ANY problems? Don't you mean MANY problems, Judy? I didn't say.

"We have some time before first period," I said. "Would you like to review my lesson plans?"

"That's okay, you can surprise me."

Conversation turned to my new home. We stood chatting about the delights of Clayville, and Judy told me that she and Bill often drove over for Tony's Pizza and to hit the liquor store. We were still chatting when Doug arrived.

"Some fine day for November," he said.

"Fine day for your first assessment," said Judy. She told him she'd be in to see him after lunch. As she walked off towards her office, Doug cursed.

"Gentle Jaysus in the garden. So much for winging it today. I'd better get something planned right quick." He jogged down the hall to his classroom while I fretted off to mine.

On the way, I passed the shrine to Mary, set in a small recess in the hall. I reached out and patted her right foot. It felt cool and smooth, like a beach rock. How many teachers had reached out to her in times of trouble? Her serene face revealed nothing.

Since my arrival in September, Judy had been nothing but friendly and helpful. But when she arrived at my classroom, she was wearing a blazer—a blazer! She might like to keep things casual, but I knew this was serious. This was my career. This was me being assessed. This mattered.

Judy slid into an empty desk at the back of the class, rested her chin in one of her hands and smiled at me. I took a deep breath in, then released it, ready to begin. But my usually boisterous students were quiet. I asked several easy questions, part of our habitual warm-up, but no one volunteered an answer. They kept their heads down, so I couldn't even catch anyone's eye.

The silence grew uncomfortable; I tugged at my sweater, feeling the heat rise. Why had I worn a turtleneck today? As I went to open a window, Judy picked up her pen and began to write. I could just imagine her assessment: "Class unresponsive. Rachel unprepared." In my misery, I realized it would also work the other way around: "Class unprepared. Rachel unresponsive."

From the window, I lurched to the blackboard and picked up a piece of chalk. Something about its familiar weight grounded me. Have fun with it, I could almost hear Dad say.

Screw the lesson plan. I quickly wrote two verbs on the blackboard: *aimer* and *détester*. Then I told the class in French that I hated peanut butter, but loved ice cream.

"Now," I said, "I want all of you to tell me about your likes and dislikes. En français, bien sûr."

I looked expectantly around the room, but no one wanted to share. The seconds ticked by. Then, slowly, like a wraith sent from the netherworld to haunt me, a long white sleeve rose. What the hell? The hand at the end of the sleeve belonged to none other than Calvin. Nervous twitch? Nope. Son of a . . .

It was impossible not to call on him. No one else had volunteered. "Oui, Calvin?" I said, my voice squeaking like a smoke detector in need of a new battery.

He put down his hand and began to speak. In French!

"Je . . . déteste . . . ."He stopped, and looked around the room. "Je déteste . . ."

I waited for him to reveal his hatred of me.

". . . français. Je déteste français."

There were scattered bursts of nervous laughter. I walked down the aisle and stopped beside his desk. He met my gaze, his chin jutting out. How to respond in front of Judy? A row of neat stitches marched along his sleeve, nimbly mending a rip, and reminding me of my conversation with his mother. Calvin Piercey would not be hauling wood on my watch.

"Non?! Tu détestes le français?" I put my hand to my heart as if in shock, then pretended to shed a few tears. "Oh, Calvin, quelle tristesse!" I was hamming it up now, mock-rubbing my eyes.

Something shifted. Calvin sat back in his chair and grinned. The boy behind him reached up and mussed Calvin's hair. By the time I walked back to the front of the classroom, the air was full of waving hands and Judy was writing furiously in her notebook. By the end of the class, I had revised Judy's assessment to: "Class responsive. Rachel undaunted."

After school, I met Judy for a debrief. She was sitting at her desk drinking tea from a mug that read "World's Greatest Teacher." I wondered how many of those were kicking around.

"I was some pleased to see the great relationship between you and Calvin," she began. "Not many of the teachers has that."

I coughed to cover my surprise. Calvin and I didn't exactly have much of a rapport.

"You know, Rachel, humour is an important teaching tool and you used it so effectively today."

"I tried to have fun with it, I guess," I said, as if that had been my plan all along.

Judy spent the next ten minutes reviewing my performance in the three classes she'd observed. She provided constructive comments on several areas that needed improvement, but said that overall things seemed fine.

As I was leaving her office, Doug was heading in. He suggested we meet for dinner to compare notes after our first review. "We'll go to Tony's," he said. "I'll pick you up at seven."

I gave him my new address and headed home, a bit giddy after my talk with Judy. I found myself wishing I could talk to Dad about my review. He would've been so interested. I would update Mom, of course, but it wouldn't be the same.

When Doug arrived, his car lights lit up the living room and I ran out to meet him.

"Some cold, b'y," he said, as I slid into the passenger seat. "Winter's coming."

Tony's was busy, but the proprietor found us a small table near the back. The red and white tablecloths were identical to those at Luigi's and I thought, with a pang, about Sheila.

After we'd ordered pizza and beer, I settled back in my chair and looked around. There was a bar on the other side of the restaurant where two women had their heads together, laughing. Their easy camaraderie made me miss Sheila even more.

"That lesson plan saved my arse today," Doug said.

"What lesson plan? This morning you said you'd have to wing it."

"I pulled out the big guns for grade eleven biology. My top-secret weapon."

I snorted. "What are you, James Bond?"

A waiter arrived with our beers and we clinked bottles.

"To probation," said Doug.

"To the end of probation," I corrected him. "So, tell me about this secret weapon."

Doug took a long drink of beer. "Ahh, some good. No more American watery beer." He put the bottle down on the table and said, "It's something I learned from my supervisor when I was a student teacher. You puts together a killer lesson plan and files it in your bottom drawer. It's there, on tap, when you needs to impress someone. Golden."

I had to admit, it was genius. "So you're prepared for when you're unprepared."

"Exactly."

The waiter came back with our pizzas and we were quiet as we began to eat.

"So how did you make out?" Doug asked after a few minutes.

"Calvin spoke French today, unasked," I said. "So basically, I'm a goddess."

"Nice."

My pizza was delicious, but huge. I had a feeling I'd be having pizza for breakfast the next day.

Then Doug said, "Can I have a piece of your pizza?" and I saw his was all gone.

"God, you can eat. Help yourself."

He slid a slice from my plate to his, smearing tomato sauce on his thumb in the process. He licked it off contentedly, then carefully picked off the mushrooms. He ate the slice, then looked with puppy eyes from me to the rest of my pizza. I nodded.

When he had finished the last bit of my breakfast, he patted his stomach. "The beast has been fed."

"*Beast* is the word for some of the grade nines," I said.

"Go on, girl, they're not that bad."

"No, they're not," I agreed, somewhat reluctantly. "Trudy and Calvin are the ringleaders; they stir the others up. Trudy was off sick today and I got lucky with Calvin."

"Ba-dum-dum."

"You know what I mean." I told him about the habitual noise levels and inattention in grade nine.

"You needs to get on top of that right quick. Show them who's boss."

I reached for my beer. "Easier said than done."

Suddenly, Doug stood up and came around to my side of the table, folding his arms. "Let's go."

"Hang on," I said. "I'm not finished."

He leaned down and put an arm on either side of my chair, moving uncomfortably close. "Rachel, get up now."

Flustered, I looked away and caught the woman at the next table staring.

"Doug, what are you doing?" I hissed. "Knock it off."

He leaned in close and I smelled a musky aftershave under the beer. Then he pushed himself back up and punched me very lightly on the arm. "That's how I would get respect if I had to. You needs to find out what works for you. Want some dessert?"

"Dessert?" I practically screamed. "How about a knuckle sandwich?"

We compromised on ice cream. Afterwards, Doug offered to drive me home, but I declined. I liked the short walk past my new landmarks and seeing my little house, with the porch light shining its welcome, as I came around the corner. I stood outside and looked up at the stars, remembering Lucille's comment that stars were stars. I wondered what Lucille was doing that evening and whether her new boarder appreciated her. But I was enjoying living on my own for the first time in my life. Spending Friday nights in Little Cove was no longer appealing, but I planned to stop by after school one day soon to visit Lucille and buy one of her rugs for Mom's Christmas present.

16

November slipped past and December arrived with the first snowfall. We watched it come down, soft and steady, outside the classroom windows. I was almost as restless as the students. When the afternoon bell finally rang, they exploded into the schoolyard. I watched from my classroom window as Calvin made a big snowball with his bare hands and chased Cynthia around my car. When he caught her, he shoved the snowball down the back of her coat. She shrieked blue murder but wore a huge smile. She grabbed his toque and sped off, looking back over her shoulder and laughing as he slipped in the snow, trying to catch up. A dump of snow could make a pair as disparate as Calvin and Cynthia find common ground.

Later, when I left school in the dark blue early evening, the snow had been cleared from my windscreen. I smiled, imagining Phonse sweeping it off with a broom. But when I slid into the driver's seat, I saw a note taped to the steering wheel: "Clayville's not far enough. Piss off home out of it."

My stomach lurched. Someone had been in my car, maybe even sat in the driver's seat to put the note there. I banged my fist on the steering wheel, and the paper split in two. I ripped the pieces off and threw them on the passenger seat.

Screw this place and the people in it. I pulled out of the parking lot and put my foot down hard on the accelerator. By the time I left Little Cove, I had fishtailed twice, scaring myself enough to slow down.

For a minute I kept my eyes on the road, the car lights drilling amber tunnels into the falling darkness. But I couldn't help but look over at the torn paper, wanting to check the handwriting. Was it the same person? And why? What had I done to deserve this treatment? When I shifted my eyes back to the road, my car had veered over to the wrong side and two headlights were coming straight at me. I swerved, then braked hard, remembering too late that you should pump the brakes on icy roads. My car spun around, then slid off the road into the ditch.

I heard a door slam, then a voice called, "Miss O'Brine?"

My driver's door opened and a wrinkled face under a red toque peered in.

"Lord thundering Jaysus," said the man. "You scared the frigging life out of me. You all right?"

I opened my mouth but no words came. The most I could manage was a thumbs-up. He reached over, undid my seat belt and helped me out of the car and up from the ditch.

I gulped in the cold air. When my breathing returned to normal, I thanked my rescuer. He introduced himself as Eddie Churchill and said that Phonse had told him all about me.

I sagged against the side of his truck. "You know Phonse."

"Know him? Sure he's my cousin and next-door neighbour, can't know him much better than that."

He reached into his coat pocket, pulling out a flashlight, which he shone at my tires. "No snow tires on 'er," he said. "No wonder you're after sliding off the road."

"The garage in Clayville is putting them on for me," I said. The day I'd bought the winter tires, the garage had been too busy to put them on and I hadn't been back since.

"No, my dear," he said. "I'm doing it the once. It's a bad road the best of times, and when it's icy, she's like the bottle. Let's push her out first."

From the back of his truck, he fetched some cardboard. We climbed back down into the ditch and he put the cardboard behind my wheels for traction.

"You okay to push?" he asked.

I nodded.

He put my car in neutral and joined me at the back bumper.

"Now then, missus," he said, "we needs a bit of the old rock and roll."

We pushed the car, back and forth, working it up and eventually out of the ditch.

Then he handed me the flashlight to hold, got the tires and jack from my car, and set to work.

"So you teaches French," he said. "I wish I could do the parlez-vous."

"It's never too late," I said.

My fingers grew numb clutching the flashlight and I changed hands periodically, shoving the cold one in my pocket. Mr. Churchill didn't seem to notice the cold. He worked methodically, whistling.

"What's that tune?" I asked at one point.

"It's called 'Sonny's Dream,'" he said. "Phonse'll know it."

Finally, he cranked the jack back down and put my summer tires and the jack in the trunk. "Put those away now when you gets home," he said. "You won't be needing them for a keen spell."

"Thank you so much, Mr. Churchill."

"It's Eddie," he said, blowing on his hands, then rubbing them together.

I opened my purse. "How much do I owe you, Eddie?"

"I can't take nothing for that," he said. "For one thing, it was a five-minute job."

"More like forty-five," I said.

"Plus, Phonse would have me head. Sure you're part of the community, now, right?"

Whoever was sending me those notes might not agree with Eddie, but as I drove slowly home through the falling snow, the words *part of the community* glowed in my heart.

When I arrived at school the next morning, Phonse was shovelling the front steps.

"Morning, Rachel," he said. "Heard about your tires. With all that travel back and forth to Clayville, you might want to ask himself to look out for you."

"Who? Eddie Churchill?"

"No, girl." Phonse pointed at the statue inside the door. "St. Jude. Patron saint of lost causes. That road is a lost cause if I ever saw one."

I hadn't fully twigged to the name when I'd first arrived. But when Phonse said "lost causes," Calvin's sulky face appeared in my mind's eye. Apart from that brief moment of participation when Judy had visited the classroom, he'd reverted to his sullen self. No wonder Patrick wasn't so keen on the statue in the front hall.

17

As the first term drew to a close, I was quietly pleased with the progress I'd made with the students. Sure, there were days I wanted to brain every last one of them, but for the most part, they were coming to respect me. Some of the older girls talked to me about their social lives. And I liked to think I was developing a rapport with them.

I had lunch duty that day and a few of the students came and sat with me, sharing stories of a weekend gathering at Bob's Cove, halfway between Little Cove and Clayville. I found myself wondering how they could possibly enjoy spending time there in the bleak weather.

"Miss, Pam was some mad at Jimmy," Roseanne confided this time. "She went mental."

"Why?"

"He hung a rat in her face," Beverley shrieked in response.

"Was it dead?" I asked.

There was a half second of silence, then the girls began whooping with laughter.

I screwed up my face. I wasn't sure what she meant but was beginning to think I didn't want to.

Roseanne spoke very slowly. "He took down his pants and wiggled his bird in her face."

"Oh," I said. "Well, that's . . ." I didn't have the words. "Excuse me, girls," I said. "I think I'm needed over at the grade sevens' table."

I fled, the girls' giggles resonating behind me. For all their isolation and lack of amenities, these girls were far worldlier than I'd ever been at their age. The first "bird" I'd ever properly seen had belonged to Jake.

Inevitably, I overheard the story repeated in the hall that afternoon, culminating with, "And then miss asked if it was dead." I closed the classroom door against the laughter.

The drive home after school took me straight past the turnoff for Bob's Cove, and on impulse, I turned down the track, despite the growing darkness. I drove a few hundred yards to the dead end. Grabbing a flashlight from the glove compartment, I walked to the cliff's edge; waves crashed against scarred rocks, then reeled back again. The wind gusted fiercely, slowing the progress of a lone seagull that screamed its frustration.

Crouching low in the wind, I scuttled down the path to the rocky beach that was the students' social club. Straight ahead were remnants of a bonfire, the charred black logs scattered like bowling pins against the white snow. Glass shards littered the beach rocks where bottles had been smashed.

I nearly dropped the flashlight when its arc revealed what looked like a body lying in the distance. As I got closer, I saw it was a large piece of driftwood. To the left was a small cave, tucked out of the wind and protected from the snow. The howling in my ears softened. The flashlight shone on discarded cigarette butts and a plaid blanket bundled in a corner. Father Frank's comment about "the vexing problem of chastity" rang in my ears as I headed back to my car.

What exactly did these kids get up to down here? Jake and I had struggled to find places to go when we started sleeping together. There'd been lots of sneaking around, including a painful experience in a boat out on the lake at my family cottage. There'd been many back-seat encounters, including, I now recalled, the night a campus police officer had tapped on the window of Jake's car and told us to move along. There was nothing particularly romantic about young love, it seemed, no matter where you lived.

18

N ear the end of term, Doug stopped by my classroom.

"Mudder's invited you for dinner on Friday," he said.

"Why?" I asked. With this invite, and the upcoming Christmas concert and staff party, it was almost like I had a social life.

"She said she's after hearing so much about you, it was time she clapped eyes on you."

I hoped her sources did not include Bertha Peddle from the store or angry Roy Sullivan.

"Geri will be there too," Doug added. "It's my birthday."

I hadn't heard Geri mentioned in quite a while, but then again, I hadn't been spending much time in Little Cove. Apart from that brief encounter at the Mardy pub, this would be the first time I'd be seeing Geri and Doug together. Doug and I had developed an easy banter, and I found myself wondering if it was the same between him and Geri.

On Doug's birthday, to kill time between the end of the school day and when I was expected at his family home for dinner, I had arranged to drop in on Lucille. She was pleased to see me, although when I mentioned my plans, she got a funny look on her face.

"So you'll be meeting Grace." It turned out this was Doug's mother's name. "Don't mention you been here," she said. "Might spoil your evening."

When I asked what she meant, she didn't answer, and instead changed the subject. Over tea she caught me up on the hookers and her daughter, Linda, who was not coming home for Christmas because she had decided to stay in Labrador.

When it was time to go, I handed Lucille a wrapped bottle of rum and she presented me with a quilt. It was all rolled up and tied with a string, but that didn't hide its beauty.

"Lucille," I said. "I can't accept this. You already gave me one when I bought the rug to send to Mom in Australia."

"That was the buy one get one free fall special," she said.

"Honestly, Lucille. I can't accept this if you won't let me pay for it."

She batted her hand at me. "Now who ever heard of paying someone for a Christmas present?"

As usual, she had the last word.

Lucille walked me out to the car and pointed the way to Doug's place.

The house was perched high on a hill; the lights of a Christmas tree blinked in the front window. I walked up a ramp that zigzagged back and forth, and knocked at the door.

Geri opened the door and said hello. Then she whispered, "In case Doug didn't tell you, his mam's in a wheelchair."

"Thanks," I said. "He didn't."

She frowned. "He never does."

She led me to a large living room where Mrs. Bishop sat by the fire, sipping a glass of red wine. She was the most elegant woman I'd seen in Little Cove. She had long black hair, with only a few streaks of grey, tied in a low ponytail. Her cherry-red lipstick matched her wool dress perfectly.

"You're very welcome here, Miss O'Brien," she said. It was the first time my surname had been pronounced correctly since I pitched up in Little Cove. I was so used to hearing O'Brine that I nearly corrected her.

"Call me Rachel," I said, then held up a poinsettia. "I brought this for you."

Geri took it and placed it on the coffee table.

"Then you must call me Grace," she said. Then she called out to Doug to tell him I had arrived.

He came through from the kitchen wearing an apron emblazoned with a picture of a Newfoundland dog, above which was written "Top Dog."

"Whaddya at?" he asked.

"Happy birthday. I wasn't sure what to get you, but I know you like to eat, and I have my own kitchen now." I handed over a container of my signature chocolate chip cookies.

"They looks good, t'anks." He leaned down and pecked my cheek. I was conscious of Geri, but she seemed completely indifferent.

"Geri, can you get Rachel a drink?" Doug said. "I'm wrassling with the cod tongs."

I hadn't heard Lucille ever mention cod tongs. Perhaps it was one of the "new-fangled gadgets" she loved to denigrate.

Geri brought me a glass of wine, and I sat on the sofa across from Doug's mother, trying to ignore the framed picture of Jesus that hung on the wall above her. His sacred heart was exposed and his sad eyes seemed to follow mine, no matter where I looked. He would totally beat me in a staring contest.

"You must be finding Little Cove a big change from the mainland," Doug's mother said.

"It has its charms," I said. "But I live in Clayville now."

"Even Clayville isn't big enough for some," she said, glancing over at Geri, who was flicking through a fashion magazine.

"Don't you miss Toronto?" Geri asked, looking up. "All those malls."

"There are things I miss, sure," I agreed.

Doug shouted from the kitchen, "Grub's up."

Geri wheeled Mrs. Bishop into the kitchen, while I followed ineptly behind. Over at the stove, Doug stood on a hooked rug that wasn't a patch on any Lucille made. Red gingham curtains hung at the large window, and the seemingly mandatory daybed was over in the corner.

I sat at one end of the table with Mrs. Bishop opposite me and Doug and Geri on either side. Doug loaded my plate with what looked like chicken nuggets topped with little hash browns. When Geri declined both, Mrs. Bishop clicked her tongue.

"I've seen more meat on Good Friday than on your bones, Geraldine," she said. "Doug's after making us a proper feast. Cod tongues and scruncheons."

Her words sank in. Cod had tongues? And if so, what were the little scruncheons? Did cod have testicles?

Geri waved her hand at Mrs. Bishop. "Sure, you knows I don't like fish."

Mrs. Bishop was watching me, so I stabbed a cod tongue with my fork and began to chew. And chew. It was cod chewing gum. Finally, I swallowed it down with water, then speared a scruncheon with my fork. I brought it close to my face for a discreet sniff. My taste buds relaxed; any cousin of bacon was fine by me.

"The scruncheons are good," I said.

"Does that mean the tongues aren't?" Doug asked.

"Don't eat them if you don't want," his mother said. "They're an acquired taste." She glanced sideways at Geri. "Sometimes a forgotten one, too."

"I like the taste," I said, aiming for diplomacy. "But the texture . . ."

"Have the small ones," said Doug. "They're less chewy."

"Still gross, though," said Geri, so I ate the lot.

When our plates were empty, Geri cleared them and fetched bowls from the cupboard, placing one in front of me. "Do you have any family in Newfoundland?" she asked.

"She's all on her lonesome down here," Doug answered.

His words had me wondering if this was a pity invite.

Doug placed a steaming casserole dish in the centre of the table. "Rabbit stew. Caught and skinned the bugger myself."

Images of famous bunnies hopped into my mind: Peter Rabbit, the Easter Bunny and old Bugs himself. I found myself wondering if it was too late to claim a sudden conversion to vegetarianism.

Doug's mother filled her bowl, then passed the serving spoon to me. I churned through the stew, ladling potatoes, turnips, carrots and parsnips into my bowl. But Doug was watching me closely, and it was his birthday, so I added the smallest bits of meat I could find. I told myself it was chicken. And I kept telling myself that all through dinner, even when I asked for seconds.

"Do you do all the cooking?" I asked Doug.

"Since my accident," said his mother. "But it's not right. I'm hiring a cook in the new year."

"You're not," said Doug.

"You'd have more free time. You could go to St. John's and see Geraldine," she said. "Not be stuck out here looking after the likes of me."

Doug and Geri exchanged glances. Doug frowned, then after a minute, he said, "You knows I don't like being in amongst the townies. And I'm not going anywhere just yet. I signed a two-year contract, remember?" He gestured across the table at me. "Rachel's got her licked though."

I froze, wondering if I had gravy on my face. I discreetly mopped my mouth, but the napkin remained pristine white.

"What do you mean?" I asked.

"Your one-year contract. How'd you swing that? Probationary is usually two."

"I asked for one year," I said. "I think they were a bit desperate, because of the . . . situation. So they said yes."

"Brigid Roche." Mrs. Bishop sighed. "Grief makes us do foolish things. Don't we know that in this house." She twisted her wedding ring and the room went quiet.

To fill the silence, I asked Geri what type of nursing she did.

"General surgery," she said. "Never a dull moment."

"Geri likes plenty of excitement," Doug said. "Even on the job."

"I likes to be on the go," she said evenly. "Nothing wrong with that. And I likes being amongst the townies. Anyway, enough about the townies, now. Why did you become a teacher, Rachel?"

"Maybe because my dad was one," I said. "He passed away in April."

"I'm so sorry," both Geri and Mrs. Bishop murmured.

"Thank you," I said simply. "His students loved him."

Doug caught my eye and gave me a little smile. For a minute, the only sound was the wall clock ticking. My mind wandered to Dad's funeral. A girl with little round glasses had clung to Mom, sobbing, "I loved him so much." Mom told me later that she couldn't decide whether to hug her or hit her.

I forced myself back to the present. "What about you, Doug, why did you become a teacher?"

"NBA never came calling." He stood up then and said, "Time for cake." He opened the fridge and removed a large chocolate cake. I found myself wondering if Geri had baked it, but then she said it looked delicious, so I decided she hadn't.

We sang "Happy Birthday," then Doug blew out the candles and cut the cake. As Mrs. Bishop passed me a slice, she said, "What are your plans for Christmas, Rachel?"

Doug answered for me. "Sure you knows she's going up to the mainland."

I didn't correct him, not wanting another pity invitation. I would be in Clayville, all on my lonesome as Doug had put it earlier. The Christmas break was less than two weeks long, too short a time to go to Australia, I'd reasoned, especially with all the plane changes. And it had seemed pointless to go back to Toronto with Mom not there and our house rented out for the year.

"Pointless?" Sheila had practically shouted down the phone line when I told her. "What about me? Don't we always go for dim sum on Christmas Eve? And who's going to carry my bags during the Boxing Day sales?"

But by the time I decided Sheila was right and I should go visit her in Toronto, there were no flights left. It would be me, myself and my fiddle having a festive little pity party.

I was tired, so when my offer to help do the dishes was gently declined, I made my leave. Geri asked if I would mind dropping her at her mother's, explaining that it was on the way.

During the short drive, we chatted about the holidays. Geri said she would be home for a few days over Christmas, but would be attending a big New Year's Eve party in St. John's. I wondered if Doug would go too. It didn't sound like his scene to me.

I dropped Geri at a small house ablaze with light, waiting, probably unnecessarily, until she went inside.

Afterwards, as I drove home, I found myself speculating about Geri and Doug. They seemed at ease with each other, but lacking in affection. Why hadn't she asked Doug to take her home? The whole thing seemed odd, but then again, as my romantic history would attest, I was no expert on relationships myself.

19

On the last day of term, the faded red-velvet curtains on the stage at the front of the gym opened to reveal a choir dressed in white robes. Stage left, seated at the piano, was Sister Mary Catherine. As the opening notes of "Away in a Manger" rang out, a dozen tremulous voices gained confidence and volume. When the song was over, the grade seven pupils arrived onstage to present the nativity. Hanging at the back of Sister's classroom, their costumes hadn't looked like much, but now, as the children took their positions, a charming tableau emerged with shepherds in bathrobes and tea towels and angels in white bedsheets and silver tinsel. The narrator took a deep breath and began. "Many people were on the road to Bethlehem, Mary and Joseph among them."

I stood against the back wall, having arrived too late to find a seat in the packed house. Phonse was next to me, leaning on his broom. My eyes roved over the audience and landed on the hookers, all sitting in a row. Lucille caught me looking and nodded. Further along, Cynthia sat with a guy in a black leather jacket. His arm was wrapped tight around her shoulder and he looked too old for her. Heck, he looked too old for me. I didn't recognize him, not even when he glanced over his shoulder. His scowl would have done Billy Idol proud.

The narrator was reaching the conclusion of the familiar story when I spotted Georgie Corrigan, coat open over her distended stomach. She must be due any day. As a homemade donkey crossed the stage pushed by Mary and Joseph, I was reminded of Georgie's comment that day in the takeout about the Virgin Mary.

When the vignette ended, the audience clapped loudly. As the curtains swung shut, the back door of the gym opened behind me, blowing in a gust of cold air, and Doug. He shut the door carefully so it didn't slam and came over to stand beside me.

"Where were you?" I whispered.

"Clayville. Patrick asked me to get the booze for the staff party," he said. "The road was right slippery so I had to take 'er slow coming back. Then I had to drop it all off at his place." He blew on his hands. "Some cold out there, too."

A woman in the back row turned around and shushed Doug. After she'd turned back around, he made a face at her, and then I made one at him. Then the curtains reopened and we turned our attention to the stage.

The grade nines were dressed in red and green, girls on the right, boys on the left. Divide and conquer? A few of the girls had tinsel draped around their necks and wrists, and Calvin was wearing a Santa Claus hat. Surely it was not possible for that disparate and discouraging group to perform a cohesive piece of entertainment.

Judy crouched down on the floor in front of the stage and held up her right hand, with three fingers raised, then two, then one.

"Knock knock," said the girls, in perfect unison.

"Who's there?" asked the boys.

"Wenceslas," came the reply.

"Wenceslas who?"

"Wenceslas bus to St. John's?"

There was scattered laughter and a few groans from the audience.

Then the boys shouted, "Knock knock."

"Who's there?"

"Wayne," said the boys, and the audience chuckled when every boy pointed dramatically at Wayne Molloy in the front row.

"Wayne who?"

"Wayne in a manger."

At that point, Wayne ran over to the nativity scene, lay down on the ground and began to suck his thumb. The laughter was longer and louder. The grade nines, Calvin and Trudy included, were enjoying themselves. I glanced over at Sister Mary Catherine, who did not seem to be amused by Wayne's antics.

"Knock knock," cried the girls again.

"Who's there?"

"Mary."

Sister stood up, fists clenched.

"Mary who?"

"Mary Christmas!" they all shouted, throwing red and green streamers out into the audience.

Sister sat back down, smoothing her habit. The grade nine class had been onstage for less than five minutes, but their performance had been enthusiastic and well received. It was a triumph for Judy.

At the end of the concert, Patrick headed to the stage to thank the performers and the audience. Then, with Sister playing along, everyone—pupils, parents and teachers—stood and sang the "Ode to Newfoundland." Doug closed his eyes and put his hand on his heart.

> *When sun rays crown thy pine-clad hills,*
> *And Summer spreads her hand,*
> *When silvern voices tune thy rills,*
> *We love thee, smiling land.*
> *We love thee, we love thee*
> *We love thee, smiling land.*

> *When spreads thy cloak of shimmering white,*
> *At Winter's stern command,*
> *Through shortened day and starlit night,*
> *We love thee, frozen land.*
> *We love thee, we love thee,*
> *We love thee, frozen land.*

I didn't know the lyrics, but the heartfelt rendition had me blinking hard. When it was over, people clapped and cheered. "That was beautiful," I whispered to Doug, my voice catching. "Like a prayer."

"Newfoundlanders are a cult, sure." He reached out and brushed a strand of hair from my face. I jerked away when I saw Sister Mary Catherine frowning at us. As soon as the audience began to disperse, she left the stage, headed in our direction.

"I'm out of here," I said to Doug. "It's too warm. I'll see you at the party." I retrieved my coat and purse from the staff room, loitering there for a while in the hopes of avoiding Sister. Then I headed to the front entrance. It had snowed lightly during the concert and everything was covered in a "cloak of shimmering white." I watched the last stragglers walk up the road, then Doug came hustling out, rubbing his fingers together in the cold.

"I left my car at Patrick's when I dropped off the booze," he said. "I'm low on gas. Can I snag a lift, maid?"

I exhaled loudly. "I hate when people call me that. It reminds me of an old maid."

"Well, you'll prob'ly end up one if you stays so sensitive," he groused. "Jaysus God tonight, woman. It's just an expression."

When we got to my car, a note, wet with snow, was tucked under the wipers. Doug snatched it up. "Ohhh, what's this? Someone's got a secret admirer."

"Give it to me, Doug," I said, my voice sharp.

He held it high above his head, teasing me. I jumped to grab it, but I couldn't reach. "Give it."

He angled it towards the streetlight, saying, "I'll just take a peek first."

"No!"

He grinned and opened the note. I found myself wondering what his reaction would be. Would he be upset on my behalf?

"Nope," he said. "Can't make anything out. I think it's in French."

"It is?" I plucked it from his hand and read: "Tu es beau."

It was flattering, if grammatically incorrect. My shoulders relaxed. Maybe I did have a secret admirer. The writing was different, more childish looking. I was pretty sure this was nothing more than a teacher's crush, but I would compare it with the others when I got home. I shoved the note in my pocket.

"So, what's it say?" asked Doug as we got in my car.

"Just that someone thinks I'm pretty. Well, handsome, if we're doing an exact translation."

"Seems like a good omen," said Doug. "You might not end up an old maid, after all."

I whacked him. "And you might not end up bruised. But I doubt it."

Patrick's house was right down by the sea. We could hear the music before we reached the bend in the road. "It's gonna be a time," said Doug. I pulled into the driveway and shut off the engine.

"When's your flight?" Doug asked.

"What fli—" Then I remembered that I was supposedly off home to Toronto soon.

"Oh, um, in a couple of days. What are you doing for Christmas?"

"I'll be around. Mudder needs me, though she denies it."

The car windows had fogged up as we sat there, and Doug drew a little Christmas tree in the middle of the front windscreen with his index finger.

"You forgot the star," I said, leaning over to add one.

"That's you," he said, his voice husky.

"Doug."

"Shhh," he said, putting a finger to my lips, the faint pressure making them tingle. He traced their outline lightly, then moved his hand to brush my hair out of my face.

Our eyes were locked on each other, and despite the chill in the air, I felt a heat rising in me. Doug leaned in and then, *thwack!* A snowball hit the back window of my car hard. I jerked my head, driving it up into Doug's face.

"Oww," he said, moving his hand quickly to his mouth.

A second snowball hit the car, and I got out in time to see two boys holding each other's sleeves for balance as they slip-slid their way down the road, their laughter ringing in the night.

Doug got out and slammed the passenger door. "Gave me a fat lip," he complained.

"Sorry." I scooped up some snow so he could hold it to his mouth.

As we reached Patrick's front door, I wondered whether Doug had been about to kiss me. Would I have kissed him back? And what about Geri?

20

At that time of year, it seemed that the main perk of being a teacher, apart from the generous holidays, was the Christmas gifts. Finally, I had my very own "World's Greatest Teacher" mug, not to mention perfumed soap, Christmas decorations, homemade jam and all the chocolate I could eat, which was a lot.

I slightly overdid it on Christmas Eve, eating an entire box. I slipped from the loveseat to the floor, cradling my stomach. "It was the Turkish delight," I wailed into the silence. A new year was just around the tinsel, and I'd learned much since September, although clearly not when to stop eating chocolate.

Eventually, I felt well enough to crawl along the floor and turn on the Christmas lights. I snuggled under Lucille's quilt and admired my short, fat Christmas tree, decorated simply with white lights and red bows. I turned out all the other lights and lay in the dark, watching the fairy lights twinkle.

Sparsely placed around the base of the tree were three items: a big box from Australia, an envelope from Sheila, and a squat and clumsily wrapped package that someone had left on my desk on the last day of the term. Sheila's envelope had arrived two weeks ago, but I'd managed to restrain myself from opening it. It would be weird not seeing her over the holidays, maybe even weirder than not seeing Mom.

I stared at the presents, looked away, then looked back again. Those gifts were begging to be opened. After a short moral struggle, I decided that, since it was already Christmas Day in Australia, I was within my rights to open Mom's gift.

I tore open the brown postal wrapping, pausing to smile at the Christmas paper featuring Santa on a surfboard. Then I dug through the tissue until my hand hit something hard.

I wrapped my fingers around it and raised it in the air. It was a boomerang. I laughed until my stomach hurt more than it had from the Turkish delight. Dad would've laughed at this gift, too. I was also pleased with the symmetry of the gifts Mom and I had chosen. She'd sent me a symbol of Australia and I had mailed her a piece of Newfoundland in the form of Lucille's rug. The package still hadn't arrived the last time we'd spoken, but I was hopeful that when she called me on my Christmas Day, she would have received it.

When I put the boomerang under the tree, my fingers brushed against Sheila's envelope and I swear it seemed to open itself, although it was me who pulled the card out. Sheila's message was brief: "Your present will arrive on Boxing Day. Please be home to accept delivery."

This would not be a problem, since I had no plans to speak of.

It seemed silly to leave the last package sitting all alone under the tree. And as I turned it over, I noticed a label: "For my fiddle girl." Ah, Phonse. It was a homemade cassette tape. I stuck it in my boombox and almost immediately recognized the tune Eddie Churchill had whistled as he changed my tires. "Sonny's Dream," he'd called it. I listened as Sonny's mother begged him not to leave her.

When the song ended, I pressed rewind.

Sonny's lamenting mother didn't sound like the women I knew. Lucille, so proud of her daughter, Linda, teaching in Labrador; Cynthia's mother, so supportive of her scholarship hopes; and even Mrs. Piercey, who wanted something more for Calvin.

I listened on repeat until I knew every word of "Sonny's Dream" by heart. When I stopped pressing rewind, the tape moved to the second track and I smiled as "Sweet Forget Me Not" filled the room. The singer was nowhere near as good as Beverley, whose voice had astonished me that night in Mardy. I carried the boombox up to my bedroom and fell asleep listening to the music.

Mom's call woke me on Christmas morning. She exclaimed over Lucille's rug, then said she'd spent her Christmas Day at the beach.

"How was that?"

"Odd," she said. "But also, wonderful. Different."

We caught up on each other's news and exchanged book recommendations. We kept it light, neither of us mentioning how much we missed Dad.

"You're not spending today on your own, are you?" Mom asked.

"No," I assured her. And I wasn't. I would have the best company: Mr. Red Wine, Ms. Paperback and my very dear friends Cashews and Chocolate.

After we hung up, I made myself a toasted bacon and cheese sandwich for breakfast and drank gallons of coffee. I tried not to think about Dad's grave under a shroud of snow with no visitors.

And really, as far as I was concerned, Dad's spirit wasn't there in the ground. It was in books and music and birds. Still, something drove me to bundle up and explore the deserted cemetery behind my house.

Most of the headstones were faded and covered in lichen, which peeked out from beneath the snow. One read simply, "Dear Mother." Others gave incredibly detailed biographical information. Many people had drowned or been lost at sea; I thought of Lucille's husband and Doug's father. On the gravestone of two brothers killed at Beaumont-Hamel, I read, "There is a part of France that will always be English." It took me a minute to decipher it until I remembered that Newfoundland had not joined Canada until 1949. Then, it hit me; people like Lucille and Phonse had basically lived through their own Confederation.

Later, I had a long bath, not even bothering to straighten my hair afterwards, moving instead directly to pyjama time. I lay in the dark, sipping red wine and watching *It's a Wonderful Life*. I drifted off, dreaming that Calvin was Clarence the angel, desperate to get his wings.

A BELL WOKE ME, and I half shouted, "He got his wings!" Then I realized it was the doorbell. The house was freezing and my neck ached from having fallen asleep awkwardly on the sofa.

"Go away," I groused, wrapping the quilt tighter around me.

But whoever was at the door kept on banging, and I remembered Sheila's advice to be home on Boxing Day. Still wrapped in the quilt, I dragged myself to the door and saw the familiar face that I loved so well. I burst into tears and threw my arms around Sheila.

"Never mind that for now," she said, pushing past me and dropping her suitcase on the floor. "I'm freezing!" She stamped her feet to shake the snow off her boots. "Now we can hug," she said. And we did.

"How did you? When did you?" I kept changing the question, finally settling on, "How was the trip down?"

"Godawful. Crying baby all the way from Halifax, spent the night in a questionable B&B in St. John's, mad taxi driver on the three-hour drive out here . . . but it was worth the nightmare to see that look on your face when you opened the door."

"How did you get a flight?"

Sheila was actively snooping now, poking in the kitchen cupboards. "Mike pulled a few strings."

Sheila's brother was a big shot at MusiCan, the national video channel, and knew all the right people. "I fly back on New Year's Day," she added, heading for the stairs.

I followed her into the bedroom and she opened the curtains.

"Is that what I think it is?" She pointed down to the cemetery, where my tracks around the gravestones from yesterday were still visible in the snow.

"Uh-huh."

"And to think I flew all this way to cheer you up because I thought you didn't know a soul down here," said Sheila.

Six days of bad jokes. Bliss.

21

"Extra-large, double cheese, double pepperoni," Sheila said to the shy waiter at Tony's. "And two more beers, please." She flashed her megawatt smile and he stumbled into a chair as he left.

"How's the job?" I asked. Sheila was a sales representative for a pharmaceutical company. Her stock answer if anyone asked what she did for a living was "drug pusher." She was made for sales; Dad used to say she could convince anyone to do anything if she tried hard enough.

"There's talk of another promotion," she said tucking her blonde hair behind her ears.

"How's Peter?"

"Do keep up, Rachel. I dropped him a month ago."

Sheila had a rule of three when it came to men: one on the way in, one on the way out, and one on the side. I operated a similar system, but mine was for books.

When the pizza arrived, we went quiet until a good dent had been made.

"Almost as good as Luigi's," Sheila said, patting her mouth with a napkin.

"I miss Luigi's," I wailed.

"Luigi misses you too," said Sheila. "That's our first stop when I break you out of this joint. Now, listen, how is everything down here, really?"

I told Sheila how pleased Phonse was with my progress on the fiddle. I complained about the impossible challenge Judy had set me, to convince the students to play traditional music at the garden party.

"Like that tape you were playing earlier?" she asked. "I loved it. I might see if I can buy some music like that for Mike."

Then I launched into a long anecdote about how I'd cracked the discipline problem with worksheets. At first Sheila listened patiently. But after a minute, she held up her hand.

"Whoa, whoa. This is all deeply fascinating, but I want to hear about Doug."

"What about him?"

"Rachel." Sheila's tone brooked no dissent.

So I told her about the moment in the car before Patrick's party—the star comment, the maybe-almost kiss, the snowball that had ended whatever might have been before it started. I left out the part about how my lips had tingled.

"I think he might . . . sort of . . . kind of . . . like me. A bit," I summed up.

Sheila reached out and patted my hand. "There you go with that huge overconfidence thing again, sweetie." We dissolved into giggles. When Sheila had regained control, she said, "Do you think you might . . . sort of . . . kind of . . . like him? A bit?"

I shrugged. "He has a girlfriend."

"Yeah, yeah, he has a girlfriend. But I thought you said there was a weird vibe."

I nodded. "Yeah. Geri seems great, but they don't seem to have much in common. And they spend virtually no time together. She lives in St. John's and hardly ever comes out this way."

I paused and lined up my cutlery. "But, you know, when Jake cheated on me, it tore me apart. I could never do that to someone else."

"You wouldn't be the one cheating."

"Semantics."

Sheila opened her mouth to argue the point, but a cry of "Rachel!" stopped her. Judy and Bill had arrived at the restaurant, and Judy was waving as they made their way across the room to our table.

"You're back from Toronto already?" Judy asked. I ignored Sheila's side-eye and introduced her to Judy and Bill, managing to duck the question in the process.

"Are you free tomorrow night?" Judy said. "You could come mummering with us."

"Mumbling?" I said.

Judy laughed. "Mummering. It's a Christmas tradition. You puts on an elaborate disguise, goes door to door, and does a little skit. And then, with any luck at all, they offers you a drink."

"Halloween and Christmas all wrapped up in one magical night," Sheila said. "Sounds excellent."

I must have looked less enthusiastic, because Judy said, "Come on, Rachel, it's fun. Music, entertainment, a few laughs." She turned to her husband. "Tell her, Bill."

"It's an excuse to get hammered," said Bill.

"It's more than that," chided Judy. "It's an important part of our heritage, a fine cultural tradition that needs to be maintained, it's . . ." She grinned. "Yeah, it's also an excuse to get hammered."

She eyed us appraisingly. "We could have real fun with you. No one would expect a mainlander to mummer. With the right disguise, they'd never guess who you were."

Bill waved his hand in the air. "One problem with your plan, me duck."

"What's that?"

"Soon as she opens her mouth, the crowd will know she's that Miss O'Brine from over to the school."

The beer I'd been drinking may have been a factor, but I rose to Bill's challenge, leaping from my chair and shouting in the broadest Newfoundland accent I could muster. "I'm a Newfoundlander, luh. Best kind, right? Proper t'ing. How's she going, b'y?"

Our waiter was on his way over but, after my little performance, veered quickly away.

"Not bad," said Bill, rubbing his chin.

"Not bad," agreed Judy. "Talk in a deep voice. You can be Jenny the Wren."

"A wren? Wasn't that a World War II women's regiment thing?"

"Ah Rachel," said Bill. "I dies at you. Judy, me darling, do us the honours, will ya?"

Judy cleared her throat, then recited a long verse about a wren on St. Stephen's Day.

I wasn't exactly sure what it all meant, but Sheila and I clapped loudly, as did the family at the next table. Judy bowed low. She was a natural performer.

"Do you think you can learn that if I writes it down?" said Judy.

"I guess so," I said.

"Great. We'd better get to our table now before we loses it, but let's talk before you goes."

Sheila and I had another beer and then, after paying our bill, stopped by Judy and Bill's table. Judy had written out lines for both of us on the back of a paper placemat. She told me I was to dress like a bird.

"Sheila," she added. "You needs to dress like a bit of a hussy."

"I thought she was supposed to be disguised," I said, and Sheila thumped me.

Judy rubbed her hands together. "It's going to be some fun. Even when Sheila takes off her disguise, they won't know who she is."

"That's me," said Sheila. "The Russian doll of disguises."

Sheila and I left the restaurant and linked arms to walk home.

"Will Doug be murmuring?" she asked.

"It's mummering," I said, displaying my new-found vocabulary. "And I don't know." Then I remembered. "Oh, crap. I kind of let him think I was going to Toronto for Christmas. I hope he's not mad at me."

"Oh my God," said Sheila. "Imagine if you had gone to Toronto to surprise me and I'd come down here to surprise you?"

"Yeah," I said. "Like 'The Gift of the Magi.'"

"But with better hair," said Sheila.

22

The next morning Sheila and I went to the coffee shop for breakfast. Although she'd been up for mummering the previous night, she was less keen today.

"Do we have to go?" she whined. "Aren't we a bit old for dressing up?"

"Wilf," I said, after we'd placed our order. "What are your thoughts on mummering?"

"The wife makes me do it every year," he said, loading a plate with butter tarts and muffins.

Sheila gave me a triumphant look. "Makes him do it, see? This poor man is forced to participate. Against his will, Rachel. I will not be forced."

Wilf put the plate on the tray with our coffee mugs. "And every year after it's over, you know what I says to her?"

"Never again?" said Sheila.

He laughed. "Nope. I says, Darling, remind me next year how much fun it was."

It was my turn for the triumphant look.

"Okay, okay," Sheila grumbled. "But what are we going to wear?"

"You needs to have a rummage over to the second-hand store," said Wilf.

After treating us to a detailed history of mummering outfits he had worn over the years, Wilf gave us directions to the second-hand store, where later that morning, we spent an enjoyable hour trying on ridiculous combinations of clothing. It was a far cry from our former shopping sessions at the mall, but just as fun.

We spent some time memorizing our lines over takeout pizza from Tony's that evening. Then we changed and drove out to Judy's.

When the back door opened, Sheila began humming the *Twilight Zone* music because whoever was beckoning us in wore a pillowcase over their head, with cut-outs for eyes and mouth. We guessed it was Judy, since it was too short to be Bill. She was sporting a plaid shirt, denim overalls and big rubber boots. She had a massive hump on her back; a tweed cap and a pair of men's gloves completed her look. She hustled us into the kitchen, where Bill sat in a wedding dress with full train. He wore a curly red wig and white gloves up to his elbows.

Bill and Judy exclaimed over our outfits.

I was wearing rubber boots and a blue coverall. I'd made wings from coat hangers and wore a balaclava to hide my face. Perched on my head, tying the ensemble together, was a tea cozy in the shape of a bird.

Sheila wore a tropical bikini top over her black turtleneck and a red skirt over her jeans. A bandana covered her mouth; dark sunglasses and a sombrero completed her ensemble. Bill was wearing a worn, white baby blanket for a veil. Once Judy fastened it over his face, he couldn't see anything. He kept stumbling and swearing softly to himself whenever he tried to walk.

We left the house and shuffled down the road.

Sheila kept whispering her lines over and over again to practise, but Bill shushed her as we approached the door of a lime-green house, and then he rapped sharply at the door.

When someone finally answered, Sheila stepped forward as instructed and shouted, "Any mummers 'lowed in?" Bill had been quite pedantic about Sheila not saying *allowed*. It had to be *'lowed*.

The door opened wider and our prospective host smiled broadly. "Lord lightning Jaysus, come in out of it 'til we gets a look at ye." Then he shouted over his shoulder, "Nettie, there's mummers after coming."

His wife came running, a dishtowel still in her hands. She waved shyly then invited us into the kitchen. Then she went to the bottom of the stairs. "Eugene," she called. "Run next door and tell Phil and Bessie to come 'round and see the mummers."

Eugene was a student at the school. With no sign of recognition, he ran past us and out into the cold, wearing only a T-shirt. His sister Darlene galloped down the stairs after him. "What crowd is this?" she asked, staring hard at us. She left the kitchen, and I heard her dialling the phone and then her breathless voice saying, "We got mummers here, come over the once!"

Within minutes a dozen people had crowded into the kitchen.

Bill began to talk in an exaggerated whisper:

'Twas on my fateful wedding day
I should have been bright and gay.
But me darling sweetheart crept away
And married a girl from Witless Bay.

Amidst laughter and clapping, Bill began to sob hysterically and fell to his knees in front of Judy, who pointedly ignored him. He clasped his hands to his enormous bosom and jerked a finger at Sheila.

"That's the hussy who stole him."

Sheila strode into the centre of the kitchen. She put her hands on her hips and wiggled them from side to side. Then, with one hand on her sombrero and the other on her heart, she spoke loudly, not bothering to mask her own voice:

> It was a shocking thing to do
> I'm a bad one, through and through.
> But please don't put the blame on me
> A little birdie made me, see?

There'd been more discussion about whether I should try to disguise my voice. Bill wanted me to hold up a sign, rather than speak. But in the end, I convinced him I could pull off an Irish brogue. As Sheila left the centre of the room, we gave each other a high-five and I took her place, wriggling my shoulders in an effort to flap my wings.

> The Wren the Wren
> The Queen of all birds
> On St. Stephen's Day she got caught in the furze.
> She dipped her wing in a pint of beer
> And bid everyone a Happy New Year.
> Although she is little, her honour is great
> So rise up now lads and give her a treat.
> And if you don't believe the words that I say
> Here's the old skipper to show you the way.

Someone grabbed my arm, but I pulled away and made for Bill and Sheila. Judy stepped forward and spoke her lines in a deep, low voice, ending with a flourish:

> *We fine mummers brave and true*
> *Have now put on a show for you.*
> *Guess who we are, go on now, think*
> *While you're at it, we needs a drink.*

We bowed to great applause. We were then offered drinks, which we slipped under our various veils and coverings, sipping with difficulty. Then we waved goodbye and headed off to the next stop. As we walked single file up the road, we talked excitedly about our triumphal appearance.

"We nailed it," crowed Sheila.

We visited a few more houses and no one guessed who we were. At each house, we had a drink. At the penultimate one, they served neat rum. I was starting to flag when we rounded a corner and saw a house with every light on and music flowing out of its open front door.

"Looks like Eddie Churchill's on the go tonight," said Bill. "Funny, he never said anything."

"We were invited," said Judy. "But I said we were busy."

"Now why would you do that?" Bill asked.

"So we could show up in disguise and they wouldn't be expecting us."

"You're a fine woman," said Bill. "Someone should marry you."

We walked up the path to Eddie's house and made our way in. People stepped aside to make room for us, and we ended up in the middle of the kitchen. I spotted Lucille and the hookers clapping time with the musicians. When the song ended, the musicians ceded the floor to us and once more we performed our skit.

"Sacred Heart of Jaysus," said Lucille. "Who are ye at all?"

I kept my gaze on the linoleum floor, anxious not to give myself away. Also, I didn't want to catch Sheila's eye, in case we got the giggles.

Lucille began prodding Bill's stomach, making him jump about.

A young man came right up close to Sheila and peered in her face. "It's that French one down to the school, right?"

Lucille circled Sheila, conducting a close inspection. "That's not Rachel," she said. "I'd stake me life on it."

"Well," said an old man standing by the wood stove. "She talks like her, but I seen that Miss O'Brine at church one time and she's right short." He put his hand to his waist. "Only comes up yay high."

I managed to restrain myself from a defence of my stature.

The young man looked down at Sheila's feet. "She's wearing heels though, right?"

Despite Lucille's protestations, the majority decided that Sheila was me. After some prolonged urging and with a nod from Judy, Sheila took off the sunglasses and sombrero. The room was silenced.

"Who knit you?" asked the young man.

Sheila, ever the wit, replied, "Aunt Pearl."

There was laughter. Then another question, "What are you doing out this way?"

"Visiting friends," said Sheila.

"We're not friends anymore," said Bill. "Since you stole my Judy." He clapped his hand over his mouth, but it was too late.

"Bill, my son," howled Eddie. "You had us fooled." He jerked his hand at Judy. "I expect this is the missus." Judy pulled off her headgear and Eddie gave her a hug.

"I needs a drink after being stuffed under that pillowcase," Judy said.

Sheila, Judy and Bill were all enjoying a drink but I was still disguised, which wasn't much fun. Then the door banged open and Doug walked in.

"Rachel," he said. "What are you doing here? I thought you went home."

I pulled off my tea cozy and balaclava.

Doug had a wounded look on his face, but before I could speak to him, Eddie passed me a beer and said, "Not bad for a mainlander."

Sheila clinked her bottle with mine. "We mainlanders are all right, once you get to know us," she said.

I wasn't really listening; instead I watched Doug go over and talk to Phonse. I started to follow him, but then Geri arrived with another woman I didn't recognize, and the pair of them went over to talk to Doug.

I turned my attention back to Sheila, introducing her to Lucille. Sheila gave her a big hug. "Thank you for taking such good care of my best friend, Lucille."

"Ah, go on with you," said Lucille. "She was no bother."

Phonse came over to talk to me. I kept looking past him for Doug, but couldn't spot him.

Sheila batted her eyes at Phonse. "I've heard so much about you from Rachel. I think you practically run that school."

Lucille whispered in my ear, "She's flirting with Phonse. You better tell her he's a . . ."

"Confirmed bachelor," I replied. "Don't worry, Sheila flirts with everyone, but she's harmless."

Lucille raised her glass to toast me. "You've come a long way since that first day you pitched up all high and mighty," she said.

I flinched. "What do you mean?"

She reached over and tugged one of my curls. "Just that you're after loosening up a bit, girl. And it's some good to see."

Eddie's kitchen was similar to Lucille's but more cluttered. Over by the stove, a rangy brown dog lay oblivious to the noise. The party was in full swing now and empty beer bottles stood beside bottles of rum and whiskey. Big ceramic bowls of chips and pretzels were filled and refilled.

Clusters of people stood talking, their heads together, and bursts of laughter would periodically fill the room. Judy was in high spirits. She and Bill were waltzing in the hall. Naturally, Sheila was surrounded by admirers. She had a knack for getting men to riff off one another, rather than compete with each other. When Doug came by, pushing through the crowd, I grabbed his arm.

"Come and meet my best friend Sheila."

But just as I introduced them, Phonse handed me a fiddle. "People are asking if you'll play. Will you?"

I took the fiddle and joined the musicians in the corner. As we tuned up, I thanked Phonse for the cassette he'd given me for Christmas.

"I don't know what you're talking about, girl," he said. "I never gave you a cassette." While I wondered who had, the accordion player addressed the room.

"The teacher's gonna join us but she only knows the one song, right?"

Phonse corrected him. "She's after picking up a few more, b'y."

I caught sight of Doug, who was no longer talking to Sheila but standing on his own, leaning up against the wall. Before I could look for Geri, the music started and I had to concentrate. It was much more intimate playing there than it had been up on stage that night, but I closed my eyes and tried to relax into the music.

After playing several songs, we took a break and I went to find Sheila. She was deep in conversation with Eddie Churchill, who was filling her in on the history of Little Cove. People kept arriving, and the house grew so crowded that the party spilled out into the cold air. I saw Geri leave with her friend but there was no sign of Doug.

Hours later, Sheila and I walked back to Judy's to share her spare bed. The stars were out and the night was cold, but there was a warmth in my heart big enough to heat the whole of Little Cove.

I was tired and wanted to sleep, but Sheila wanted to do a party debrief. She was convinced that Lucille and Phonse would make a cute couple.

"Really?" I said. "I can't see it."

"Well, I'll tell you who doesn't make a cute couple," she said. "Doug and Geri. They barely spoke all night."

"Maybe they had an argument?" I said.

"No," said Sheila. "It wasn't like they were mad at each other. More like"—she yawned and rolled on her side—"indifferent."

I thought about how Geri and Doug had been apart all evening. Maybe Sheila was right.

"Sheila," I whispered, but she was fast asleep.

23

On New Year's Eve morning, Sheila and I sat on opposite ends of a loveseat, sipping tea. "I can't believe you're leaving so soon," I said.

"Relax," she said. "I'm not leaving until next year."

"Ha ha, well that's tomorrow. But speaking of next year, any resolutions?"

She put down her mug and stretched. "The usual, exercise more and eat less." Then she snagged the last chocolate chip cookie from the batch I'd baked earlier that morning. "So listen, what can we do in this joint that doesn't involve alcohol?"

"It's New Year's Eve! Who are you and what have you done with Sheila?"

"Seriously. I need to go to bed early. The taxi arrives at ridiculous o'clock tomorrow morning. I'd like to drive out to Little Cove in the daylight, break into the school and maybe have some fish and chips."

"Deal. Well, maybe not the break and enter part. I have a key. But I hope you've had a good time, Sheila."

"Rach, I've loved every minute of it. And best of all has been seeing you so content. When I saw you playing the violin the other night . . ."

"Fiddle."

"Whatever. You fit right in with that music."

She reached out and touched my hair, which I hadn't straightened in days. "I love these curls, you never used to let them go. You're happy here, Rachel."

I smiled. "I guess I am."

Then she smacked her forehead. "Wait, no! You're really happy here. Don't you dare try to stay here any longer than June. You're on a one-year contract and that's final, missy."

"Sir, yes sir. Now, since you've eaten all the cookies, should we head out to Little Cove?"

"Yes, and I want to see the school. Whenever I think of you down here, I imagine Anne Shirley breaking a slate over Gilbert Blythe's head. I need to update that image. At least to the 1960s."

She stood up and stretched. "Oh, and since I didn't get to chat to Doug much at the party, call him and ask him to meet us for fish and chips."

"But I've never called him before."

"So?"

Who could argue with that logic? But when I called, his mother said he had gone to the cabin for a few days, hunting with a friend.

"Hunting, like, for real?" Sheila asked when I told her. I didn't dare mention the rabbit stew.

Half an hour later, we were in the car, heading to Little Cove. When we came across two hitchhikers, I slowed down to pull over. I had recognized Sam Sullivan, from grade ten French. My heart sank when I realized he was with Calvin Piercey. Still, I couldn't exactly pull away now.

"What are you doing?" Sheila said. "Didn't your mother ever teach you about stranger danger?"

"Relax, I'm the only one who would qualify as a stranger around here."

"Well, strange, anyway," said Sheila.

The car door behind me opened and the two boys scrambled into the back seat. "H'lo, miss," they said.

"Boys, this is my friend Miss Murphy, who's visiting from Toronto."

Sheila twisted in her seat. "For God's sake, don't call me that. Makes me sound like an old bag."

Calvin snickered.

"It's Sheila. Now tell me, boys," she said. "How do you find Miss O'Brien as a teacher?"

I held my breath as Calvin spoke.

"I don't like French."

"What is it with boys and French?" Sheila asked.

He shrugged. "Don't see the point of it."

"Well," said Sheila. "It can help you get a job with the government or the RCMP or Air Canada . . ."

"I wants to join the RCMP," Sam piped up.

"And are you taking French?" Sheila asked.

"Oui," said Sam.

"Good for you," said Sheila. "French could give you a real advantage."

"I might have to drop it next year though," he said. "Dad don't want me wasting time on it."

My brain began to fizz as I remembered Doug's suggestion a few months back that I start a French club. That might be a way to snag more students and help those who weren't already taking the subject. A remedial English club had been a spectacularly bad idea. But a French club was a great one.

"Where can I drop you boys?" I asked.

"By MJ's takeout please," Sam said. "We can walk the rest of the way from there."

"Ah, le takeout," said Sheila. "C'est bon." She shifted in her seat to face the boys again. "See how I used my French then? You never know when you'll end up needing it. Like, say, if your best friend's a French teacher and you're trying to impress her so she'll buy you lunch."

They grinned. No one could resist Sheila's charm. We said goodbye to the boys in the parking lot, then went into the takeout.

There was no sign of Georgie at the cash register. Her mother took our order, and when I asked after her, she said, "She's after having the baby. My first grandson."

It was hard to read her expression, so I simply asked how Georgie was doing. But Sheila quizzed her on the baby, asking for name (Alfie) and weight (six and a half pounds and "right as rain").

After we'd eaten, we got back in the car and made the short trip through Little Cove. I pointed out the gas station, the church, the school, Lucille's house and the wharf. I did not drive as far as Bertha Peddle's store on principle.

"It's cozy," Sheila said. "I love the coloured houses. But I totally get why you moved to Clayville. Can we go to the school now?"

I turned the car around and we headed back. I unlocked the front door of the school and we went inside. Naturally, Sheila headed straight for the nearest male, rubbing the toes that protruded from his marble sandals.

"Thanks to St. Jude for favours received," she intoned.

"Great name for a school, eh?" I said.

"It kind of works."

"The patron saint of lost causes?"

"And hope," said Sheila. "The patron saint of hope."

"Says who?"

"The patron saint of nagging, also known as my mother."

"Huh," I said. "I guess if you think about it, hope is the flip side of lost causes." I made a mental note to inform Patrick.

"Where's Doug's classroom?" asked Sheila after I'd given her a brief tour.

"Why?"

"Just want to get a better feel for him."

"What are you, psychic?" But I led her down the hall and into the classroom. I leaned against the blackboard, while she wandered around, trailing her fingers along the rows of desks. Then she joined me at the front of the room and hovered her hands over his desk.

"I'm sensing some unresolved sexual tension here," she said, ducking when I threw a brush at her. It bounced on the desk, sending clouds of chalk into the air.

"You saw him with his girlfriend the other night."

"Yeah," said Sheila. "I saw them spend every minute of the party apart. I saw him unable to take his eyes off you when you were playing the violin."

"Fiddle," I said.

"Fiddlesticks," she replied. "Something is *not* going on with those two."

"Sheila, she's really nice."

"So are you, honey," said Sheila.

"Well, thank you," I said. "I only wish I could say the same for you."

"Hey!" She threw the blackboard brush back at me.

We bickered our way to the staff room, where I introduced Sheila to Patrick's beer fridge. "Bitchin'," she said. "Let's have one for the road."

"Well, it is New Year's Eve."

We settled in at the table and clinked bottles. Sheila shifted in her chair, took off her boots and put her feet in my lap. "You know, there's one thing you haven't asked me about since I got here," she said.

I picked at the label on my beer bottle. "I know."

"Last chance," Sheila said. "I'm going home tomorrow."

I twirled a strand of my hair and looked out the window.

"Okay," I said. "Have you heard from Jake?"

"Yup."

"Has he asked about me?"

"Yup."

"Are you going to answer every question like that?"

"Yup."

"Seriously," I said, pinching her ankle.

"Ow." She removed her feet from my lap. "You can't touch me, miss, I'm telling the principal."

"Sheila, talk."

"He's not going out with that . . . bitch anymore. He said he messed up. He said he was an idiot."

"He got that right," I said.

"Yup."

We finished our beer and I put the empties in the box beside the fridge.

"Rach," Sheila said. "He asked me how he could get in touch with you."

"Did you tell him?"

"I wouldn't do that unless you were on board with it. Oh, and he also belatedly offered to pay for my ruined dress. You know, the one that doubled as a swimsuit."

As we headed for the door, she added, "Should I have given him your number?"

"Nope."

24

Even though Sheila had only spent a few days with me, I was lonely after she left. As I made the first commute of 1986, I felt a pang when the morning DJ played Paul Young's "Every Time You Go Away." It was all very well having Wilf at the coffee shop, but I needed to make some friends in Clayville. I changed the radio station, although it didn't matter much. The turnoff for Bob's Cove was coming up, and as soon as I passed it, I would lose all reception.

I'd once asked Lucille how she managed to get radio reception, and she told me that she had a booster antenna on top of her house. It was only when Sheila and I spent the night at Judy's that I'd discovered cable TV existed in Little Cove. Judy said Lucille didn't have it because she wasn't much for television herself and didn't want boarders hanging around in her living room every evening.

As I turned into the school parking lot for the new term, my stomach flip-flopped. I was looking forward to seeing Doug. We hadn't spoken much at Eddie Churchill's party. When I reached my class-room, Doug was there waiting for me, which I took as a good sign.

"So you didn't go home for Christmas."

It was an accusation. Doug's arms were folded across his chest, his face pinched.

"No."

"And you didn't tell me?"

"I didn't tell anyone."

"But then you shows up to the party, mummering, and ignores me all evening."

"I didn't ignore you. I wanted to talk some more, but then Phonse asked me to play. Besides," I said, "I called you a few days later. Your mother said you had gone hunting."

"Oh, forget it." He brushed past me. "I don't know why I cares anyway."

"Doug, wait," I said, but he kept on walking.

I rubbed my eyes in frustration. Then, worried I'd smudged my mascara, I went to the women's bathroom. As I repaired my eyes, I spoke to my reflection in the mirror.

"I don't know why *I* care either. He's got a girlfriend, anyway."

"Is that you, Rachel?" a voice called from one of the cubicles. "Who are you talking to?" A toilet flushed and Sister Mary Catherine emerged.

"Would you believe, Sister," I said, "I'm talking to myself. I thought I was alone."

I made to leave, but she positioned herself in front of the door.

"We are never truly alone," she said. "God is always with us. He sees what you do." Her eyes drilled into mine. "And so do I."

I put one hand on the wall for support.

"My dear, I have seen you and Mr. Bishop together." She spat the last word out like a bit of spoiled fruit. "I think that young man may be developing feelings for you. We can ill afford another scandal at St. Jude's."

"There's no scandal."

"Good," she said. "But I'm asking you to remember your position as a Catholic teacher, all the same."

Years of Catholic schooling had taught me there was only one acceptable answer.

"Yes, Sister."

So, Doug was mad at me again. What else was new? I put any thoughts of him aside and went to see Patrick about setting up a French club. Doug would not be getting any credit for the idea from me.

"Excellent idea, my dear," he said. "I loves how you gets stuck right in."

I paled at the thought of how differently the conversation might have gone if I'd raised the possibility of a remedial English club. Patrick suggested I announce the club right away at assembly.

Ten minutes later, I gripped the podium and looked out at the student body, filling them in on my plan. The general vibe in the gym was boredom. Cynthia was sitting near the front, eyes down, fiddling with her pencil case.

"We'll meet at lunchtime on Wednesdays," I said. "Everyone's welcome, even if you aren't studying French. We'll look at French culture: food, music, films. And I'm going to try to bring in some guest speakers."

No one looked at me. No one cared.

"Does anyone have any questions?"

No one raised a hand.

"We'll do role plays, too. Ordering in restaurants, job interviews . . ." I was boring myself at this point. "So I hope to see many of you there!"

My first lesson after assembly was senior French, a class mostly made up of girls. I unrolled a picture of Francis Cabrel, all long hair and moustache, and pinned it to the bulletin board. "In French club next week, we'll listen to the music of Francis Cabrel, but today I thought I'd give you a taster."

I inserted the cassette. "This song is called 'Je l'aime à mourir,' which basically translates to 'I love her to death.'" I waited for the collective swoon and was not disappointed. I pressed play and we listened to Cabrel crooning about his lover.

"Oh, miss, what does it all mean?" asked Beverley in a breathless voice.

"You'll have to come to French club to find out."

After class I asked Cynthia to stay back. She hadn't done her homework and just before Christmas had failed a pop quiz. It was sloppy, careless work: missing accents and incorrect subject-verb agreements. I was disappointed because she'd been my star student. When I asked her about it, she refused to meet my eye.

"I forgot to study," she said.

The old Cynthia wouldn't have needed to study. She would've known the material cold.

"Are you sure you're all right, Cynthia?" I asked.

"Best kind, miss."

"It's just that—"

"Oh, miss," she pleaded. "Can I go please?"

"See you at French club?"

"I can't be bothered with that foolishness," she said.

I tried not to let her comment sting.

Two days later I held the first meeting of the French club. The posters I'd pinned up in the halls hadn't enticed many members. A few girls in my senior French class showed up, but not Cynthia. I gave them each a ditto sheet with the lyrics for two Cabrel songs and we listened to them a few times. By the third time around, Beverley was singing along. Then we broke down the lyrics.

As I'd hoped, seeing grammar and vocabulary in a song helped bring the language alive. We finished with some role play about music; the girls concocted dialogues about visiting a music store and talking about favourite bands. Despite the chatter as the girls filed out, it didn't feel like much of a success. Five girls who were already interested in French had joined the club. I would have to up my game if I was going to get better attendance.

The following week I marched into school laden down with plastic containers, dishes and cutlery. Phonse met me at the door, relieving me of some of the load. "Staff party?" he asked. "Mr. Donovan never said nothing."

"French club," I said. "The way to a student's brain is through their stomach."

I visited each homeroom before the bell, handing out chocolate chip cookies to everyone. I told them if they came to French club, there'd be even more food on offer.

At noon, I cleared my desk and covered it with a red-and-white checked tablecloth. I stuck a small French flag in a vase and sliced a loaf of white bread, next to which I put a bowl of jam. I poured apple juice and grape juice into clear plastic cups, and for the pièce de résistance, I placed a cake in the middle of the table.

The five girls who'd come to the first meeting were back, along with a few students from grade nine. Sam loitered in the doorway but sheepishly joined the others when I beckoned. I pretended to be a waitress, handing each of them a menu/vocabulary list. The specials were a poor man's version of croissants and jam, red and white wine, and *gâteau*. Beverley joined in straight away, asking for red wine and a croissant. With some coaxing, the others gradually followed suit. By the end of the session, most had ordered something *en français* and all of them had eaten my wares.

"Miss," said Tim, a boy in grade nine. "Any of them cookies on the go or wha?"

"They were more of a bribe . . . I mean treat."

"They were some good, though."

"Tell you what, if you bring a friend along next week, I'll bring a double batch of cookies."

Sam stayed behind to help clean up, stacking the empty plastic cups. I told him I had a guest speaker lined up for the next meeting. "It's a corporal from the Clayville RCMP. So I know you'll want to come along and hear him."

"Yes, miss," he said. "Merci!"

Pleased with the little progress I'd made, I assigned no homework at all that afternoon. I was taking the evening off, and so could my students. But, as I tidied my desk at the end of the day, I heard shouting in the hall.

"Where's that goddamn meddling blood of a bitch French teacher?"

As the footsteps came closer, I looked around in desperation. Then I grabbed my pointer and stood behind my desk. Into the classroom charged a tall man wearing jeans and construction boots, a baseball cap on his head. It was Roy Sullivan.

"You and that Quebec crap," he raged. "You got no right to tell my son what to do outside school hours. Batter to Jesus, luh."

"S-sorry, I don't know what you mean," I said.

"Sam's after saying he can't help me out on Wednesday because he's got French club. You got no right to keep him here at lunchtime. We wants him home. Plenty of small jobs to be done in the off season, before fishing starts up again."

"I thought it might help him with—"

"With what? The RCMP?" His mouth twisted. "I'm after

184

telling him a dozen times to give up with that foolishness. Don't you be encouraging him, you hear? He'll be fishing with me, like I fished with my fadder and him with his fadder before me. Stay the hell away from my son."

"Roy?" Patrick strode into the room. "What's all the commotion?"

Sam's father flicked his hand at me dismissively. "This one needs to keep her oar in her own boat." And he strode past Patrick and out the door.

I sank down in my chair, still clutching the pointer and shaking.

"Christ on a bike," said Patrick. "That man's a hard ticket." He sat down on a desk and smiled at me. "Listen to me now, Rachel. Judy and I are right impressed with this French club. Don't mind that arsehole."

The next morning Sam came to see me. "Miss, I'm some stunned. I forgot I needs to help out at home on Wednesday so I won't make the RCMP talk."

"Your father came to see me," I said, gently.

He blanched. "Sorry, miss. Was he right mean?"

"He feels strongly about fishing, I guess."

Sam's face sagged. "I hates it, miss. I'm not like Dad, or me brother. I gets right sick out at sea." He wiped his mouth with the back of his hand, then said, "I don't care, I'm still coming. I can, can't I?"

"You're welcome any time, Sam," I said.

I was heartened by his fleeting smile, but I was also worried about what would happen if Sam did come back next week. I didn't want to experience a repeat visit from his father.

25

Even though Doug was still acting cool towards me, he was my go-to for advice on local customs, so I ambushed him in his classroom the next morning.

"Can you talk to me about fishing, please?"

He tossed his pen down and folded his hands behind his head. "What about it?"

I filled him in briefly on the tirade from Sam's father.

"Don't mind him," said Doug. "That man's as crooked as sin. Never seen him smile, not once."

"But what is it about fishing? Why do they make kids do it, even when they don't want to?"

"Don't go tarring us all with Roy Sullivan's brush," Doug said. "Dad didn't make me fish. Took me out and showed me the ropes, sure, and I was glad of it. But he would've been all right with me going off to do something else, too."

"But you like fishing." That had been clear when he'd taken me out in his boat.

He nodded. "Yes, girl. Loves a bit of fishing. It's as much our religion as the Church. There'll be men fishing these waters as long as there's cod swimming in them. But it's hard graft, and even before Dad died, I didn't want it. And after . . . well, I wouldn't do that to Mudder."

I pictured his glamorous mother in her wheelchair. "Doug, what happened to your mother? I mean, if it's okay for me to ask."

The corners of his mouth drooped. "I'll tell you all about it sometime," he said. "But not now." He looked at his watch. "Bell's about to go."

I was glad to hear that he'd confide in me sometime about his mother. And it seemed he wasn't mad at me anymore.

"Thanks for the talk," I said. "Remember when you said Newfoundlanders were a cult?"

He nodded.

"Well, you're my guru."

He laughed. "I'll add it to my list of skills."

I gave him a little wave and had reached the door when he said, "Hey, fiddle girl, how d'you like that cassette I made you for Christmas?"

So Doug had given it to me. I liked the cassette even more now that I knew its provenance.

"I loves it, my son."

Doug threw back his head and laughed. I danced all the way back to my classroom. If Newfoundlanders were a cult, I felt ready to join.

It had been freakishly mild for several weeks, but halfway through the first lesson of the morning, the snow began to fall, thick and fast. By mid-morning Patrick had called the buses back, and by noon the students were gone. I was brushing snow from my car when Patrick came outside, sliding towards me in his shoes.

"Road to Clayville's shut," he shouted above the wind. "Lucille says you can stay with her." He gestured out at the road where the gravel had disappeared from sight, and added, "You might be better walking up if you can bear it. The roads are bad here too."

I locked my car and left it, trudging up the hill towards Lucille's. The wind was impossible; the snow swirled in every direction, blowing down my neck and under my top. When I'd reached the halfway mark up the hill, Eddie Churchill pulled in, the chains on his tires crunching in the snow. He reached across and opened the passenger door. "Hop in," he shouted over the wind.

"Some weather, wha," he said. "I'll get you up to Lucille's." He added there'd been a bad accident on the Clayville road right before the RCMP shut it. "Best to sit tight."

Lucille was at the kitchen table smoking when I went in, stamping my wet boots on the floor. "You don't need a storm to come visit, you know," she called. "I'll put the kettle on."

Over tea, she told me that her daughter Linda was now engaged and we talked about wedding plans for a while. After I yawned a few times, Lucille suggested I go up to my old bedroom and have a lie-down.

"It's that kind of day, girl," she said.

It was strange to be back in my old room. I lay on the bed and wrapped a quilt around me. The wind screamed at the window and its panes rattled right back. I didn't think I'd sleep, but I woke later, freezing in the dark. When I tried to turn on the bedside lamp, it didn't work.

Downstairs, Lucille was working on a crossword by the light of three candles.

"Power's out," she said. "I allows the wind knocked down some lines. I never made it to the shop, but there's bread and bologna. Fancy a drop?"

She went to the cupboard and took down a bottle of rum and two glasses. I drank mine with warm cola; Lucille took hers neat, smoking steadily as we worked our way through the bottle and the crossword. I hadn't eaten much and the rum went straight to my head. On my way up to bed, I had to hold onto the bannister with one hand, a candle flickering wildly in the other.

The moon shone bright through the lacy ice whorls on the window. I drifted off, dreaming of Doug. We were waltzing at the pub in Mardy and he was whispering "Fiddle girl" in my ear.

I woke, what seemed minutes later, to the sound of pots banging in the kitchen. The smell of breakfast cooking enticed me down the stairs.

"Power's back on," Lucille said. "I'm cooking up a feast."

We stuffed ourselves on bacon and eggs, and toutons with maple syrup. I asked for seconds of the toutons. As Lucille obliged, she gleefully reminded me how I'd turned my nose up at the fried bread dough the first time she'd served it.

When we were finished eating, I offered to do the dishes, so Lucille sat with a cigarette while I washed up. When the last pan had been scrubbed, I told Lucille I was going for a walk.

She wrinkled her nose. "In this weather? You best watch out for rot holes."

"What are they?" I asked.

"Soft spots in the snow that you could fall into."

"Maybe the roads are plowed," I said.

"Hmph. They won't have got out this far so early in the morning."

As usual, Lucille was right. Snow lay thick on the road and the brightly coloured houses were muted under a heavy white trim. Plumes of smoke rose straight in the air from many of them. Abandoned cars lay buried under a thick white duvet.

The cold seeped through my boots, and it wasn't long before I turned back towards Lucille's. Nearing the path that led to the wharf, I heard shouting. Someone in a light blue coat ran towards me, hands waving in the air. It was Belinda.

"Miss," she cried. "It's Ruthie, Calvin's dog. She's trapped."

I hurried down the path and we ran towards the wharf together. Twice I had to grab Belinda's sleeve to catch my balance. As we reached the wharf, I saw the dog paddling frantically out in the bay between two large slabs of ice. Calvin was at the end of the wharf calling to her. When we arrived at his side, he latched on to me.

"Miss, can you save her?" His voice caught. "I tried twice to get out there, but the ice is breaking and I don't know how to swim."

Instinct kicked in and I ran to the steps that led from the side of the wharf to the frozen sea. Thankfully, someone had shovelled them.

"No, miss," Belinda yelled. "It's not safe."

"We can't just leave her," I shouted back.

Belinda called out that I should wait and she'd go get help, but I was already at the bottom of the steps. The ice was windswept, and as I shuffled along, I could hear a crackling beneath me. I edged towards the dog, holding my breath, as if that would somehow make a difference.

"Rachel!" The cry cut through the cold air. "Get the hell back here!"

Doug was standing beside Calvin on the wharf.

"I'll be right back," I called.

Then Calvin shouted, "Good girl, Ruthie. Miss is coming to save you."

I slid carefully over to where the ice ended and the open water began. I squatted down, making a clicking noise to try and coax Ruthie towards me. She paddled over, whining frantically. I grabbed her collar and tried to pull her out, but she was too heavy. She began thrashing about, her paws making the water churn.

I called her over again and tried to grab her around her torso, but my mittens slid right off her icy coat. She thrashed away from me, bleating now like a lamb.

"Come on, girl," I crooned.

She splashed back again, her movements more frantic, her whining louder. I lay down on the ice and tried to pull her out, but again lost my grip. She drifted away, paddling more slowly now and quietly whimpering.

"Don't give up, girl," I pleaded, standing back up and looking around desperately.

"Miss, do something!" yelled Calvin.

I jumped in.

Doug screamed my name as the cold water hit me like a fist. Ruthie splashed over, paws scratching my face until I pushed her away. My hands were numb already, but I managed to grab her collar. She licked my face repeatedly.

I dragged her towards the hard ice, then treaded water, pushing up on her bottom. Her front paws clawed at the ice, bits of it rasping off. I was starting to lose the feeling in my legs. The only way I knew they were still moving was that I wasn't going under.

Finally, with a sudden heave, Ruthie got purchase and scrambled jerkily out of the water. Then she shook herself violently, the freezing water hitting my face like bullets. Not that it mattered; I was up to my neck in it. Without a backwards glance, Ruthie charged across the ice in the direction of the wharf and Calvin.

I didn't watch the reunion; instead, I concentrated on my own exit. I was used to hoisting myself out of swimming pools—it was a point of pride for me to never use the ladder. So when I pressed my sodden mittens into the ice, I expected to push myself out right away. But my arms wobbled, then gave way. I tried again, but it was no use.

My eyes darted to the wharf, where a crowd had gathered. A man in a red coat was gesturing wildly. Beside him was a bald man I knew to be a parent, though I couldn't remember whose. I didn't see Doug.

My breathing quickened as my predicament became clear. My coat was soaking wet and heavy; like Ruthie with her fur, it was dragging me down.

I shucked my mittens off, then clawed uselessly at my coat buttons. My fingers refused to work. I stretched my arms up onto the ice and flutter-kicked to try to get out. I was too bulky, too wet.

Back at the wharf, Doug was pushing through the crowd with a coil of rope slung over one shoulder. He clambered down the steps, followed by several men. Doug lay on his stomach and began elbowing his way across the ice, the others following. Eddie Churchill and Phonse were behind him. When Doug was about fifteen feet away, he stopped, as did the others. Then each of them grabbed the ankles of the man in front of them; all the way back to the wharf they formed a human chain.

Doug raised himself to a squatting position and threw the rope at me. It landed about a foot away.

"I can't reach it," I called, trying to keep calm.

He pulled it back towards him. The second time he threw it, the rope landed inches from me. I clawed at the ice but my fingers would not close around it. When I shook my head, there was shouting from the crowd on the wharf. Doug pulled the rope back and cinched the end of it around his waist. Eddie Churchill held the other end.

"Rachel!" Doug sounded hoarse. "I'm going to crawl over and pull you out, okay?"

I nodded, my teeth chattering. Doug inched over to me. His face was white, his eyes wild. He reached out and grabbed my hood, tugging and tugging until my chest breached the ice. Half strangled, I lay on the ice, breathing hard.

"Jaysus God tonight, woman," he said, his voice shaky. "You're after giving us all a fright."

Then he untied the rope and secured it around my waist. "All right, b'ys," he shouted. "I got her."

Behind him the men began tugging. I tried to crawl with the rope, but mostly I let myself be dragged. It was slow going. Doug was beside me, elbowing his way across the ice, his eyes never leaving mine. When we finally reached the steps, he pulled me up and into his arms, muttering, "Thank Christ."

Then Eddie jostled him aside, shouting instructions. Hands joined to form a chair and I was hurried up the steps to the wharf. Then Eddie hoisted me into his arms and carried me carefully up the path to Lucille's. Doug and a few others walked behind us, their voices high as they replayed the rescue.

"More guts than brains, wha?" said Eddie as we arrived at Lucille's door.

She appeared, all cross at the commotion until she saw the state of me. "Jaysus, Mary and Josephine," she said. "What's after happening?"

"Lu-Lucille," I managed to spit out. "I'm sorry."

The men all talked at once, trying to fill her in. One of them patted my shoulder awkwardly. "Christ on a bike," he said. "Thought you was a goner." Doug gave him a dirty look.

"Bring her in the kitchen quick!" Lucille shouted at Eddie. "And get that wet coat off her. I'll get some quilts."

Doug followed Eddie inside and fumbled with the buttons, then pulled my coat off and threw it on the floor, where a pool of red water began to form as the dye leached out. Lucille came out of her bedroom with a pile of quilts at the exact same time that Judy burst through the door.

Suddenly, I remembered that Dad's lighter had been in my coat. I fell to the floor and clawed at the pockets, but they were both empty. I stammered my thanks to Eddie and Doug, shoulders heaving as I held back the sobs.

"Judy and I got her now, b'ys," said Lucille, ushering the men out the door. I could hear Doug asking to stay.

Judy patted me on the back. "It's just the shock," she said. "You're grand." Then she stripped off the rest of my clothes, Lucille wrapped me in quilts, and they sat me beside the stove to warm up.

"How long do you reckon you were in the water, Rachel?" Judy asked.

I said I didn't know. "We won't put you in the bath," said Lucille. "It might be too big a shock for the system. I'll make a hot water bottle for you." She bent down and peered at me more closely.

"What's after happening to your face? It's scratched up like a chicken pen."

"The dog," I said. "Her way of saying thanks, I guess."

"Well, she must be feeling better, Judy," said Lucille. "She's got her sass back."

The kettle had boiled and Lucille now filled a hot water bottle for me and put it on my stomach over the quilt. "Now, let's move you to the daybed and I'm going to fix some hot soup for you."

She and Judy helped me hobble over to the daybed. Judy sat down beside me while Lucille started banging pots and pans about on the stove.

"You okay?" Judy asked.

I nodded, shivering.

"Thank God for that," she said. "When I asked you to find a way to reach Calvin, I wasn't expecting anything quite so dramatic."

I managed a little laugh.

Lucille now brought over two steaming mugs of tea. Judy put her own on the floor and held mine up so I could sip it. Before I'd made much progress, Lucille filled another mug with pea soup and brought it over. I was able to curl my fingers around the handle and slowly drink it.

"Where's Doug?" I asked.

"I sent him to check if the roads were cleared," said Lucille. "He was all for getting an ambulance, but I allows you're all right now, aren't you?"

I nodded.

Eventually, the two women helped me upstairs to bed. Lucille piled so many quilts on me, I was rendered immobile. I lay there, listening to her walk back and forth from the kitchen to the living room every time the phone rang, which was about ten times more often than I'd ever heard when I lived there. At various points I heard Lucille using the words *foolish, cracked* and *grand,* all of which I interpreted as descriptions of me.

When I awoke later, Lucille was sitting on the edge of the bed. I told her I was feeling much better. She gave me one of her robes to put on, then helped me back downstairs to the daybed. Then there was a shuffling in the hall, and Calvin came through to the kitchen. He stood awkwardly in the doorway, hands thrust in his coat pockets.

"I wanted to say t'anks, miss."

I managed to right myself to a sitting position and patted the daybed. "Come sit down. How's Ruthie?"

"Ah, miss, she's the best kind. Lying by the stove now, with me mudder fussing over her. And she's chewing the biggest bone you ever saw." His voice cracked. "T'anks for saving her, miss."

He sat down, hands coming out of his pockets. His bony wrists were at least two inches from the sleeve ends. He rubbed his hands up and down so hard on his cords I thought sparks might fly. Then he reached into a pocket and dropped something into my lap. It was an intricately carved bird. I turned it over, marvelling at the detail—the beady eyes, the richly feathered wings.

"Where did you get this?" I asked. "It's beautiful."

"I made it." He looked at me sideways and smiled shyly. "I likes to mess around with wood. Me grandfadder taught me." His eyes lit up as he spoke of his hand-me-down tools and how he loved to carve wildlife.

"You're awfully good at it."

"Better than the French, right, miss?"

"Un peu," I said.

Lucille had gone upstairs to fetch more blankets and now came back into the kitchen with Doug in tow. "Look who I'm after finding, lurking about in the hall, making a mess with his snowy boots," she said.

Doug raised his eyebrows when he saw Calvin sitting beside me.

"Now then, Doug," Lucille said. "How long do you think Rachel was in the water?"

But Calvin answered first. "About five minutes, I'd say."

"That's not so bad," said Lucille. "I allows she'll be right as rain soon enough."

"Plows are out in Clayville," Doug said. "With any luck, they'll get out this way later. I could run you home, Rachel."

"No!" Lucille's voice was sharp. "She's not leaving this house tonight. I wants to keep an eye on her. I think we could all use a cheer up, though. Rachel, are you up for a kitchen party?"

I gestured at my borrowed robe. "I'm not sure I want to wear this in company."

But Lucille said she had some clothes belonging to Linda that would fit me just fine.

"Miss," said Calvin. "Will you play the fiddle tonight? We listens outside the Mardy pub sometimes."

I held up my reddened hands. "I don't think I can tonight, Calvin."

I DIDN'T REALLY WANT a party, but Lucille said people wanted to come see me. The hookers came, and Eddie Churchill and Phonse, and Judy and Bill, and even Calvin's mother, who took my hands into hers, rubbing them to try to heat them up.

"T'anks for saving Ruthie," she said. "She means the world to Calvin."

Phonse patted my head. "You must be wore out, girl. Rest up, sure."

Judy and Bill waltzed around the kitchen while others took it in turn to play a tune or sing or recite. About an hour into the party, Doug walked in carrying his mother in his arms. "I couldn't fit the wheelchair through your door, Lucille," he shouted across the room.

"Grace!" Lucille fought her way through the crowd. The two women looked at each other for a good minute before Lucille reached up and stroked Doug's mom on the cheek. "My God, girl, it's some good to see you."

"I decided I could get out more," she said. They made space for her on the daybed beside me, and she accepted a glass of wine. "What a brave thing you did," she said.

"More like foolish," said Lucille. "Now Grace, give me a minute to pass 'round these sandwiches, and then I wants a chinwag."

Lucille had told me to avoid alcohol, but my glass was on endless refill of soft drinks. People I didn't know squeezed onto the daybed on the other side of Grace to chat. Some praised my bravery; others lamented my foolishness. When Lucille returned, I bragged to her that someone had called me a chucklehead.

"They think I'm funny!"

"They thinks you're stunned, more like," she said.

"I s'pose it's a fine line sometimes," said Grace.

Then Lucille bent down and whispered in her ear. Grace nodded and Lucille called Doug over and asked him to carry his mother into the living room. "It's been too long," Lucille said. "We needs to catch up, and there's too much of a racket in here."

I held Doug's beer while he moved his mother. He came back and sat beside me. We didn't say much, just sat in companionable silence. At some point, I noticed his arm was around my shoulders.

Late in the evening Roy Sullivan arrived with a case of beer on his shoulders. "Where is she?" he asked, moving through the crowd. He put the case of beer at my feet. "Sorry about that bust-up," he said.

I managed not to ask which one.

"You got some courage, girl," he said.

I asked Doug to open the case of beer and he handed one to Roy, who twisted off the cap and passed it to me, then opened another one for himself. It was against Lucille's advice but I clinked bottles with Roy, then said, "You know what courage is?"

"What?"

"Stepping away from a family tradition that doesn't work for you. Following your own dream. That's real courage."

Doug inhaled sharply and pinched my waist, but Roy Sullivan held my gaze for what seemed like a long time. Then he nodded and took a long swig of his beer.

26

The day after the rescue, I felt well enough to drive myself home to Clayville. Lucille insisted on sending a food package with me—a loaf of her bread and a jar of pea soup. I told her I was good for milk.

On my return to school on Monday, the students all wanted to talk about the weekend. When I suggested we do so *en français*, they were less keen all of a sudden.

I perched the little bird that Calvin had given me on my desk beside my stapler. Calvin's behaviour was impeccable in class these days, but never again did he participate; he endured. It was obvious to me that he wasn't going to pass French again this year, and after asking around the other staff members, it seemed that the same held true in other subjects.

While researching scholarship possibilities for Cynthia in the library, I found a file folder labelled "Careers." I flicked idly through dog-eared brochures for various apprenticeships, a few universities in the Atlantic provinces, the RCMP and the Canadian Forces. Tucked at the very back of the folder was a brochure for an arts college in Nova Scotia. After reading it, I went to find Judy.

"High school is wasted on Calvin," I said. "He's seventeen, he could leave if his mother would let him." I waved the brochure at her. "I found this in the library. Did you see that wood carving he gave me?"

Judy took the brochure and set it on her desk, barely glancing at it. "Calvin can't go to arts college," she said. "Not in Nova Scotia, and not anywhere else. But there's a trades college in St. John's where he could study carpentry."

"No! Calvin's too talented to be a carpenter."

"I wasn't really thinking about Calvin," Judy said. "Calvin needs a trade so his mother is satisfied he'll earn a good living. She needs that guarantee."

"Judy, you're a genius!"

"I know," she said. "But can you remind Bill?"

"So, I can look into this trades college?" I asked.

"For what it's worth," she said, "you have my blessing. But that's not the one you'll need."

I phoned the trades college in St. John's and had a long conversation with its director. A few weeks later, a large package arrived in the mail for me, and I asked Calvin to see me after school.

He knocked on my classroom door, his face wary.

I beckoned him in, and when he sat down at my desk, I filled him in on the trades college.

"I think it would be good for you. You don't need a high school certificate to apply."

Calvin didn't answer. I waited until he had finished cracking every knuckle, then I passed him the big envelope.

"Take a look," I said. "And I talked to the director. The main focus is carpentry, but they have some courses in furniture making, wood carving and . . ." My voice dwindled away. Calvin was sitting on the chair beside my desk, holding the unopened manila envelope away from his body. Then he slid it back across the desk to me. "T'anks, miss, but Mudder wouldn't like it. She wants me to get my certificate."

"You would get a certificate," I said. "A really useful one."

He scuffed his shoe back and forth against my desk. I fought the urge to tell him to knock it off.

Then he said, "It's no use, miss."

"What if I talked to your mother?"

The scuffing stopped. "You'd do that? For me?"

"Especially for you."

He ducked his head, but I thought I saw a smile. "T'anks, miss."

"C'mon," I said. "I'll drive you home. And you know what else, Calvin?"

He shrugged.

"They have a basketball team."

Calvin directed me to a small house, in a row of three, about halfway to Mardy. Mrs. Piercey was outside, brushing dirty clumps of snow from her path. She approached my side of the car and I wound down the window. "Is Calvin in trouble?" she asked. "What's he done?"

"He's not in trouble," I said. "I was hoping to speak to you about his future."

She beamed. "Aren't you grand?"

When I got out of the car, Ruthie nudged my leg. I gave her a good pat, then she raced around the car and jumped on Calvin. The pair of them headed towards a faded grey shed at the bottom of the yard.

"That's Calvin's workshop," Mrs. Piercey said. "He spends all his free time in there making things."

She invited me inside her home, removing a sewing basket from the table. I thought about those neat stitches on Calvin's shirt. Her handiwork, like her son's, was flawless. She moved quietly about the kitchen, putting on the kettle and fetching tea bags, mugs and tinned milk.

When she sat down beside me and poured the tea, I took a glossy brochure out of the envelope and laid it on the table. "The trades college in St. John's has been in touch with the school," I said. "They're looking for students for their carpentry program."

I slid the brochure towards her. She tapped her fingers on it, but didn't pick it up.

"You don't need a high school diploma. So even if Calvin doesn't pass"—I bit my tongue to keep from saying *again*—"this year, it wouldn't matter. He could leave St. Jude's and start at the trades college in September."

Mrs. Piercey was looking out the window, so I kept talking to the teapot.

"They do some wood carving courses and there are grants for exceptional candidates. I told the director about Calvin's nature pieces and he's so eager to meet him."

Mrs. Piercey's gaze slipped to her mug. It was time to try a different approach. "Then again, maybe this is all just a passing fancy for Calvin."

She looked up, her face animated. "Passing fancy? More like his passion. His grandfadder taught him when he was still a child. He just took to it, you know?"

I tried not to react when she picked up the brochure, but crossed my fingers under the table.

"Did you say the director was in touch with the school?"

I nodded. The director had been in touch with the school. On a phone call that I had initiated, but she didn't need to know that.

Mrs. Piercey wore a pair of reading glasses on a gold chain around her neck. She lifted them now and balanced them on her nose. She read the brochure cover to cover. Then I took out the various application forms and laid them on the table. Our heads were bent together over the paperwork when Calvin came in, with Ruthie right behind him. His mother got up, twisting a tea towel in her hands.

"Miss O'Brine's been telling me all about this carpentry course in town. I was wondering if you—"

But she got no further as Calvin lifted her in his arms and twirled her around the kitchen to her delighted protestations.

27

At the next parent-teacher get-together, a steady stream of people gathered to speak to me. Most of their children weren't studying French; they wanted to talk about the dog rescue. Cynthia's mother beamed as she finally managed to squeeze through the crowd.

"You're popular tonight." She wrapped her sweater protectively around her narrow frame and said, "We're some proud of Cynthia. Imagine her going off to university next year."

"Is that still the plan?" I asked.

"Yis. Most definitely."

I brushed non-existent lint from my dress to buy some time, then said, "It's just that Cynthia's work has been . . . a little up and down lately." In truth, there was no up, it was all down.

Mrs. O'Leary frowned. "Is she not keeping up with her French either? I'm after telling the other teachers I'll have her by the scruff when I gets her home. She's been out beating the paths too much."

I said I thought Cynthia could still achieve her targets if she knuckled down and got back to work.

"If?" said Mrs. O'Leary. "If? Sparks are gonna fly when I gets her home."

The next morning Patrick called a brief staff meeting before school started.

"I wants your views on Cynthia O'Leary," he said, "before I writes the letter of reference for her scholarship applications."

"Her latest French exam was terrible," I said. "She didn't answer most of the questions."

"Same with biology," said Doug. "She's after taking a real nose-dive."

Around the table, it was the same story. The golden girl was shining much less brightly.

"She will reap what she sows," said Sister Mary Catherine.

Judy threw her a filthy look, then said, "She's got such a bright future ahead of her, Pat. We can't let her throw it away."

He turned his palms up. "I'm after meeting with her parents twice," he said. "She's got them drove mental. She's gone right wild since she took up with Ron Drodge."

"Who's he?" I asked.

"He's too old for her is what he is," said Doug.

Patrick cleared his throat. "He's Brigid's brother. The teacher you replaced."

I remembered Lucille telling me how Brigid's brother had been driving the car when her husband, Paul, died in the accident.

"That fella has been trouble since the day he was born," Sister said. "Rotten through and through."

There was silence. Maybe everyone else felt the same as me about Sister's judgmental nature.

"Anyhow," said Patrick. "Let's focus on Cynthia's school work."

We talked for a few more minutes around the table, and all agreed that unless Cynthia's former work ethic returned, and soon, there would be no need for Patrick to write a letter of reference.

"I could try speaking to her," I offered.

"I wish you would," said Patrick.

That afternoon, I asked Cynthia to stay behind after class.

She grimaced. "I'm wanted at home."

"It won't take long," I said, moving to close the classroom door.

She slumped in her desk, playing with a gold chain around her neck, zigzagging the heart pendant back and forth.

"I'm worried about you."

Cynthia folded her arms over her chest.

"You seem to be giving up on school. Your marks have slid right down. University might be—"

She cut me off. "Don't matter. I can get a job in the fish plant."

"I thought you wanted to leave Little Cove and go to university."

She didn't answer, just kept zigzagging the heart until I wanted to rip it from her throat.

"Cynthia," I tried again. "It seems like you're throwing away your future for some guy who'll probably drop you in a few months."

Her face hardened. "Ron wouldn't do that."

"How do you know?"

She gave me a scornful look. "You wouldn't understand. Can I go now?"

"Listen to me. You're so bright. You could do anything. What happened to wanting to be a French teacher?"

"Is that why you asked to see me? Because you wants me to be like you?"

Something about that sneer on her face made me lose my cool.

209

"Don't throw your life away for some jerk." I put my hand over my mouth.

She jumped up, her eyes wild.

Before I could say anything else, she was halfway out the door. "It's none of your business what I does outside of school, miss. Just leave me alone."

I followed her down the hall, reaching the front door in time to see her climb into a red Camaro that revved its engine, skidded on the icy gravel, then roared up the road away from Little Cove.

The day was capped off with a note tucked under the wipers of my car when I left later that evening. More of the same. I crumpled up the note and got in my car.

28

After our failed talk, Cynthia began missing school more than she showed up. There were only a few days left until the Easter break, and I found myself wondering if she would bother coming back before then. But on the last day of school before the break, she was standing by my car in the parking lot when I came out.

"Miss, can I talk to you?"

Then I noticed mascara had run all over her cheeks and dried, like little railroad tracks cutting through a field.

"What is it?"

She glanced around the empty parking lot. "Could we talk in your car?"

Tears and the need to confide in someone privately. Just like that, I knew.

Stunned, I held open the passenger-side door for her. Then I went around to my side and got in. She stared at the dashboard, biting her lip. Patrick was always going on about what a credit Cynthia was to the community. I thought of Georgie working in the takeout. I didn't want Cynthia to miss out on any opportunity that might still be available to her.

"How late are you?" I asked when the silence became unbearable.

She gasped. "How did you know?"

"Lucky guess," I said. "When was your last period?"

Her face twisted as if she was in pain. "I'm not sure." She looked down, playing with a button on her jean jacket.

"Have you told your mother?"

"No, miss, she'd kill me, she would." She pressed her hands down on her still-flat stomach. "What's going to happen? When Georgie got pregnant, she had to leave school."

"Have you told Ron?"

She slowly moved her head side to side. "He don't want kids. Oh, miss, what am I going to do?"

"Do you want to keep the baby?"

"I . . . I don't know. And I won't be able to graduate," she wailed.

"Cynthia." I kept my voice as even as I could. "This might be hard to hear, but I'm not sure that would've happened anyway. Your grades have slipped and you've missed so much school."

She exhaled, loud juddering breaths. "I knows. But I was talking to Mr. Donovan, and he said if I really buckled down, I might still be all right. Not for a scholarship, but just to get my certificate. But now . . ." A sob escaped from her mouth.

"Look," I said. "You have options. You could keep the baby. Or you could have it and give it up for adoption."

"But either way, I wouldn't be able to finish school." She chewed her nails and I was reminded of Georgie's, bitten to the quick.

NEW GIRL IN LITTLE COVE

I'd seen Georgie in Clayville last month, struggling to push a baby carriage through the snow. Little Alfie was fast asleep, under a hand-knit blanket. After I'd admired him, I'd asked Georgie when she might return to school.

She reached in to adjust his blanket. "I'm not," she said. "I couldn't leave him."

Cynthia bounced her knees up and down so hard the car began to shake. I looked out the window at the school where I was employed to uphold church doctrine. "There's one other possibility," I said.

"What, miss?"

"You could make it go away."

"What do you mean, miss?"

I took a deep breath. "You could get rid of it."

She inhaled sharply, like she'd stepped on a tack. "Miss, I could never do that. It's a mortal sin."

A mortal sin. It sounded so archaic. I'd certainly never uttered those words in my life. But religion seemed to have a stronger hold on the students at St. Jude than it had ever had on me.

At that moment, the red Camaro drove into the parking lot, circling like a shark. Cynthia rubbed her eyes roughly, then opened the door and got out. Then she leaned back in and said, "Miss, promise you won't say nothing. Please. I'll tell Ron you were having a go at me about missing school. He'll wonder why I was in your car."

"Don't leave it too long, Cynthia," I said. "You want to keep all your options open."

The car door slammed and she ran for the Camaro. I pounded my fist on the steering wheel. Dammit! Her future was now well and truly screwed. Then fear dropped into my stomach like a stone into a well. I had kept my words somewhat ambiguous, but

Cynthia had figured out that I meant abortion. What if she told someone what I'd said?

There was only one person in whom I felt I could confide, but Sheila had just left for a two-week holiday in Mexico. Would Doug be sympathetic? I drove over to his place to find out.

"I need some advice," I said when he answered the door.

"You okay?"

"Not sure."

He hollered to his mother that he was going out and we got into my car. Then he directed me away from Little Cove and past Mardy too. After about ten miles, we turned off onto a dirt road that led to the sea, as so many of those little roads seemed to. I turned off the engine and we got out of the car.

"Bartlett's Cove," he said. "I loves it here, especially in the summer."

We walked carefully over the icy beach rocks as they skittered beneath our feet. We sat down on a large pile of boulders, about twenty feet from the water. The waves scraped the shore and Doug waited while I tried to find the right words.

Finally I spoke. "I may've messed up. One of the girls at school is pregnant and came to me for advice."

"Who?"

"I promised I wouldn't say."

He was quiet for a minute and I imagined him running through the list of probable suspects in the school.

"What did you say?"

"I ran through a bunch of options with her."

"Like what?" Doug asked.

"Keep it, give it up for adoption . . ."

He nodded. "That's about the size of it."

I jumped down from the boulder and picked up a small beach

rock. I threw it towards the sea, but it bounced short. "I also mentioned abortion."

Doug whistled softly. "Trying to get yourself fired?"

I kept my gaze focused on the horizon.

After a minute, he asked, "Do her parents know?"

I shook my head.

"Don't get too involved, Rachel," he said. "Don't take her to town."

"What do you mean?"

"It's bad enough you mentioned it, but don't help her get one, if that's what she decides. She'd have to go to St. John's. And it's not guaranteed. A committee of doctors would decide. I'm not sure, but I think parents needs to be involved if she's a minor."

"How do you know so much about it?" I asked.

"They does them at the hospital where Geri works."

My heart was slamming against my chest now. But I had to know. "What do you think about it?"

"I think you were right foolish to talk about abortion with whoever this girl is, and you teaching in a Catholic school."

"That's not what I mean. What do you think about abortion?"

"Why do you care what I think?"

I climbed back on the boulder and sat beside him, hugging my knees. "I just do."

Doug shifted on the rock. "I don't understand women at the best of times. But I can't imagine what it would be like carrying a baby you didn't want."

"Meaning?"

"Meaning, men can't get pregnant so we don't get to decide. It's down to the woman to do that."

I felt my shoulders relax.

"So, what do we do now?" Doug asked.

"Wait and see," I said. "Maybe it's a false alarm."

"I hope so," said Doug. "For everyone's sake."

I got up, rubbing my arms.

"We going?" Doug asked.

"I'm cold."

"I'm hungry. Let's go to Tony's," Doug said.

An hour later, we arrived in Clayville and parked in front of Tony's, where there was a lineup out the door.

"Damn, I was really wanting pizza," Doug said.

Then a family walked out the door, the father carrying two pizza boxes, the two kids chattering excitedly.

"We could get takeout and eat at my house," I suggested.

"Excellent idea, girl."

Back at my place, Doug poured wine while I grabbed plates and glasses from the cupboard. Just before we sat down, I went to the living room and put on the cassette he'd made me.

"You never did tell me what happened to your mother," I said, handing him a napkin.

A shadow passed over Doug's face. "She tried to kill herself."

"What?"

"After Dad drowned, in the run-up to the funeral, she took to walking up above Little Cove, at the rocks near the end of the bay. She was out all hours, didn't eat, didn't sleep. And she fell out with Lucille something bad."

"Why? What happened?"

Doug topped up his glass. I put my hand over mine to stop him refilling it. "Dad and Lucille's husband drowned on the same day. They were out fishing together and a bad storm came up. They didn't have a chance."

I thought of the gravestones in the cemetery out back, documenting all the lives lost at sea.

"Mudder got it into her head that John, Lucille's husband, had convinced Dad to go out even though a storm was brewing. That Dad didn't want to go and felt forced into it. It wasn't true. If Dad didn't want to go fishing, he wouldn't have gone. He was his own master."

"But why did they go out if a storm was coming?"

Doug drained his glass. "That was all part of Mudder's revisionism. That storm was not predicted: it came from nowhere. Seven men drowned up and down the coast that day and tons of boats were wrecked. They held a joint funeral for Dad and John. At the wake afterwards, Mudder caused a right old scene, said John had killed Dad and Lucille had blood on her hands, too. She said she'd never speak to Lucille again."

"And when did . . ." I tried to think how best to phrase it. "When did she have her accident?"

"She disappeared from the wake and threw herself off the rocks up above. Lucky not to be killed. She claimed she slipped, but I don't think anyone believes that. When she got out of hospital, she became a recluse. My aunt comes every day to help out. That party at Lucille's after you rescued Ruthie, I think that's the first time she's left the house in five years, apart from hospital appointments and such."

When the pizza was gone and the wine bottle was empty, Doug slid another bottle from my wine rack. "Grab your glass," he said. "Let's go sit somewhere more comfortable."

I turned over the cassette, then joined Doug on the loveseat, where we sat and talked for a while. Then "Sweet Forget Me Not" began to play on the boombox and he pulled me to my feet and took me in his arms. We danced slowly around the room, Doug bending low and singing softly. When the song came to an end, we kept dancing. Doug tilted my chin up, looked in my eyes and smiled. Then he pulled me gently back over to the loveseat.

"Rachel," he said, his voice soft. He put a hand either side of my head and stared at me for what felt like a long time. Then he leaned over and I closed my eyes, waiting for what I knew would be a kiss this time.

Then the phone rang.

"Don't answer it," he whispered. I waited for the answering machine to kick in.

"Rachel," my mom's voice was weepy and small. I pushed Doug away and rushed to pick up the phone.

"Mom, what's happened, are you okay?"

I mouthed "sorry" to Doug. He poured himself another glass of wine and picked up a newspaper from the coffee table.

Mom was talking but I couldn't understand what she was saying through the sobs. And then I heard her say "one year," and I felt a lump blocking my throat.

"It's one year. He died one year ago today," she whispered.

"No, Mom," I said. "It's tomorrow." Like that would be any comfort to her.

"It *is* tomorrow in Australia." Her sobs came in huge waves. I sat down on the floor and murmured, "It's okay, it's okay," when clearly it wasn't.

"I needed to talk to someone who knew him, someone who"—she choked, but carried on—"who loved him as much as me."

I wanted to reach through the phone line and grab her and never let go. Even though Mom and I had never been close, even though Dad had been the glue between us, I understood her grief.

"Tell me a Dad story, Rachel," she said, cutting into my thoughts. "Please."

It was as though by asking, she had pushed all my memories away. I couldn't think of a single one. But then my gaze fell on a framed photo on the mantelpiece—the three of us at the cottage, Dad wearing binoculars around his neck.

And I remembered. Mom was lying on the dock, sunning. I was sitting in the shade reading. Dad was watching birds, then he came nearer to Mom, closer and closer, raising his binoculars to his eyes. Dad was a keen birder, and his favourite joke was to pretend that Mom was a rare bird. This time, he'd outdone himself, talking in a stagey, heightened whisper, like some nature show host.

"I'm very close now," he'd said softly. "We have to be quiet; we don't want to startle her."

By this point, the binoculars were practically touching Mom's nose. "Yes, folks, it's the lesser spotted cuckoo bird." And Mom looked up, shading her eyes and laughing, saying how old his joke was, almost as old as him. And Dad leaned over to kiss her.

"Remember the lesser spotted cuckoo bird?" I said.

Mom half laughed, half cried down the line. "Yes!" And as I sat there, back to the wall, hugging my knees, she told me the story that had just played out in my brain, much better than I ever would have. Gradually, warmth crept into her voice, and by the end, she even gave a little laugh.

"That's exactly what I needed, Rachel. That's a perfect Dad story. I went for a long run today and I listened to Vivaldi. That's how I marked the day."

"That's good, Mom," I said. "Can we talk again tomorrow?"

"Of course. Love you."

"Love you too."

"And Rachel," she whispered. "Thank you."

I hung up the phone. "Sorry, Doug," I said. "That was my mom and—"

But he was passed out, glass of red wine still in his hand, tilting dangerously towards the floor. I gently removed it and tried to wake him, but he was out cold. Even when I clattered dishes in the kitchen, he didn't stir. Eventually, I went upstairs to bed.

The next morning, when I went downstairs, Doug was where I'd left him. He was awake, although not very, holding one shoe. He scratched his head and looked around blankly.

"Me and red wine," he said. "Deadly."

"I know someone else like that," I said. "My mother."

I picked up his other shoe and handed it to him.

"I needs coffee," he said.

"You don't drink coffee."

"Well, I needs something."

"It's Good Friday," I said. "I doubt Wilf's is open."

Doug groaned. "Oh, Christ, the Stations of the Cross."

"What?"

"Just be glad you lives in Clayville away from Father Frank," he said. "I needs to get home right quick."

I offered to drive him, but he said he was bound to get a ride if he hitchhiked. After an awkward hug at my front door, he was off.

29

I didn't tell Doug that it was the anniversary of Dad's death. I'd been marking anniversaries privately all year—his birthday, Mom's birthday, their anniversary, the date he was diagnosed—on and on and on. Today was the big one. I couldn't decide if it was important or meaningless. Maybe all that mattered was that Dad was gone, not the date that he left.

I wandered around my house, restless and out of sorts. I took a package of red licorice out of my kitchen cupboard, threw on a coat and went to the cemetery, where I sat shivering on a bench and eating. Licorice was Dad's favourite candy. I'd snuck a few into his suit pocket in the coffin before the funeral. When the licorice was all gone, I went home, took out the fiddle Phonse had gifted me and played Vivaldi while the tears streamed down my cheeks.

Lucille phoned on Saturday evening to invite me for Easter dinner the next day. I'd spent Friday and Saturday on my own, so I gladly accepted. She said her knee was bothering her and would I mind coming early to drive her to Mass. I hadn't been to church since I moved to Clayville, but for Lucille, I would make the effort.

On Easter Sunday morning, I straightened my hair for the first time in ages and wore a dress under my trench coat. I drew the line at a bonnet.

Lucille was waiting for me at her gate when I drove up. She limped over to my car.

"Arthritis," she said when I asked what was wrong. "What's after happening to your hair?"

My hand rose to pat it. "I straightened it. Why? Does it look bad?"

"Different."

"Different good or different bad?"

"Different is all." She'd clearly forgotten that I used to straighten it every day when I lived with her.

We were early, but the lot was full so we had to park across the road.

"All these part-timers," Lucille said, shaking her head. "Christmas and Easter and the odd wedding or funeral. It's not right." If they were part-timers, that made me a temp at best.

Then Lucille said, "Lord Blessed God. I never thought I'd see the day." I followed her gaze and saw Doug manoeuvring his mother's wheelchair up the stairs of the church.

Mass seemed to go on forever. During the homily, I peeked back to look for Doug, but Lucille elbowed me back in line.

As we walked out afterwards, many parents and some students wished me happy Easter. Lucille squatted by the wheelchair, talking to Grace, while Doug and I waited beside them. I worried about Lucille's knees.

"I loves your hair, Rachel," Doug's mother said. "What are you after doing to it?"

"I straightened it."

"I likes the curls better," Doug said.

His mother snorted. "Sure what do you know about hair?"

Judy and Bill walked down the church steps and came over to join us. "Wonderful grand to see your mother out and about," Bill said to Doug.

Judy tugged at my sleeve. "Can I have a quick word?"

She led me away from the others and said, "Probably not the best place to raise this." For a minute I panicked that somehow she'd found out what I'd said to Cynthia.

"I'm away at a conference for the next few days," she said. "I wanted to talk to you about your teaching contract."

"Is there a problem?"

"Lord, no, the very opposite. I spoke to Pat on Thursday and frankly neither of us can imagine this place without you. Do you know there's two grade nine boys considering French next year after that RCMP talk you arranged?"

"Wow, that's fantastic."

"I knows you don't have to say anything yet," Judy said. "But unusually, you're on a one-year contract. Any idea what your plans are for next year? We'd love you to stay."

I looked down the road towards the school, unsure how to respond. "I didn't really think things through when I took this job," I said. "It was kind of impulsive."

Judy cocked her head, looking at me. "You always kept your reasons quiet."

"I needed to get away. The plan was to get a year's experience, hopefully get some good references . . ."

She held up her hand. "That won't be a problem. The word *glowing* springs to mind."

I felt my cheeks grow warm. "Thanks. The logical thing would be to go back home at the end of the year."

"Logic is overrated. Try listening to your heart."

I glanced over to where the others stood chatting and caught Doug looking. We held the gaze for what seemed a long time, until Lucille bawled over to me, "We leaving today, missus, or wha?" and the spell was broken.

"Can I think about it?" I asked Judy.

"Of course," she said.

I walked over to join Lucille, already weighing my options.

As soon as we entered Lucille's house, I smelled Jiggs Dinner. I helped her set the table, and when we sat down to eat, I piled my plate high with boiled potatoes, turnips and carrots and salt beef.

"I see you missed out the cabbage as usual," said Lucille.

In an effort to distract her from my dietary transgression, I remarked on Grace's attendance at church. "Doug told me about the storm that killed his dad and your John," I said. "It sounded terrible."

She shook salt furiously on her meal. "It was hard old times for lots of people. It gets easier, but I'll never stop missing my John. I still talks to him all the time." She patted her mouth with a napkin, then added, "It's some good to share memories with people who knew him well."

It reminded me of what Mom had said. She needed to talk to someone who had loved Dad, too.

"And now," said Lucille, bringing me back, "I can talk to Grace about him, thanks to you."

"Why thanks to me?" I asked, then put another forkful of food in my mouth.

"Sure you're the one got her out of the house."

I was mid-chew and gestured my lack of comprehension.

"The first time she left her house in years was the night she come here for the party after you nearly drowned yourself trying to save that frigging dog."

I ignored her use of the word *trying* and said, "But why did she care about Ruthie?"

"It wasn't the dog, girl. It was the rescue. That day will stay in people's memory, Rachel. In your own way, you took on the sea, and you won. And those days are to be celebrated around here. Once Grace left her house that evening, I think she realized what she'd been missing hiding away at home all those years. I guess Mass was the last barrier she had to break through. Now she's done it, and that's down to you."

After dinner, Lucille washed the dishes while I dried. The radio was on low, emitting a steady flow of jigs and reels.

"What's happening with your contract?" Lucille asked, handing me a soapy pan.

"What do you mean?"

"I wondered if you might stay on next year."

"That's what Judy was asking me after Mass today."

"Course she was. They're lucky to have you. What did you say?"

"That I'd think about it."

"Hmph," said Lucille, whatever that meant.

When the kitchen was tidy, Lucille made tea and we sat back down at the table. She brought me up to date on the hookers and Linda's wedding plans, while I half listened. It was all very familiar, sitting there while Lucille talked the ear off me, but after a while, I realized that something was off. Then it dawned on me. There was no ashtray on the table, and the spot over the stove where Lucille kept her cigarettes was bare. She hadn't smoked the entire time I'd been there.

"Did you quit smoking?" I asked.

"Yes, girl," she said. "Thought you'd never twig to it. I asked

Linda about a birthday present, and she said the only thing she wanted was for me to give up the smokes."

I jumped up from her chair and hugged her tight.

"Jaysus, girl," she said. "You nearly spilt me tea."

I glanced around the once familiar kitchen to see if there were any other changes. There was another tear in the linoleum and a new rug was tossed on the daybed. It consisted of wide stripes of blue and green, with a big splodge of yellow in one corner at the top. When I admired it, Lucille was dismissive.

"Pah," she said. "I ran out of blue and green rags, so I had to add that yellow bit. The sight of it's got me drove off me head."

"Well, I love it. It's like an abstract painting—all sea and forest and sun."

"You're cracked, my dear. Cracked." She laughed. "Abstract painting, I never heard the like. Wait 'til I tell the girls."

But when it was time for me to leave, Lucille thrust the rug into my hands. "Take it," she said. "You got me thinking." She gestured at the yellow splodge. "Maybe that's hope."

30

By chance, I had discovered that the Clayville district high school had a swimming pool that members of the public could use outside of school hours. I'd been swimming my whole life. As a toddler, my photo was in the local newspaper, accompanying a fluff piece about children's swimming lessons. At university, I worked as a lifeguard. I was even asked to swim competitively, but for me, swimming had always been about release and solitude. I might have started out angry or sad, but as I worked my way up and down the pool, my mind would clear and I would begin to relax.

To gain access to the swimming pool, I had to write my name and address in a dog-eared red book and pay the attendant five dollars for ten weeks of swimming. It seemed a pretty fair deal.

I changed quickly and pulled on my goggles, slipping into the pool. A used adhesive bandage floated past; I scooped it up and put it on the side. In the lane next to me, a woman in a bright orange swimsuit was doing lengths, and before I knew it, we were matching each other stroke for stroke. When I came out of the shower later, she was in the change room, and we chatted briefly as we dried off and dressed. She introduced herself as Maggie Vincent and it turned out that she was a history teacher at the high school. We agreed to meet at the pool the following Friday.

By the time I got back to my place, I was starving. I made a cup of tea and grabbed a cookie while I contemplated dinner. Then the phone rang.

"Rachel?" The voice was tremulous and I didn't recognize it.

"Yes."

"It's Biddy." I could almost hear the pain in her voice.

"Has something happened?" I asked, putting down my mug and tensing. "Is it Lucille?"

"No," said Biddy. "It's me." These last two words were almost whispered.

"What is it?" I asked.

"We hit a moose."

"You hid a moose? I don't understand."

"Eddie Churchill was driving me into Clayville this morning and there was a moose in the road and, well, we hit it."

"Oh my God, are you all right?"

"A bit banged up," she said, adding that her head had been knocked against the car window. "And I'm right worried about Eddie. He's gone off to St. John's in an ambulance and they won't tell me nothing because I'm not his next of kin."

I thought about kind Eddie Churchill, how he'd put on my winter tires and told me I was part of the community, and how he'd helped get me off the ice after I rescued Ruthie.

"Rachel," said Biddy, then hesitated. "I hates to ask, but they says I can go home if someone comes to collect me and I wondered if . . ."

"I'll be right over, Biddy. Where are you?"

"Emergency. I don't think I fits that description, but that's where I'm to. I wants a proper cup of tea and I wants to go home."

I grabbed my coat and purse and ran out to my car. Within minutes I had found the Clayville hospital and followed the signs to the emergency entrance. It was a small hospital, and I was later to learn that the emergency department was really only for minor injuries. Anyone seriously injured was taken directly to St. John's.

Biddy was sitting up very straight on a chair in the waiting room. Her face was grey, so that her birthmark looked less livid. There was a huge goose egg on her forehead. Her right arm was in a sling and she looked absolutely exhausted.

A middle-aged nurse was sitting beside Biddy, and as I approached, she stood up and said, "Are you the next of kin for Mrs. Cormack?"

Before I could say anything, Biddy answered.

"Yes," she said. "This is my niece Geraldine I was telling you about." She gave me a look.

"Oh," the nurse said, suddenly more interested. "Mrs. Cormack . . ."

"*Miss* Cormack," Biddy corrected.

"Miss Cormack is after telling me that you works at the hospital in St. John's. Do you know Patsy Fowler?"

For a minute I was flummoxed. How much lying was required, and what sort of medical knowledge was I meant to have?

Then Biddy whimpered, "I wants to get home."

I wasn't sure if it was a clever distraction or a genuine need, but either way, the question was forgotten. The nurse said that Biddy had a suspected concussion and needed to be watched for the next twenty-four hours. "Of course, you'll know that," she said. "And she got a bit bashed around so she's got these"—she thrust a bottle of pills at me—"painkillers."

I glanced at the label—one every six hours—then asked, "What about her arm?"

"Doctor thinks it's just a bad sprain, but we wants her back here on Wednesday for a check. But she's not to use it in the meantime."

"Not like I could if I wanted to," said Biddy. "I'm trussed up like a turkey, sure."

She stood then, making it clear it was time to go. I walked alongside her, staying close but not wanting to touch her, afraid of hurting her. When we reached my car, I helped her into it, then pulled the seat belt gingerly around her arm and buckled her in.

"So it looks like you need someone to stay with you tonight," I said.

Biddy frowned. "My sister's gone to St. John's with Lucille for a wedding. They won't be back 'til Sunday afternoon."

"What about Flossie and Annie?" I said.

"They're gone to the wedding too."

"Never mind," I said. "I'm coming to stay with you. It'll do me good to have a weekend in Little Cove," I lied. "It's been too long."

"You're not," said Biddy. "A young one like you don't want to be fussing over me in your free time."

"I am," I said. "And that's final. We'll stop at my place so I can get some clothes and things and then we'll head out to Little Cove."

Biddy was quiet as we drove through the empty streets of Clayville. My little house was ablaze with light, and despite the circumstances, I took a minute to admire it. I helped Biddy out of the car, and she winced when I accidentally brushed her arm. Once we were inside, I settled her on one of the loveseats and told her to relax while I put the kettle on. Then I ran upstairs to throw some clothes and toiletries in a bag.

When I came back downstairs, Biddy was standing at the mantelpiece.

"Is that one of Lucille's?" she asked, gesturing at the rug hanging on the wall.

"She gave it to me when I moved out," I said. I still felt a bit bad about my hasty departure even after all this time. "Do you think Lucille was annoyed when I moved out?"

"I don't think so. You're not carrying around guilt about that, are you?"

"Maybe a little." Even lapsed Catholics tended to keep at least some carry-on baggage.

"My dear," said Biddy. "Lucille is my best friend but she'd try anyone's patience on a full-time basis. I loves spending time with her, but I also loves closing the door behind her to be all alone in me own house." Biddy seemed to have put into words my exact feelings about Lucille.

She went back to the loveseat and sat down. "I think you did well to get your own place." Her eyes darted around the room. "And it's right cozy here, girl, although that's a funny old place to keep your milk, if you don't mind me saying." She pointed at the can of milk that had been sitting on my mantelpiece for months.

The kettle began whistling, so I grabbed the can and went to the kitchen. I made a pot of tea, and put fresh milk in a little jug but also opened the evaporated milk just in case. Then I put some cookies on a plate. I wanted to make a bit of an effort. Sheila and Doug had been my only visitors thus far. I decided that I would invite Maggie Vincent, the teacher I'd met at the pool, over for coffee soon. It was past time to make a few local friends in Clayville.

I sat down beside Biddy and poured the tea, glad I'd tidied up the evening before. It was only me, and I wasn't a complete slob, but sometimes I let things slide. Often there would be empty tea-cups and magazines strewn around. My mother would've been horrified.

Biddy sipped at her tea. As expected, she went for the tinned milk. She said she wasn't hungry, but after a few minutes reached for a cookie. Their one-hundred-percent-irresistible success rate remained intact. She took tiny bites and chewed for ages between each bite, until the cookie was gone. Then she told me about the accident.

She said it had been foggy, but Eddie was careful, not driving too fast. "But the moose come out of nowhere, as they does."

Apparently, Eddie slammed on the brakes, "Which probably saved us," she said. Instinctively, she reached up and gently patted her goose egg.

"Were you wearing a seat belt?" I asked.

She tutted. "Course I was. It might've been a bit loose, but I was wearing it."

She said Eddie hadn't been wearing his. "He never does."

"Will he be okay?"

She clasped her hands together as in prayer. "They wouldn't say much because I'm not a relation. I expect Phonse will know. I'll check with him when we gets back to Little Cove."

I took that as a hint and cleared up, putting the tray on the kitchen table. Seeing the two kinds of milk side by side, I decided to pour fresh milk into a flask to bring to Biddy's. I might be roughing it out there, but I wasn't going back to tinned milk. A girl had her limits. At the last minute, I grabbed the cookie jar as well.

I drove slowly, partly because I was now terrified of hitting a moose—something I had never before even contemplated—and partly because of the potholes that jolted us on our journey.

Biddy's house was unlocked. I readied myself to shove the door, but it glided easily open.

"Phonse is after fixing that door for me," Biddy said as I followed her inside. It was dark and cold in the kitchen.

She sighed. "Fire's gone out in the stove."

"You sit down in the rocking chair," I said. "I'll light the stove."

"There's a knack to it," she said. "She's a temperamental old thing." She gestured at the wood and kindling stacked neatly against the stove. "You needs a few blasty boughs."

I took a quilt from the daybed and tucked it around Biddy. "I'm used to temperamental old things," I said, smiling. "We have an old stove at our cottage back home that we use when the power goes out."

With Biddy instructing me, I was able to get the fire going. The room quickly began to warm up.

"I could turn on the heat too," I said.

"Heat?" said Biddy. "That is my heat. I never bothered getting anything else installed when the others around here did. I figured it was only me, and when the stove's going, it's warm enough. When I was a youngster, we used to take an old brick to bed that was warmed up on that very stove and then wrapped in a pillow case. Now I takes a hot water bottle. Progress," she cackled.

"It must've been so different in Little Cove back then," I said.

"In some ways, sure," she said. "But lots is the same. Lucille and I in and out of each other's houses. Annie and Flossie tagging along after us." She frowned. "Those two used to be real trouble, but they came around in their widowhood."

"What do you mean?"

"Ah, I'd best not tell tales out of school," she said. Annoyingly.

I sat down at the kitchen table and we were both quiet for a minute. Biddy instructing me in how to light the stove had reminded me of the last time I'd been at our cottage. Dad had been lying on the sofa in front of the bay window, watching the wind move the trees and the rain pelt the lake. I'd been putting the finishing touches on a pizza, which Dad had requested, even though we all knew he wouldn't eat any of it. Mom was in the bedroom working.

Then the power went out and we were immediately plunged into darkness. Mom came out and got the flashlight from the kitchen drawer. She held it over the stove while Dad talked me through how to light it. We'd even cooked the pizza on top of the stove and Dad had managed almost a whole piece, saying it was the best he'd ever eaten.

Mom and I couldn't face going up to the cottage after Dad died. It had sat empty all summer, and then our handyman shut it up for the winter. But lately, I'd been missing it, and Sheila and I had made plans to spend some time there in the summer.

I got up to put more wood in the stove, then asked Biddy if there was anyone I should call. "Do you have a number for where your sister's staying in St. John's?"

"I don't want them fussing and worrying when they're meant to be enjoying themselves at the wedding. She'll be home on Sunday and you can get home then."

"Trying to get rid of me already," I said.

Biddy asked me to call Phonse. "He might have some news about Eddie," she said.

Tacked to the wall beside her telephone was a faded list of names and numbers. I noticed Lucille was at the top and Brigid Roche's name had been scratched out. I found Phonse's number, but there was no answer.

"He might be over in Mardy playing tonight I s'pose," she said. "We'll try again tomorrow."

We sat and chatted idly until Biddy said she was tired. I helped her undress, then settled her in bed, plumping pillows and adjusting quilts. Then I made her a hot water bottle. Her eyes were closed when I returned with it, but she opened them and smiled.

"I usually reads before I goes to sleep, but I don't think I can manage it tonight," she said.

"What are you reading?"

She pointed to the bedside table and I recognized the book immediately: *Light a Penny Candle*. I'd read it last year, enjoying the gentle writing and the story of two girls whose lives were entwined. I hoped Sheila and I would be friends for life the way Elizabeth and Aisling were, although preferably without all the drama.

"I could read you a chapter," I offered.

Biddy smiled. "That would be grand, Rachel."

I dragged the rocking chair in from the kitchen, wrapped myself in a quilt and began to read.

31

I woke in the middle of the night, still in the rocking chair. My watch told me it was two o'clock. Some nurse I'd turned out to be. I gently roused Biddy, who grumbled that she was fine and told me to leave her be. So I went to the kitchen, put some wood in the stove and curled up on the daybed under a quilt.

Biddy's voice woke me in the morning. She wanted help getting out of bed. I asked her if she wanted me to take her to the bathroom.

"My God, girl, I'm not that far gone," she said. She climbed slowly up the stairs and I tried not to fret. But twenty minutes later, she was back, hair brushed and a smell of minty toothpaste about her. She needed help to get dressed, but that was all.

I was desperate for my Saturday morning coffee fix, but settled for tea. I set to work on breakfast, after turning on the radio. Soon enough I was singing along with the folk music they played.

"Nice to hear a young one singing in this house," said Biddy. "I miss Geraldine. She don't come home much these days."

I kept my attention fixed on the stove while I digested this information. "Maybe she's really busy at work."

"Yes girl, I allows. But I think she also got the taste for life in town now. I never sees her with Doug anymore. He's a bayman through and through. I don't think that was ever a love match."

I joined Biddy at the table, dishing up eggs and cutting up the bacon for her. She ate left-handed and seemed to manage well enough. After breakfast, she asked me to phone Phonse, but again there was no reply, and she began to fret.

"Maybe he's at the school," I said. "I could drive down and see. Will you be all right on your own for ten minutes?"

She batted her hand at me, which I interpreted as a yes.

Phonse was not at the school, but Doug was. He said Little Cove was abuzz with news about the accident and asked me how Biddy was doing.

"I'm driving Phonse into St. John's this afternoon so we can get Eddie."

"So he's okay?"

"Broken arm and pretty banged up, but he'll live. His truck is totalled, though."

"From hitting an animal?"

"Have you ever seen a moose? They're huge." He gestured with his arms.

"It's good of you to pick up Eddie."

"He'd do the same for me. Eddie Churchill is our unofficial taxi service. He's driven Mudder around for years when I'm not able."

I thought about all the times I'd seen Eddie driving Lucille and others around. A good man.

"I guess Elsie will be back tomorrow to take over," said Doug.

"Who's Elsie?"

"Biddy's sister." He paused, then added, "Geri's mom."

Ah.

"Doug, why wasn't Biddy invited to this wedding that half the ladies in Little Cove seem to be attending?"

"Not a clue."

"You're no good for gossip."

Doug gave me a funny look. "When your own mudder is a constant source of gossip," he said, "you learns right quick it's a hateful beast. Besides, who says she wasn't invited? Maybe she was and she didn't want to go."

Thinking about what Biddy had said about closing the door and having time to herself, that possibility seemed more likely. But Doug was right, it really was none of my business. And nor, I realized ruefully, was the torrid history of Flossie and Annie. Chastened, I said goodbye and told him to drive carefully.

"I always do."

"And give my best to Eddie."

When I returned to Biddy's house, she was delighted to hear that Eddie was coming home so soon. After lunch I asked if she'd mind if I went for a walk.

"I'm so much better today," she said. "You could go home, sure."

"Nope," I said. "I'm staying until the reinforcements arrive."

It was a bright warm day, so I walked down the path to the wharf and leaned on the side for a while, staring out at the sea. Heading back up to Biddy's something glinted in the sunshine. I stooped down and picked up a silver whistle on a thin, red string. It was too dirty to put in my mouth to see if it worked, but I shoved it in the pocket of my jeans.

Back at Biddy's I caught her doing the dishes one-handed. I scolded her and took over.

"I'm getting right jittery sitting here doing nothing," she said.

"It's called recuperation," I said. "And since I'm apparently a nurse," I winked at her, "you'd better follow my orders."

She sat down at the table, and I quickly washed the few dishes and left them to dry in the rack. Then I fished the whistle out of my pocket and gave it a quick wash too.

"Look what I found coming up the path," I said, putting it on the table in front of her.

She picked it up and examined it closely. "Oh, that'll do nicely for my treasure box if you don't want it."

Intrigued, I asked her to explain.

"Go on out to that cupboard in the front hall," she directed. "Have a rummage 'til you finds a wooden box. Bring it here to me 'til we goes through it. That'll keep us occupied."

I did as instructed and found the box under a bag stuffed full of wool. Back at the table, Biddy told me that as a young girl, she'd always been fascinated by found treasure, bringing old bits of coloured glass or seashells home from the beach.

"I never stopped collecting things," she said. "Of course, if I knows who it belongs to, I gives it back. I once found Judy's engagement ring. She'd been beside herself, lying to Bill that she'd taken it into Clayville to get the diamond polished and wondering what she'd do if it never turned up."

Biddy reached into the box and pulled out a red mitten.

"I found this about three years ago out on the road. I left it on my fencepost for a few days, but no one claimed it, so I washed it and put it in here. Look at those stitches," she said, holding it up. "They're perfect. Whoever knit this is right crafty."

She put the mitten on the table and dug into the box again. "Of course, I favours shiny things. Bottle caps, bits of jewellery. I'm like a magpie." Then she looked down at her sling and laughed.

"A magpie with a broken wing, hey. Oh, I dies at myself sometimes, girl. Good thing I lives alone."

Her face was animated now and it seemed to me that the goose egg was shrinking.

"Oh, my dear," she continued, "I've found all sorts of things. People knows to come see me if they've lost something. Between me and St. Anthony, things tends to turn up."

"What's St. Anthony got to do with it?" I asked, thinking, Does everything have to come back to religion in Little Cove?

"And you a teacher in a Catholic school," she said. "Shocking lack of knowledge." But when I looked up, she was smiling. "St. Anthony is the patron saint of lost things."

Was there a patron saint for lapsed believers? I silently wondered.

"Dear St. Anthony, please look 'round, something's lost and must be found," she intoned.

I must've rolled my eyes because Biddy tutted and told me that the prayer was absolutely known to work. "You try it the next time you loses something, girl. Go on, now, say the prayer for me so I knows you'll be ready if you needs it."

"Dear St. Anthony, please look around, something's lost and must be found," I said, somewhat sulkily, I realized. But thankfully Biddy wasn't really paying me much attention. She was delving back into the box.

"Some nights when I'm here on me own, I turns on the radio and then I gets the treasure box out. I likes to imagine stories about all this stuff."

Now I was interested. "Stories? That's wonderful, Biddy. Why don't you write them down?"

"Oh go 'way with you, girl," she said. "You're talking nonsense now. Write them down? Sure who'd want to read them?"

"Me!" I said.

She shook her head. "No girl. The treasure box stories are for my own amusement, no one else's."

"But, Biddy," I began.

"The only stories I tells are in the rugs I hooks," she said. "And that's final."

It seemed Biddy could be as stubborn as me.

She reached into the box again.

"I found this when the snow melted," she said. "It was on the path down to the wharf. I don't recognize the initials and it don't seem to work no more, but it's real silver."

I was half paying attention and half thinking about a book of Biddy stories, but when I saw what she'd placed on the table, my hand went to my mouth.

"What is it, girl?" she asked.

I wiped tears from my eyes. "It's mine," I whispered.

"J.O'B.?" Biddy said, puzzled.

"Joseph O'Brien," I managed to say. "My dad."

"Oh my dear," she said, reaching over and patting my hand. "St. Anthony, you see?"

I placed Dad's lighter on the palm of my hand, tracing the engraving with the index finger of my other hand. As hokey as it sounded, especially to this non-believer, the return of the lighter seemed like a blessing.

32

If I hadn't come to stay with Biddy, I might never have been reunited with Dad's lighter. I said as much to her and offered to take her for fish and chips as a reward.

"What a treat!" she said. "I never has that." She gestured out the window and I saw it had begun to rain. "But I'm not sure I wants to brave that weather. Could you get takeout?"

I said yes, as long she promised not to set the table.

The first person I saw in the takeout was Cynthia, sitting with her mother at one of the booths. Mrs. O'Leary called me over and we chatted briefly. I tried to catch Cynthia's eye but she stared resolutely down at her plate.

Then I joined the lineup to order. Even though there were three people in front of me, Mrs. Corrigan bellowed, "What can I get you, Miss O'Brine?" from behind the pass-through.

I bellowed my order back and the people in front of me shuffled to the side so I could pay.

"You're some good to be looking after Biddy," said Mrs. Corrigan, wiping her hands on her apron and coming out to stand by the cash register, where Belinda was ringing up my bill.

"She and Lucille have been good to me ever since I arrived," I said. "It's the least I could do." Besides, I added to myself, thinking again of Eddie Churchill, I'm part of the community.

"How's Biddy getting on?" she asked.

Was it my imagination, or did everyone in the takeout seem to lean in to hear my answer? I thought about what Doug had said about the gossiping, and how Biddy valued her privacy so much.

"She's fine," I said, falling back on the O'Brien code. "Just fine."

Biddy raved about the fish and chips and said she must treat herself more often. She was much livelier that evening, going so far as to ask for a drink of sherry. Naturally, I joined her. It would have been rude not to.

But when it was time for bed, she asked if I wouldn't mind reading her another chapter, which I gladly did. I knew there was a second Maeve Binchy book out and I resolved to buy it for Biddy if I could find it in Clayville. And, if not, then heck, I'd been in Newfoundland for almost eight months, maybe it was time to check out St. John's.

I slept on the daybed again that night. It was warm and cozy in the kitchen, and despite Biddy's obvious improvement, I wanted to be within earshot if she woke in the night.

The next morning, I woke early and looked around Biddy's kitchen, really looking. There was a stack of books beside the daybed where I lay and the treasure box was still on the table. Biddy's tea set, neatly organized up on a shelf, was bone china. Three hooked rugs lay on the floor: one in front of the wood stove, one by the daybed and one at the entranceway. I was lying under the most gorgeous quilt I'd ever seen, although clearly, I would never admit that to Lucille.

The ringing phone interrupted my inventory taking and I answered quickly, not wanting to wake Biddy.

"Hello," I half whispered.

"Who's that?" said a voice I didn't recognize. "Where's Biddy?"

"It's Rachel O'Brien," I said. "Biddy's still asleep. I'm . . ." I thought about what Doug had said about not gossiping. "I'm visiting her this weekend."

"Visiting?" The voice was incredulous. "This is Elsie, her sister."

"Oh," I said. "I wasn't sure who I was speaking to. I'm staying with Biddy this weekend because I didn't want her to be on her own, after the . . ." I paused, wondering how best to phrase things.

"I'm after hearing about the accident. Sounds like she'll mend just fine. Normally, there's nothing Biddy likes better than being on her own," Elsie said. "But I'm glad you were able to stay with her."

"It's honestly a pleasure," I said.

"Hmph," came the reply. "We're coming back to Little Cove as soon as we can, you tell her," said Elsie. "And I'll see to her then."

After I hung up, I poked my head around the doorway of Biddy's room. She was awake and I asked her if she wanted tea in bed.

"My dear," she said. "What luxury, yes, please. And this is nonsense now, but are there any of them cookies of yours on the go or wha? They're some good."

Ten minutes later, Biddy and I were having cookies and tea for breakfast, she in her bed and me in the rocking chair. I looked up at one point and Biddy had a big smile on her face.

"What's got you so happy?" I asked.

"I just realized that for the first time in fifty years, I don't have to go to Mass this morning," she said, gleefully. "I'm too poorly."

"Oh," I said. "I thought you were feeling better."

She smirked, and snuggled back under the covers.

"You know," I said. "If you're not feeling well, maybe I need to stay with you. Just in case."

"Not a chance, my dear," she said. "You needs to show your face. People knows you're out here and, as a teacher, you needs to set the example."

She was sounding remarkably like Father Frank, it seemed to me.

That afternoon, I packed my bag and tidied up the kitchen and Biddy's bedroom while she dozed by the stove in the rocking chair. Then the door flew open and Lucille burst in, followed by Geri and a woman who looked like an older but very well-preserved version of Geri. Biddy woke at the noise and held her one good arm out. Lucille ran over and patted Biddy's shoulder and stroked her cheek, and then settled on a chair beside her, asking how she was and what had happened, and scolding her, saying that if she'd come to the wedding with them, then none of this would have happened in the first place. By the time Lucille stopped for breath, Biddy looked exhausted.

Geri was examining Biddy's head and adjusting the sling. Then she filled the kettle and put it on to boil. Elsie sat down beside me on the daybed and introduced herself, asking how Biddy was doing. I gave her a quick summary and showed her the bottle of pills, then began to gather my things to slip away quietly.

"Rachel O'Brine!"

I turned, expecting Lucille to be telling me off about something, but it was Biddy speaking. She crooked her finger at me and I went back over. When I bent down, she stroked my cheek and said, "You're a star, Rachel. Thank you so much. Now go on home and enjoy some peace and quiet in that cozy house of yours."

And I did.

33

A few days later during morning break, Judy burst into the staff room, her face white. "Cynthia's missing. Do you know where she might be?"

I shook my head, then followed her, wordless, to Patrick's office, where he was deep in conversation with a tearful Mrs. O'Leary. Her bloodshot eyes were locked on Patrick; she barely registered us entering the room.

"I hates to say it," said Patrick, "but do you think she went off somewhere with Ron?"

Cynthia's mother accepted his proffered tissue. "That's what's got me so worried." She dabbed at her nose. "I went to see Ron. He said she left his place last night in a right state. He figured she'd come home, but she didn't. I went to bed early with a headache and when I woke up . . ." She was silent for a minute and when she spoke again, her voice was fierce. "I frigging well knew he'd drop her. I kept telling her but she wouldn't listen."

I leaned against the wall listening to the discussion, wondering first whether Mrs. O'Leary knew that Cynthia was pregnant and second whether she actually was. I had promised not to say anything, but the fact that Cynthia was missing changed things. I beckoned Judy out into the hall.

"I think Cynthia might be pregnant."

Her face crumpled. "How do you know?"

When I briefly explained, her face grew stern. "Why didn't you tell me?" she said, then went back into Patrick's office, shutting the door in my face.

When no one came out, and the bell rang signalling the end of break, I went back to my classroom. The day passed slowly. At lunch I went to the staff room, but no one was there. After school, I went to Judy's office, then Patrick's, but there was no sign of either of them. At a loss, I drove home, wondering where Cynthia might be and hoping she was okay.

That evening, Patrick phoned and told me that Cynthia had been found unconscious on a bench in Clayville Park, following an overdose of sleeping pills.

"Oh my God," I said. "Is she all right?"

"They're after pumping her stomach. It looks like she'll be okay, but they're keeping her in for now."

"Patrick," I said. "I'm sorry I didn't tell anyone about the pregnancy. Cynthia made me promise."

"You did what you thought was right," he said.

"But was it?"

His heavy sigh whooshed down the line. "There's nothing right about any of this. Don't drive yourself mental with shoulda woulda coulda."

"I think Judy's pretty mad at me."

"Cynthia's a relation of hers," Patrick reminded me. "So I

expect she feels responsible. Which, by the way, she isn't. None of us are. Cynthia's in the Clayville hospital for now, but she might be transferred to St. John's for a psychiatric consultation. She's asking for you. Do you think you could go see her tonight?"

"Sure," I said. "As soon as I hang up." Until recently, I hadn't even been aware of the Clayville hospital and now I was heading back there for the second time in less than a week.

Cynthia had been admitted so I went up to the reception desk to find out her room number. The young clerk looked up from her gossip magazine. I gave her Cynthia's name, and as she checked her log book, she said, "Be good for Diana to have a friend on the inside."

"Sorry?"

She tapped the magazine cover. Just below the picture of Andrew and Fergie was the caption "A friend for Di?"

Sheila and I had risen early to watch Diana and Charles get married. I was hopeful, gushing about the dress and the train. But Sheila had watched between her fingers, saying "It's doomed" over and over until I had to hit her with a pillow. I hoped Fergie would bring Diana some joy and said as much to the receptionist. She nodded her agreement, then pointed me in the direction of Cynthia's room.

Just past the nursing station, I began to feel light-headed. Meeting Biddy in the waiting room was one thing; visiting Cynthia as an in-patient was something else.

I stopped at a fountain and braced myself against the wall for a minute before taking a drink. When I reached Room 17, I paused at the doorway and peeked in. The lights were dimmed, except for one directly above Cynthia, which glinted on her glasses. Her face was whiter than the sheets, and her hair was uncombed and dirty against the pillow.

I waited until she opened her eyes.

"Hi, miss," she said softly. "I'm some stunned."

"No, you're not." I sat down on the chair beside her bed as tears began to roll down her cheeks. I pulled a tissue from the box on the tray table and passed it to her. She poked it up under her glasses, dabbing at her eyes. Then she balled up the tissue in her hand, sniffing.

"You were right," she whispered.

I felt no satisfaction at hearing this. "About what?"

"Everything," she croaked. She broke down again and I waited until her sobs subsided. "Ron's after dropping me, miss. He says I'm too young and foolish for him."

I patted her arm. "I'm sorry. But he was so much older than you."

What was it with girls who fell for the bad guys? I'd never understood it, although Sheila had dabbled on the dark side when we were younger.

"Where did you get the sleeping pills?" I asked.

"Ron had them in his bathroom, I guess on account of the car accident last year." Cynthia chewed at the ragged skin of her thumb. "Everything's ruined," she said. "I gave up school for nothing."

"Never mind," I said. "Concentrate on getting better. Think about the baby."

"I lost it." Her voice was flat; I couldn't read her feelings.

I took her hand in mine. "That's hard. But maybe you can come back to school."

"It's too late for this year," she said. "Mom asked Mr. Donovan and that's what he said."

"There's always next year," I said, but she dropped her gaze.

I put the box of tissues on her lap. "Things will seem brighter soon," I said. "I'm sure of it. Can I bring you anything from the store?"

"No," she said. "Mam's coming in later with a few things." Then she closed her eyes.

"I'll leave you to rest," I said, getting up to go. I walked briskly down the hall, my pace quickening as I neared the exit. I pushed the buzzer to open the hospital doors, staggered around the corner of the building and retched repeatedly, until there was nothing left to come up.

The entire time I'd been in Cynthia's hospital room, I kept pushing the memories away and they kept flooding back in. Now, I walked woozily to my car, sagged into the driver's seat and let them surge over the breakwater.

I had been in my bedroom, two weeks after the disastrous graduation party, flipping through the photos of that evening. I hadn't even known my mother had sent them off to be developed. I lingered over a photo of Sheila and me. We were laughing so hard, our eyes were squeezed shut.

In the next photo, Jake had his arm slung around my shoulder and I was smiling up at him. It was probably taken shortly before that girl showed up. Looking at it made me nauseous and I'd ripped it into pieces. Then I felt my breakfast rising up and ran for the bathroom.

After I threw up, I wet my face and looked in the mirror. It was the second time that week, and suddenly I had a horrible thought. I counted back the days to my last period. It couldn't be. I was on the pill. I ran back to the bedroom and checked the little dial. I hadn't missed a single day. People often talked about how the pill was only ninety-nine percent effective. I guess someone had to be the one percent.

Now, sitting in my car outside the Clayville hospital, I remembered how I'd reached for the phone to call Sheila, my hands shaking as I tried to dial. Thanks to her job, Sheila knew her way around the medical profession. She arrived less than an hour later with pamphlets, phone numbers and a tub of chocolate ice cream.

Mom was out, so we sat in the kitchen with two spoons, passing the ice cream back and forth.

Eventually Sheila said, "What's the plan?"

I picked up the brochure for the abortion clinic and waved it weakly in the air.

"Are we telling Jake?"

I loved her for saying *we*. But Sheila's mother was even more hard-core Catholic than mine. "Are you sure you want to be involved with this?" I asked.

"Rachel," she said. "Do you not remember that we got married in kindergarten? Sickness and health, babe, 'til death do us part. My mother may be a living saint, but I'm on the other side of the divide. So I repeat, are we telling Jake?"

"No," I whispered.

"Good," she said. "Makes it cleaner."

Two days later, Sheila drove me to the clinic. She checked me in, sat beside me in the waiting room and filled in various forms. My hands were trembling so much I barely managed the signature. Sheila walked the completed paperwork back to the desk, then came back and talked about her annoying boss. She shared the latest pop-star gossip she'd gleaned from her brother Mike and mused aloud as to which of the three men in her current rotation was on the rise and which was about to be cut loose. None of it was new, but all of it helped.

When a nurse with squeaky shoes called my name, Sheila enveloped me in a hug. "I'm staying right here until you're done," she whispered.

Later, when I was cleared to leave, Sheila insisted on coming home with me. We walked wordlessly upstairs. I took off my sweatshirt and let it drop to the floor, crawling into bed in my sweatpants and top. I was somewhere between bulky and empty.

Sheila plumped pillows and smoothed sheets. She fetched me a glass of water and put it gently on the bedside table. Then she went to the other side of the bed and crawled in beside me.

"Do you want to talk about it?" she asked.

"No," I squeaked.

She stroked my hair. "How are you feeling?"

"Crampy."

She propped herself up on her elbow. "The nurse said that's normal, though, right?"

I fell asleep watching Sheila watch me, her normally sunny expression sombre. When I woke in total darkness, she was asleep beside me. I nudged her awake.

"I fell asleep," she mumbled.

"Me too." My teeth were chattering. "I'm cold."

Sheila threw back the covers. "Well, I'm boiling." She turned on the bedside light and got out of bed.

I pulled the covers higher, shivering.

She came around to my side of the bed and rested her hand on my forehead. "You look awful and you're burning up."

"Oh God," I said. "I think I just peed the bed."

But when Sheila pulled back the covers, we both gasped at the blood.

"Don't move," she said. "I'm calling an ambulance."

Even as I was telling her not to, I felt myself slipping away.

When I woke up the next day in hospital, Mom was sitting in the chair beside my bed, her face grave. She leaned forward and squeezed my hand too tightly. "I can't lose you, too," she said, her voice fierce. "Why didn't you tell me?"

We both knew she would have tried to stop me. "I didn't want you to worry," I lied.

"That's my job," she lied back. It had been mostly Dad's job and we both knew it.

She let go of my hand and rubbed her eyes. I wondered how long she'd been there.

We listened to machines being wheeled down the corridor and the occasional announcement over the PA system. After a while, Mom spoke again.

"Does Jake know?"

"I didn't see the point of telling him since we're broken up."

She touched the cross on her necklace, then said, "How did you let this happen, Rachel?"

"I was careful, Mom," I said. "I was on the pill."

She frowned. For her, that was almost as bad.

I could bear all those memories, even though I hoped they would someday be buried under a scab that I would never pick off. But one memory was seared in my consciousness, one I couldn't forget, no matter how hard I tried. It had happened during my convalescence at home.

After I was discharged from the hospital, Mom and I developed a habit of watching videos late into the night. One night, Mom decided to open a bottle of merlot. I was forbidden to drink because I was on antibiotics, but Mom kept refilling her wine glass until the bottle was empty. Then a dog died in the movie, and she started crying, becoming maudlin about Dad. She worked herself into such a state that I, the invalid, had to help her upstairs and into bed. I flicked the light switch off and was closing the door when she said, "It's a good thing your father's dead, Rachel. Otherwise this whole thing with you and your procedure"—she spat the word out—"would've killed him."

I knew it was the wine talking, but if she had slugged me, it would have hurt less. I left her room and drove straight to Sheila's for the night. Mom and I spent the next few days avoiding each other. Then I saw the ad for the job in Little Cove and lunged at it.

It was the word *Newfoundland* that had clinched it. New. Found. Land. Somewhere to start over.

But now here I was in Newfoundland reliving my past. I started the car in an effort to dislodge the memories, and headed home. It was funny, but the physical distance that existed between Mom and me seemed to be bringing us closer. I found myself wondering what our relationship would be like when her sabbatical was over and she came home.

As I pulled into my driveway, I remembered that Mom was due to call me. I wasn't in the greatest shape to speak to her. The phone was ringing when I opened the door and I debated not answering it. But in the end I did.

"Rachel?"

I sagged down on the loveseat at the sound of his voice.

"How did you get my number?"

"Your uncle gave it to me."

"What do you want, Jake? I really don't have anything to say to you. I'm going to hang up now."

"Wait!" His voice was pleading. "Hear me out. I deserve that at least."

There were two years of photos that to the casual observer would confirm a happy couple: Jake and me at a hockey game, Jake and me skiing, Jake and me at the cottage. We had ticked every item on the list of great Canadian date activities.

"Fine," I said. "Let's hear it."

"I screwed up, Rachel. I don't know what I was thinking."

"Clearly, you weren't thinking of me, Jake," I said, my tone becoming more sarcastic as I warmed up. "Oh, no, wait. That's not exactly right, is it? You *were* thinking of me. You were thinking I was too sad all the time, remember?"

There was silence at the other end.

"I mean, God forbid that a girl whose father has just died be sad, right, Jake?"

"I'm sorry, Rach. It was a stupid, crass thing to say. It was my first experience of death. Your father meant a lot to me too."

"No!" I stood up abruptly. "You do not get to use my father's death to justify your insensitive and selfish comments. And you sure as hell don't get to use it to justify cheating on me."

In slow-motion replay, in my mind's eye, I saw the girl go down the steps and push Sheila into the pool and all the mouths of the guests forming perfectly round *O*s.

"It was over before it began." Jake's tone was pleading.

I wanted to tell him how much he'd hurt me, but I was afraid that if I kept talking, I'd end up telling him about the abortion. I hung up, and right away, the phone began ringing again. I pulled the jack out of the wall, sat down in the rocking chair and rocked back and forth, back and forth, long into the night.

34

Two days later, I found a sealed envelope in my cubbyhole in the staff room. I opened it to find a typed letter requiring my attendance at a meeting with Patrick after school. My neck prickled. I'd never been summoned this way before.

Patrick's face was grave when I knocked on the open door to his office.

"You wanted to see me?" I said quietly.

"Shut the door please, Rachel."

The window in Patrick's office overlooked the parking lot. I sat down and waited while he stared out of it. I could see nothing going on out there, but Patrick seemed mesmerized. When I could bear it no longer, I broke the silence.

"I went to see Cynthia in the hospital."

His gaze left the window and settled on me. "It's Cynthia we needs to talk about. I'm after receiving a formal complaint about you."

"From Cynthia?"

"No."

There was another long silence, then he said, "Jaysus, girl, you messed up. I don't think I can help you with this one."

"W-what?" I said. "What is it?"

"I'm told you counselled Cynthia to have an abortion. Is that true?"

I began to shake. "I didn't counsel her to do anything. I mean, I gave her a few options."

He cut me off. "Abortion is not an option for Catholics, Rachel, as you well know. The Church views it as a mortal sin. Father Frank is adamant that this has to go before the Board. And I'm inclined to agree with him."

"But how did he . . ."

"How it was found out should be the least of your concerns right now. But Father Frank went to visit Cynthia in the hospital. That poor girl is racked with guilt and I expect she confided in him."

"But she didn't have an abortion, Patrick," I said, my voice rising. "She lost the baby."

"That's not the point." He drummed his fingers on the desk. "It's not what *she* did, it's what you, a teacher in a Catholic school, apparently said. I expect your employment will be terminated. We'll speak no more of this for now and you are not to discuss it with anyone. That's all." He picked up a folder on his desk and began to carefully examine its contents.

I walked out numb, then shut the door and leaned against it, eyes smarting, breath jagged. Phonse was mopping the floor a few feet away and looked up. I couldn't face him, so I ran the other way, outside to the parking lot.

There was a man, baseball cap pulled low on his face, standing beside my car. When he saw me, he walked quickly away. A parent? I ran to my car and found a note under my windshield wiper. I quickly read it. More of the same.

Infuriated, I started running after the man. I was gaining on him when he looked over his shoulder and saw me. He started running, too. Then he darted across the road, heading towards a field. I started to cross the road after him, but there was a screech of tires and the blaring of a horn, then Eddie Churchill's brand-new pickup truck stopped inches from me.

He jumped out of the car with the engine still running and grabbed me by the shoulders.

"Jaysus Christ," he roared. "You trying to get yourself killed?" His fingers were digging into my shoulders and I whimpered. He released me and ran a hand through his grey hair.

"Sorry, girl," he said. "I'm a bit twitchy after that accident I had. What's got you all riled up?"

"He put another note on my car," I said. "I just want to know why."

"Who?"

I pointed across the road. The man had stopped when the tires screeched, but now he began to run again.

"That's Ron Drodge. Hard case, that one. What's the note say?"

Wordless now, I handed it to him. "When are you going to start listening you mainlander bitch? Frig off back home," it read.

I told Eddie I'd been finding notes like that on my car all year. "The little bastard," he said. "I'm ashamed of him. Come on, get in the truck."

We drove back to the school and Eddie came inside with me. "I think we should tell Patrick," he said.

"No!" I didn't want to see Patrick right now.

"Well, someone needs to be told," said Eddie.

"Someone needs to be told what?" said Doug, who had appeared in the hall.

Eddie handed him the note. "Ron Drodge left this on her car this afternoon." He jerked his head at me. "She says she's had a few of these notes."

Doug read the note. "Let me get my keys," he said.

"Where are you going?" I asked.

"To have a chat with Ron."

By now, I was shaking and couldn't face the drive back to Clayville. "Can you drop me at Lucille's?" I asked.

"She's gone to Clayville," said Eddie. "Drove her there meself."

"I'll bring you to our place," said Doug. "Mudder would love to see you."

During the short journey to his house, he kept starting to speak, then stopping. He brought me inside the house and called out to his mother.

Grace wheeled herself into the hall and her face lit up. "Rachel, grand to see you," she said. "We can all have tea."

"I needs to go out, Mudder," said Doug jingling his keys.

"Off you go, then," she said. "Rachel and I can manage without you just fine."

"I can make the tea," I said. "If you give me some direction."

I put the kettle on and Grace told me where to find mugs and milk. The water splashed onto the burner as I poured.

"Sorry," I said. "I've got the jitters."

"Bad day?" she asked

She looked so sympathetic that I ended up telling her about the note and how Doug was gone to talk to Ron.

"I don't understand why he hates me so much," I said. "I've never even met him. I've been getting these notes since my first day of teaching."

Her expression changed. "Oh, Doug never told me that."

"I didn't tell him," I said. "I didn't tell anyone."

"No one?" Her tone was one of surprise.

"I didn't know who it might be, so I was afraid to tell anyone."

My dear," she said, "I'm some disappointed to hear that all of Little Cove was a suspect in your eyes. Do you not trust any of us?"

I looked down at my lap. Why hadn't I told anyone about the notes? Had I really suspected everyone?

"I'm sorry," I said. "I wasn't thinking."

"Well, never mind," she said. "But if you'd mentioned it to Lucille, she would've sussed the culprit right quick. Anyway, I'm not surprised it was Ron. He's bad news. I expect he was doing it for Brigid."

"Why?"

"I don't know. Perhaps in his mind, you took her job."

We'd drunk our tea and Doug was still not back, but I was suddenly anxious to leave Little Cove. I said goodbye to Grace and she put her arms up for a hug.

"I'll never forgive Ron for doing that to you," she said. "You were an innocent party."

As I walked down the road to get my car from the school, I found myself wondering how much longer I could lay claim to that label around here.

35

Over the next few days, I dragged myself through lessons. Every time there was a knock on my door or a note on my desk, I felt sick. The wait was over when Judy arrived at my classroom all business and said that Mr. Donovan wanted to see me and she would cover my class. So, this was it. I was about to be fired.

I grabbed my purse from the back of chair in case I was asked to leave immediately. Through the open doors of the other classrooms, my fellow teachers were carrying on as normal. Doug was sitting on the edge of his desk talking to his class. He stopped talking, and the class laughed in unison. What had he said? I wondered. Sister Mary Catherine's room was silent. The students were diligently working and she was at her desk, reading.

I knocked on Patrick's door, then stuck my head in.

A woman who looked a few years older than me sat opposite him. She had wavy blonde hair and violet eyes. Her skin was so pale I could see blue veins running beneath it.

"Oops, sorry," I said. "I'll come back later."

"Come in, Rachel," said Patrick. His face was red and blotchy under his beard. "Come and meet Brigid. She was the French teacher here before you."

"Hello," she said softly.

"I've heard so much about you," I said. And we both blushed. "I didn't mean it like that."

She inclined her head slightly. "It's all right."

Then she said to Patrick, "I'll be off. I'll wait to hear."

Patrick walked around his desk. "I'll see you out, Brigid." When they reached the door, he called over his shoulder. "Sit tight, Rachel, I'll be right back."

After a minute I saw them in the parking lot. Patrick walked Brigid to her car. He leaned into the window and talked to her for a few minutes. He waited until she drove away, then he looked up at the sky for a minute before walking slowly back towards the school.

"Christ on a cracker," he said, sitting down heavily in his chair. "Sorry about that. She pitched up here just now to ask for her job back. Said she heard you were on a one-year contract."

"What were you going to talk to me about?"

Patrick picked up a big ring of keys from the desk, weighing them in his hand. "I don't know. I was hoping to come up with a plan, but now Brigid's complicated things. I told her I had to confirm your intentions seeing as you're the incumbent now."

"But what about Father Frank?" I asked, faint stirrings of hope rising in my heart.

"I don't know," said Patrick. "I needs to have a word with him and now we got this complication. I don't think he'll want Brigid back, but I didn't know what else to say. I couldn't exactly tell her I was waiting to hear if you'd be fired."

I rubbed my eyes. "So you're still waiting to hear?"

He nodded.

We sat in bleak silence while dust motes danced between us in the light from the window. At lunchtime twenty students had shown up for French club, including a few first-timers. Behind Patrick on the bulletin board was a draft poster for the garden party. I hadn't yet gotten the students to agree to play, but felt I was wearing them down. I'd played with them again at the pub in Mardy a few weeks back. And what about Calvin? How would he get on at the trades college in September? Would Cynthia bounce back? All these people I hadn't known a year ago now mattered desperately to me. My thoughts had just turned to Doug when the bell rang so loud in Patrick's office that I jumped.

"Patrick," I said. "I know I screwed up, but I would really like to stay on next year."

He looked bleak. "It's out of my hands, Rachel," he said.

I nodded and said goodbye.

That evening Patrick called me at home. "Father Frank doesn't want you back next year," he said. "I can't find a way to go against him. You'll finish out the year. It'll be non-renewal of contract, rather than termination. I managed to get that much out of him."

"Thank you," I said, then added, "Are they really giving Brigid the job over me?"

"That has yet to be determined. I'd ask you to say nothing about any of this, please."

I hung up the phone and flung myself on the loveseat, wondering how running off with a priest compared with my supposed sins.

36

At school the next morning, Judy greeted me with a friendly smile. It was the first sign of a thaw since the debacle with Cynthia.

"You've an appointment in the library," she said. "Yes, I'm covering your first lesson, again."

"Thanks," I said. "But why does Patrick want to see me there?"

"It's not Patrick," she said. "It's Father Frank."

Walking slowly down the corridor towards the library, I understood how a condemned prisoner might feel. I stood outside, hand on the doorknob, and tried to regulate my heart rate. Then I took a deep breath and went in.

Father Frank was sitting at one of the study tables. His folded hands rested on a manila envelope.

"Good morning, Father," I said.

He didn't reply, merely indicated that I should sit down opposite him.

"Miss O'Brine," he said, "I do not like to have my instructions ignored."

I folded my hands together and waited for the lecture.

"The first time we met, I underlined the important role you would play in the lives of our young people and the moral code of conduct you were expected to display."

I bowed my head. It killed me to admit it, even to myself, but he was right. However much I might not agree with some of the teachings of the Church, the contract I'd willingly signed required me to uphold them.

"If it were up to me," he continued, "you would be leaving St. Jude's today. However, there are some complications now associated with this situation."

I waited for him to raise the subject of Brigid.

"I've had written confirmation that the archbishop will finally be visiting our parish this summer."

I looked up.

"A great deal of work needs to be done before then," he added.

"I see, Father," I lied.

He tugged at his collar, revealing a nick from his razor. "I don't appreciate being blackmailed," he said, sharply.

"I'm sorry, Father, I don't understand."

He tapped the envelope in front of him. "Two of the Holy Dusters paid me a visit last night," he said. "Lucille Hanrahan and Biddy Cormack. For some unfathomable reason, they are very fond of you. They made quite the impassioned case for you to remain in our parish."

"But how did . . ." His frown silenced me.

"My dear," he said, in a tone that made clear this was not a term of endearment. "One thing you must be aware of by now is that Lucille Hanrahan knows every blessed thing that goes on in this parish."

He put on a pair of reading glasses and removed a sheet of paper from the envelope. "This is a list of the 'miracles'"—he looked up at me over the glasses—"not a word I would choose, but the miracles you are alleged to have performed." He read:

> *Rescued a drowning dog.*
> *Helped a young man find a vocation.*
> *Ended a feud, returning a woman to her community.*
> *Reminded the community about hope.*

He put down the note and took off his reading glasses. "Now I must say, I was unaware that this community needed reminding about hope. And I would add that you are encroaching on my territory with that last one."

He replaced the note in the envelope. "According to Lucille, the Holy Dusters have downed their mops. She says they won't do a tap of work unless I agree you can stay."

A grin threatened to bloom on my face, but I managed to suppress it.

"So, can I, Father?" I asked. "Stay?"

He nodded.

"Thank you, Father."

"One more thing, now, before you go. I've told Lucille and Biddy that if anyone ever gets wind of this blackmail, the deal is off. Not a word is to be spoken, do you hear me? Not even between you and Lucille."

"Yes, Father." Then I remembered Cynthia.

"Father, what if Cynthia—"

"She told me you said 'get rid of it.' Is that correct?" His face was puce.

I nodded.

"I've told Cynthia you must have meant adoption. If anyone ever suggests otherwise, you are to deny it."

"Yes, Father." I would have to let the hypocrisy slide.

"Now, I'm going down to see Mr. Donovan in his office. You are to give me ten minutes and then you go see him. Good day to you, Miss O'Brine."

He shut the library door, quite firmly, I thought. It was almost a slam.

I waited until I was sure he was a long way down the hall. Then I stood up, raised my hands in triumph and cheered. Quietly, of course. After all, I was in the library.

This time, when I knocked on Patrick's door, I was less nervous. He motioned to the chair and I sat down. Then he spread his hands on the desk.

"It seems Father Frank is in a bit of pickle. He doesn't want Brigid back here. It was a shocking scandal for the Church and he wants no part of it, especially since the archbishop is coming for a visit this summer. The fact of the matter is, he thinks if you leaves, Brigid could have a claim on the job."

"I see." So this was how Father Frank was spinning it.

"I understand Father Frank has spoken to you."

I nodded, biting my lip.

"It seems you are viewed as the lesser of two evils."

Let's face it, I'd been called worse. "So I can stay?"

Patrick's face was serious. "Father Frank has decided that since Cynthia lost the baby, the issue is moot."

"So, you *are* saying that I can stay?"

He scratched his beard. "Yes, but by Christ, Rachel, don't ever be so foolish again. You won't be so lucky next time."

"I won't. Thank you, Patrick. And I'm sorry about all of this."

His face softened. "Well, you made a holy mess of things, girl," he said. "But I'm glad you're staying."

He stood up and held out his hand. I thought about how he'd helped me tame the grade nines, how he'd supported the French club and defended me against Sam's father, how every single time I went to him for help, he backed me. I thought about his school socials, his beer fridge, that first day when we'd exchanged fish puns.

I stood up, ignoring his outstretched hand, and went in for a hug.

When I left school that afternoon, Brigid was leaning against the side of my car. She held her hand to her eyes, shielding them from the sun.

"Patrick says you're staying." Her voice was tremulous.

"Yeah."

She bit her lip. "He says he'll help me find another job. That a fresh start would do me good."

"It's good advice," I said. "That's why I came here. For my own fresh start."

"Ron said to tell you he's sorry about the notes. He's as stunned as they come, but in his way, I guess he was trying to help me get my job back. I think he blames himself for all my foolishness with the priest." With a sad wave of her hand, she went to her own car and drove away.

I went straight up to Lucille's, delighted to find Biddy was there as well.

"I came for a chinwag," I said.

"It's grand to see you, girl," said Lucille. "I'm just making tea if you wants a cuppa."

I did. I sat next to Biddy on the daybed.

"So you're staying on at St. Jude's next year," Lucille said, with a completely guileless expression. She handed a cup of tea first to

Biddy and then to me. "That's grand, girl. You does a great job there."

"We're looking forward to the garden party next month. We're trying to choose which quilts and rugs to sell to raise money for the church," Biddy said.

"Biddy, Lucille," I said. "I know I haven't spent much time with you all since I moved to Clayville, but since I'm staying on next year, I'd like to become a hooker."

Lucille choked on her tea and Biddy blessed herself.

"What did you say?" Biddy asked.

"I mean, would you teach me to hook rugs in September?"

"We'd be delighted, Rachel," she replied. "I'm sure you'll pick it up right quick."

Lucille seemed less confident. "We'll start you off on a real easy pattern, girl."

She might have been joking, but I decided to book a private lesson with Biddy before attending an official hooking session. I did *not* want to hear one more person say "not bad . . . for a mainlander."

37

Biddy's mention of the garden party focused my mind on the task Judy had set for me all those months ago: get the students to play traditional music at the party. Perhaps I could have forced their hand. It was a school event, they were students, and I was their teacher. But I didn't want them to play because they were "made to." They got enough of that already. Instead I made a few phone calls, first to Sheila and then to her brother Mike.

The following week I asked Beverley, Roseanne and Jerome to stay back to see me after school.

"It's about the garden party," I said.

They groaned in harmony. Beverley said, "Miss, please, we really don't want to play that old music there."

"Do you all know what MusiCan is?"

"Miss," said Roseanne, "how backwards do you think we are? We watches the music videos every afternoon. While we're doing our homework, of course."

"Good," I said. "My best friend's brother is a hot-shot producer there. He's going to be in St. John's next week and I invited him down to hear you guys play."

They were now listening far more attentively than I'd ever seen them do in class.

"He's interested in all kinds of music. Of course, I would love it if you guys played traditional music for him, but it's up to you. Mike said if he likes what he hears, he might be able to get a recording session at a studio in St. John's."

Roseanne and Jerome's faces lit up, but Beverley was skeptical. "What's the catch?"

"You have to play traditional music with me at the garden party." More groans.

"One set," I said. "That's all."

"But why would MusiCan come to Little Cove?" Beverley persisted.

"Because I told Mike how amazing you guys are. And because I've known him since he was three years old and I have lots of dirt on him." The Holy Dusters weren't the only ones skilled in blackmail.

The three of them laughed. "We knows not to cross you, miss," said Jerome.

"If we does the garden party, will you definitely play with us, miss?" asked Roseanne.

"I wouldn't miss it."

"We needs Phonse, too," said Roseanne. "He's a legend."

"Sure you knows he'll do it if miss asks him," said Beverley. "He's got it right bad for her." She began humming "Je l'aime à mourir" and Jerome and Roseanne fell about laughing.

"He does not have it bad for me," I said. This was nonsense and they knew it. Phonse was the grandfather of music, for all of us. "We're friends and he teaches me the fiddle. But I'll ask him."

When I asked him later, Phonse agreed immediately. "I'm right proud of you Rachel, getting the youngsters excited about our music." He cleared his throat. "It's grand, girl, just grand."

They were far from excited about the music, but I didn't let on to Phonse.

MIKE FLEW DOWN to St. John's and made his way to Clayville. I had offered him my sofa for the night but he declined. "Rach, I'm on expenses," he said. "I've booked myself into a motel. Apparently, there are no hotels in Clayville. I might struggle to max out on this trip."

"You can buy me dinner," I said.

Over pizza at Tony's, he talked excitedly about a punk band he'd seen in Halifax. Then he said, "But my taste is as eclectic as ever. I love the stuff Sheila bought me when she was down."

"And how is my lovely Sheila?" I asked.

He grinned. "She just broke the heart of a good friend of mine."

"That's my girl," I said. "And Mike, next time can you bring her down with you? I would love her to hear Johnny's Crew." I filled Mike in on Beverley, Jerome and Roseanne.

"Who's Johnny, then?"

"I have no idea."

Mike walked me back to my house. I pointed out the local highlights: the few stores, the café, the library. "Jesus," he said, "talk about a small town. I think I'd die if I had to live here."

"If you think this is small, wait until you see Little Cove," I said.

The next day Mike drove out with me to spend the day at St. Jude's. I made him do double duty, speaking to the French club about MusiqueCan, the Québécois arm of MusiCan. I took him to lunch at the takeout for fish and chips. After school, he sat in on a practice session I'd organized with Johnny's Crew to go over the garden party set list. As we tuned our instruments, Mike set up a portable tape recorder.

I watched him from the stage as we worked our way through the songs. His head was nodding in time to the music and he was grinning. When we took a short break, the students went outside to get some air and Mike came to sit beside me on the edge of the stage.

"These kids have really got something," he said. "They're crazy not to stick with that traditional music. It's killer."

"Could you talk to them?" I said. "They won't listen to me, but you're the cool dude from MusiCan."

When the trio came back in, Mike asked if he could talk to them about their heritage. He turned on the tape recorder and asked if they had any favourite pieces of Newfoundland music.

Beverley said, "Sonny's Dream."

"Oh, I love that one, too," I said.

Mike turned off the tape recorder. "Do you mind?" he said, in faux anger. "I'm trying to conduct an interview here." The students lapped it up.

Mike started the tape again and asked Beverley why it was her favourite song.

"It makes me think of my brother," she said. "He moved out to Alberta two years ago and he hasn't been home since." Beverley looked off in the distance for a minute. "Every time I sings that song, it makes Mam cry. But the thing is, she loves to hear me sing it. She says the tears make her feel closer to Rick."

Jerome said he liked the sea shanties because his grandfather used to sing them to him when he was a young boy. "When I plays those tunes, I remembers him. And, if I ever has kids . . ."

"Chance would be a fine thing," Beverley whispered to Rose-anne and they giggled behind their hands.

"When I has me own youngsters," Jerome corrected himself, "I wants to do like Grandfadder and sing to them."

Roseanne said she liked songs with humour. "I could be that poisoned about something," she said, "but if I starts singing 'Lukey's Boat' or 'The Rattlin' Bog' or a song like that, it lifts my spirits, you know?"

Mike started giving me the eye and jerking his head towards the door. I could take a hint.

I went to cool my heels in the staff room and Doug was there. "Sounding good down there in the gym, fiddle girl. You going out with your buddy tonight?"

"No, he's taking a taxi back to St. John's. He has a flight out early tomorrow morning."

"Good. I'm cooking dinner for you."

"Sure, it'll be good to see your mom. How is she?"

"She's grand, but I thought I'd cook at your place, if that's all right."

"So I get stuck with the dishes, huh? Genius."

"I'll see you about seven o'clock," he said.

When I got back to the gym, the students were packing up. "Mike said to tell you he'd see you outside," Beverley said.

"Did you play him some of your rock music?" I asked.

Beverley looked sheepish. "Actually, miss, we're going to do Newfoundland music instead."

"But with a twist," interjected Jerome.

They had trialled speedier versions of some of the songs that afternoon. I hadn't joined in because the pace was too quick, but it had been fantastic. I told them I thought their twist on the music was the way forward. "They'll be wanting your autograph soon."

"Go on with you, miss," said Beverley, but she and Roseanne exchanged a giddy look.

Mike was sitting on the front of my car when I got out. "God, the air out here is fantastic," he said. "No smog."

"You should see the stars," I said.

As we drove back to Clayville, I asked Mike how he'd magicked the students into playing traditional music.

He chuckled. "I played them a recording of a group playing a Newfoundland folk song and asked them what they thought. They were very complimentary."

"Who was it?" I asked.

"It was them! I guess it's the first time they've heard how good they are. I'm coming back down with a cameraman for the garden party."

"You are?"

"They are seriously good, Rachel," he said. "They could be the next big thing."

I dropped Mike at the taxi company and hugged him goodbye. "Sheila is counting the days until you're back," he said.

At some point, I was going to have to let Sheila and my mother in on the news that I was staying on for another year. I wasn't looking forward to either of those conversations.

38

Doug arrived at my place laden with grocery bags and a bunch of wildflowers. I put the flowers in a jam jar and placed it on the table. Then I asked if I could help cook.

"It's a one-man job," he said. "Dead easy. Steak and Caesar salad. Maybe some garlic bread."

"I'll pour the wine," I said. "Red or white?"

"Any beer on the go?" he asked. "I don't want to pass out tonight."

I opened a beer for him and put it on the counter near the sink, while he washed the lettuce. He asked how the music session had gone, and I shared Mike's comments about the band.

"They are pretty good," he said. "I talked to your buddy this afternoon. He seems like a good guy."

"He's Sheila's brother and he's the best."

"I thought that was me?"

"Ba-dum-dum."

We carried on chatting while Doug cooked, then sat down to eat. The steaks were somewhere between rare and perfect, the salad tart and crispy. We were so busy talking, we forgot to put the garlic bread in the oven, but neither of us cared.

"Rachel O'Brine," Doug said, putting down his fork and looking at me. "You're a hard one to pin down."

"What do you mean?"

"I think you enjoys my company."

I agreed that I did.

"But you don't let me in."

"Says the man sitting in my kitchen, drinking my beer."

He raised his bottle. "Touché. I've made a few mistakes this year, Rachel. It was foolish to get annoyed about Christmas," he said. "Your best friend was down and I guess you wanted to spend time with her."

"Exactly."

"But the notes? How could you not tell me about them? Mudder says as far as you were concerned, everyone was a suspect. Not me?"

"Well, you do have a prior misdemeanour."

He scratched his chin. "Not following."

"Wait here." I ran upstairs to my bedroom and searched my underwear drawer until I found the note he'd left on my car after I'd thrown up in his boat. On the way back downstairs, I reread the part where he'd said I'd get my sea legs. Looking back on the year, it felt like I had. On land anyway.

"Exhibit A." I waved it in front of him.

"You kept it all this time?"

I blushed and made a mental note not to show him the pink ribbon he'd removed from the ceiling the first time we met. We left the dishes on the table and went to the living room.

"Doug, you say I don't let you in, but as far as I can tell, you have a girlfriend."

He started to speak but I held up my hand. "Let me finish. Remember I told you about Jake cheating on me?"

He nodded.

"Even now, when I think about that girl arriving at my house, I get upset. It was so humiliating. I mean, I'm completely over Jake, but I did love him and he really hurt me."

"I'm sure he did."

"I don't want Geri to get hurt like I did."

Doug put down his beer. "Geri's not going to get hurt," he said. "Well, not by us, anyway. She's got a boyfriend in St. John's, and I think it's time people knew that."

"I don't understand."

"Geri and I were together but it ended last summer. She loves living in St. John's and I hates it there. She's into fashion, night-clubs, the big city."

"And you're just a bayman with simple pleasures," I teased.

He nodded. "Nothing wrong with that."

"Yes, but why don't people know about her boyfriend?"

Doug patted the space beside him. "Come over here, fiddle girl." I moved closer and he put his arm around me.

"We were the only two in our graduating year that went to university," he said. "And so people thought we were this golden couple . . ." His voice trailed off, but after a minute, he continued. "It's like there was this expectation of us being together. From Mudder, too. I never told you the whole story about Mudder's accident."

There was another long silence. I waited for him to continue.

"Geri found Mudder after her fall. She was in a bad state. Could've died. The tide was coming in, so Geri wouldn't leave her until the search party found them. So they formed a strong bond. Mudder treats Geri like a daughter. Although it's more like the prodigal daughter now because Geri isn't around much anymore."

"But why did you tell me she was your girlfriend?" I asked.

"Nope. I never did."

I thought back over the year, trying to pinpoint the moment I'd decided they were a couple. Then I remembered that first night at Biddy's when Geri arrived and Biddy had said she was Doug's girlfriend. And the look on Geri's face when Biddy said it.

"Huh," I said. "I guess you didn't."

Then I remembered the weekend I stayed with Biddy after her accident. She had told me that Doug and Geri weren't a love match. Had she been trying to send me a message in her subtle way? There was the quite the history of me and misunderstandings during my year in Little Cove. I guess there was room for one more.

Doug spoke again. "Geri thought it was best if we let people down gently. She pretends she's working every weekend and I hates town, so no one expects me to go in to see her."

It was getting dark in the living room, but neither of us made a move to turn on the lights.

"Anyway, last week I told Mudder about Geri." He laughed. "I should've told her ages ago. She said she was some glad we came to our senses because we weren't a good match. And I told her I'd found a better match."

"Who?"

He kissed my nose. "You. Right from the first day when I saw you slammed up against the blackboard."

"Now there's an image I'd like you to forget."

"And you're so sparky."

"What am I? A battery?"

"See!" he said, pointing a finger at me. "Like that, I loves those little zingers. And your enthusiasm. You makes things happen." He pulled me in close and finally kissed me. Then he released me and whispered, "You makes me happy."

I took his hand and led him upstairs to my bedroom. But once we crossed the threshold, I hung back.

"Let's take it slow," Doug said. "I wants it to be special." He picked me up and carried me over to the bed, then lay down beside me, stroking my hair.

I thought of that time he'd taken me fishing, how his strong hands had steadied me when I jumped into the boat. I put my hand to his cheek and felt its softness. Then he took my hand and brought it to his mouth, kissing my fingers.

"You okay?" he whispered.

Was I? I thought about the last time I'd been with Jake, and the aftermath. For what seemed a long time, I didn't answer, just stared at Doug.

But then I nodded and leaned in to kiss him. Then he was kissing me back and I slowly undid the buttons on his shirt. I ran my hands over his chest, pausing to examine a cluster of freckles on his shoulder. I wanted to map every bit of him. I pulled my T-shirt off and Doug propped himself up on his elbow and traced the outline of my bra with his finger. Then we were tumbling into each other, headlong, full tilt, down, down into the deep.

Afterwards, we lay in each other's arms, sleepy and content.

"I s'pose you'll be going back to Toronto for a bit once school ends," Doug said. "I finally got you and now you're leaving."

"Not for a while," I said. "I want to see my mom but she's not back until August. Come with me. We could do a road trip."

"Not in your car," said Doug, dropping a kiss on my shoulder.

"It would never make it. And I'll bring you to the cabin. There's no electricity and no one for miles around."

"And we'll go to our cottage," I said. "Mom and I haven't been up since Dad died. But we can make new memories there."

"It's a good thing we're teachers," Doug said, pulling me close. "We needs the whole summer to fit all these plans in."

39

The school year was over and it was time for the garden party. As I drove towards Little Cove, the sun was weak in the sky, overpowered by thick, grey clouds.

"Please don't let it rain," I said on auto-repeat until I pulled into the parking lot. The schoolyard was a frenzy of activity. A group of senior boys, supervised by Patrick, were in the midst of lugging large trestle tables and chairs into the gym, where tea and baked goods would be served, courtesy of the local women. Just outside the gym doors, picnic tables and chairs were arranged for a refreshment area. Meanwhile, Eddie Churchill and Roy Sullivan were reinforcing a makeshift outdoor stage for the musicians: Phonse, Johnny's Crew and me.

I found Doug in the staff room. When I fretted about the weather, he smiled and said, "Sure, it wouldn't be a garden party without a passing shower."

He was on bingo duty, and after sneaking a quick kiss, jogged off to the gym to set up the PA system. I wandered around looking for Mike. He'd left a message on my answering machine to say that he and the cameraman would meet me at the school.

I went back outside, passing a variety of local people setting up booths to sell baked goods, jams, quilts and other handiwork. Elsewhere students finalized educational displays.

After a few minutes I headed back inside and found Mike in the gym, chatting to Doug, and gave him a hug. He introduced me to the cameraman.

"Are you in charge?" asked the cameraman. "It's too dark outside, we won't get anything in the can."

"If you don't like the weather, stick around," I said, glad of the chance to use the local saying. But then I had to explain the joke, thereby rendering it unfunny.

"Don't you worry, my son," said Patrick, who had arrived for the tail end of the conversation. "The sun'll be splitting the rocks before you knows it."

As ten o'clock approached, I headed to the parking lot entrance for ticket duty. There was no gate and half the community was already inside setting up, but a few people began to trickle in, handing me their tickets.

"Hiya, Miss O'Brine," said Georgie, walking with Charlie, who was pushing their son in a stroller. Mrs. Piercey stopped to say hello and I forgot to ask her for a ticket.

Ten minutes later, the flow of people was so thick that I gave up, abandoning my post. Every inch of the schoolyard was full of people. Georgie took Alfie out of his stroller; he squirmed in her arms and she handed him off to Charlie.

"Take him, will ya? He got me drove with his wriggling."

Charlie took him, giving Georgie a kiss on the cheek. Then he went to inspect the booths, jiggling his son expertly.

"Did you hear I'm staying on next year?" I asked Georgie.

"Yis, everyone's right pleased."

"I was thinking about trialling a French class in the evening, for people who wanted to earn a credit. I really hope you'll join. Mr. Donovan says your French is excellent."

She was watching Charlie over at the stalls. I followed her gaze to where he was talking to Sister Mary Catherine. The nun reached up to chook Alfie's chin and he batted his fist at her wimple.

"I don't know," Georgie said after a minute.

"Well, think about it," I said. "It might get you back to your studies."

She fiddled with an earring. "Not that bothered, now," she said. I made a promise to myself to follow up with her in September, then headed to the French club display, where Sam and Darlene were straightening a poster.

"Bonjour, mes amis," I called and they responded in French. I complimented them on their stellar display. A range of project work lined the table along with some RCMP and other federal agency brochures in French. There were tourist flyers for Saint-Pierre et Miquelon, a French colony off the coast of New-foundland. I hadn't even known it existed until Sister Mary Catherine mentioned it. I had immediately gone to see Patrick about organizing a school trip there in the spring. "My God, there's no stopping you," he'd said.

Cynthia's mother walked by, and I reached out and touched her arm.

"How's Cynthia?"

Her face fell. "I wish she was here. I miss her some lot."

"I do too, Mrs. O'Leary. I'd like to get her back to school in September."

"If she ever comes home. She's gone to live with her sister in Halifax. She's got a steady job at a restaurant there."

"Oh, that's—" I faltered, unsure what to say.

"She says she likes the money."

I could see it would be hard to argue with that. I headed over to the stage, where Beverley was organizing the instruments and the microphone. "Miss," she said. "We're after changing the band's name. It's the Forget Me Nots now."

"Sweet," I said and she laughed.

I kept on wandering. I could hear Doug calling the bingo numbers into the PA system in the gym. I passed a wheel of fortune where Belinda Corrigan and a few other students were placing bets. Bill was in charge of spinning the wheel.

"Try your luck, Rachel?" he said. "You, too, could be a winner."

"I already am, Bill," I said.

Eddie Churchill was giving wagon rides to younger children, his placid horse ignoring their squeals of delight.

In every direction, I saw familiar faces. In Toronto, you could walk all day and not meet a soul you knew. I was glad I no longer lived in Little Cove, but I was gladder still that I'd be back teaching in September.

I browsed the handicraft displays, passing table after table, until I came upon a collection of wood carvings and looked up into the face of a smiling Calvin Piercey.

"Calvin, you look so happy."

"Last day at St. Jude's, right?" He grinned. "Starts at the trades college in September."

There were several bird carvings on Calvin's table and I examined them one by one, holding them up and turning them in the light before making my final decision.

"I'd like to buy this one for my mother."

"Ah, sure, take it, miss," he said.

"No," I said. "You must treat me like any other customer."

"Five dollars, then. It's a puffin, miss."

I decided that when I gave it to my mom, I would tell her it was a lesser spotted cuckoo bird.

Biddy was in charge of the next booth over, and after I selected four rugs and three quilts, she wouldn't sell me any more. "There'll be none left for anyone else," she chided.

Two of the senior boys had organized a games arcade for the youngest children. I stopped to watch the action at a fishing booth, where a little girl was about to haul her pole back, to see what she had caught. A boy of about four years old who was waiting his turn tugged my sleeve and asked, "Are you that French nun?" There was still work to be done out here, clearly.

I hadn't seen Doug's mother arrive, but she was deep in conversation now, with Mrs. Piercey at one of the tables. They both waved at me when I went past.

There was just time to put my purchases in the back of the car before Patrick mounted the stage to introduce the band.

We began the set with "Four Strong Winds." At first the various activities carried on, but soon most people gathered around the stage to listen. As the music grew livelier, couples began to dance on the grass in front of us. Eddie Churchill waltzed past, a nimble Lucille in his arms.

Beverley and Roseanne were very much in charge, taking it in turn to announce each piece and engaging in light banter with each other and the crowd. I felt a bit sorry for Jerome, but he didn't seem to mind. Phonse and I concentrated on avoiding the camera. Whenever it panned across the stage, we would turn our backs, laughing.

"We're bound to end up on the cutting-room floor," I said.

"Proper t'ing," he replied.

We worked our way through a varied repertoire of traditional ballads and sea shanties. For our final number, Beverley had chosen

"Sweet Forget Me Not." I spotted Doug in the crowd, sitting at a table with Judy and Bill. He looked up and smiled, and the bow felt a little lighter in my hand as Beverley began to sing:

She's graceful and she's charming, like the lily on the pond
Time is flying swiftly by, of her I am so fond.
The roses and the daisies are blooming 'round the spot
Where we parted when she whispered, "You'll forget me not."

As the final notes hung in the air, there was prolonged applause and whoops of delight. We stood in a row at the front and bowed. I was smiling so hard it hurt. Phonse asked me to hand over my fiddle and Roseanne escorted me off the stage. I went and sat beside Doug, and he squeezed my hand under the table and told me how wonderful I was. Which was kind of wonderful.

"Now then, my dears." It was Beverley, back on the stage. "We got one more song for yez. It's dedicated to Miss O'Brine."

I looked up warily. This had not been in the script.

"It's a French song that she taught us and it's called, 'Je l'aime à mourir,' which kind of means, I loves her so much I could die."

Jerome leaned into the microphone. "Or, like we says around here, miss, we loves you some lot."

I could feel tears pricking my eyes as Beverley sang. Her accent was perfect. Afterwards, the three musicians came to my table and I gave each of them a hug. "I'm going to miss you guys next year," I said.

"If we're playing in the pub, will you join us?" Roseanne asked.

"Definitely," I said, "but you might be out of my league by then." I pointed to Mike, who was coming over to talk to them.

It was getting warmer, and the tea and cakes had been replaced by beer. Patrick came to join our table for a drink.

"Well that was a fine finish to the year," he said, clinking glasses all around. "I don't know how we could ever top that."

"I've got all summer to think about it," I teased.

By five o'clock the crowd was mostly gone. A faithful crew of students along with Eddie, Phonse, Patrick, Judy, Bill, Doug and I cleared up the grounds. By the time we were done, I was exhausted. I arranged to meet Doug at Tony's later and, car laden with booty, I pulled out of the school, heading for Clayville.

Just past the Little Cove sign, something made me pull over. I crossed the road and stood where I had ten months earlier. Sunlight flirted with the waves. Boats swayed in the water, and I could see a few men squatting on the wharf near the stairs I'd scrambled down to rescue Ruthie. I looked up above the wharf and found Lucille's house, remembering my first night there and all the evenings I'd shared with her and the Holy Dusters. They were good women. Finally, my eyes alighted on St. Jude's, the school where, even though I was the teacher, I'd learned such important lessons.

There was a scrabbling noise behind me, and when I looked over my shoulder, it was Phonse, up above on his bicycle.

"You lost?" he shouted down at me, grinning.

"Nope," I said and happiness surged inside me. "I'm found."

ACKNOWLEDGEMENTS

Almost ten years ago, I sat down and wrote the opening chapters of what would become *New Girl in Little Cove*. Following countless rejections and a few near misses, I shelved the manuscript. But Rachel and the inhabitants of Little Cove kept nudging me, so I entered the 2019 Caledonia Novel Award. When my opening chapter was long-listed, I had six days to completely rewrite the novel. A subsequent short-listing convinced me to try one last time.

There are 389 inhabitants of Little Cove; I wouldn't be surprised if an equal number of people, on both sides of the Atlantic, supported me on the journey to becoming a published novelist. I couldn't possibly name all of you, but heartfelt thanks to my fellow writers and friends who've cheered me on, particularly the Law Girls.

Enormous gratitude to my brilliant agent, Hilary McMahon. When I discovered she was the daughter of Newfoundlanders, I dared to dream. In our first phone call it became clear that Hilary cared about my characters as much as I did. The fact that we share a similar taste in books and now swap recommendations is an unexpected bonus.

Thank you to everyone at HarperCollins Canada. I'm hugely indebted to Janice Zawerbny, who acquired my book. Her sage editorial comments and guidance helped make the story a much better one. Thanks also to Natalie Meditsky, my ever-patient production editor, and to Catherine Dorton and Sarah Wight for stellar copy-editing and proofreading, respectively. Gratitude also to Susan Swinwood and the team at Graydon House Books.

My brothers, Barry and Sean, provided helpful comments on an earlier version of the novel as well as constant encouragement. My cousin Ann Martin read several drafts and gave invaluable advice on the Newfoundland dialect, place names and folk music. Ann delighted everyone at my wedding reception when she sang "Sweet Forget Me Not," which might be why it features in this novel.

Three women deserve particular mention; you could say they're my Holy Dusters: Bobbi French, Ellen Goldstein and my sister Siobhan. I met Bobbi and Ellen online via the comment section of Betsy Lerner's blog. In no time, I was swapping chapters and lamentations with both. Each was an excellent beta reader and a constant source of much-needed mirth. Bobbi's feedback on all things Newfoundland was especially welcome. I look forward to holding her novel in my hands one day. It's quite possible that Ellen has read more drafts of this book than me. Without her ALL CAPS emails of encouragement during the Six Day Caledonia Crisis (as I have come to call it), I doubt I would have met the competition deadline. Siobhan is my sounding board, my dial-a-therapist, and my biggest cheerleader. She too has read multiple drafts over the years and her constant counsel to "Keep the Faith" buoyed me during the tough times.

ACKNOWLEDGEMENTS

Much love to my children, Ben and Rebecca, who are apparently proud of me, and gave me space and time to write, especially during the Caledonia Crisis when they ate sandwiches for dinner every night. Even more love and gratitude to my husband, Nigel, who supports my writing in every possible way, not least financially, and whose constant refrain has been "Don't give up." I'm so glad I didn't.

Finally, I was inspired by the handiwork and instructional videos of Deanne Fitzpatrick at www.hookingrugs.com.